"Who are you?" Dr. Pulaski asked.

"My name doesn't matter," Kira Nerys said. "And I don't have a lot of time, so please listen to me. I would like you to come with me to Bajor."

Pulaski frowned. "I've already been through this with Gul Dukat. I'm afraid I can't leave the station."

"He doesn't have to know," Kira said. "I'll smuggle you down there and I'll bring you back."

Pulaski held up her hand. "I'm sorry," she said.

"No." Kira clenched her fists. "I won't take no for an answer. I won't. We need you."

STAR TREK
THE NEXT GENERATION®

DOUBLE HELIX

BOOK TWO OF SIX

VECTORS

DEAN WESLEY SMITH
&
KRISTINE KATHRYN RUSCH

Double Helix Concept by John J. Ordover and Michael Jan Friedman

POCKET BOOKS
New York   London   Toronto   Sydney   Tokyo   Singapore

An *Original* Publication of POCKET BOOKS

POCKET BOOKS, a division of Simon & Schuster Inc.
1230 Avenue of the Americas, New York, NY 10020

STAR TREK is a Registered Trademark of Paramount Pictures.

A VIACOM COMPANY

This book is published by Pocket Books, a division of Simon & Schuster Inc., under exclusive license from Paramount Pictures.

ISBN: 0-671-03256-9

First Pocket Books printing June 1999

10 9 8 7 6 5 4 3 2 1

POCKET and colophon are registered trademarks of Simon & Schuster Inc.

Printed in the U.S.A.

For Jim and his great crew—
Ken, Debbie, Chris & Kathy

VECTORS

Chapter One

Terok Nor. Its name was as dark as its corridors. He actually found himself seeking the light, but carefully. Oh, so carefully. Sometimes his cloak malfunctioned, and he was seen. Partially, like a heat shimmer across desert sand, or an electronic memory buried in an old computer. But he was seen.

He didn't dare make that mistake here. The General didn't tolerate mistakes from his agents.

He stood in the shadows just to the left of the main entrance to a place called Quark's Bar. The area the Ferengi bartender had called the Promenade lay before him, turning away to the right, bending with the shape of the station design. The walls were gray, the floors gray, everything was gray. The Cardassians had made no effort to decorate this place. Even the bar seemed dismal.

He shuddered and drew his cape around his body.

He was glad he wouldn't have to stay here too long. This Terok Nor reminded him of his prison cell. He had lost too many years of his life there. He had spent too much time staring at gray metal walls, dreaming of escape. The metal walls, the ringing sound of boots against hard surfaces, the stench of fear—impossible to hide, even though the Cardassians kept their Bajoran prisoners separate from the rest of the population—permeated the place. If he shut his eyes, his other senses would find nothing to distinguish Terok Nor from that hideous cell, from that prison he had finally left. The prison had changed him—made him bitter, made him wiser, made him more careful.

Oh, so careful.

Two Cardassian guards walked the wide passage. Their gray skin matched the depressing decor. The only thing that seemed wrong to him was the heat. By rights this station should have been as cold as its walls, but it wasn't. The heat was thick and nearly unbearable. He didn't know how anyone could stand being here for long. The heat also accentuated the smells: the processed air, the unwashed bodies, the Rokassa juice wafting out from the bar. The sensations were almost too much for him.

He reminded himself that Terok Nor was the perfect testing ground. Two races, living in close proximity, with others coming and going. Their petty differences didn't matter. That one race kept the other prisoner, that one made the other labor in uridium processing were merely details. The important factor was much larger.

Terok Nor was the perfect testing ground for the

General. A closed system, for the most part. But anyone entering the system—or departing the system—would leave a record. A trail he could follow, should he so choose.

He didn't choose at the moment.

Now he was most interested in Terok Nor itself.

To his right in the bar, crowds of uridium freighter pilots and crews shouted and laughed, the sounds echoing off the high ceilings. A few moments before, he'd been in there sitting at the bar, watching.

Waiting.

Trying to stay cool and block out the uridium smell with the odor of one of the pilots' Gamzian wine. But it hadn't helped, and besides, he couldn't see that well or hear that clearly with his cloak on.

A clang from the far end of the Promenade caught his attention. One of the Cardassian guards had dropped his phaser pistol, then grabbed the wall as if for support. The other guard bent over him, then glanced from side to side, as if worried that a Bajoran might see and take advantage.

He was too far away to hear their words. The first guard shrugged the other off. The second guard picked up the pistol and spoke on his communicator. Two guards who had apparently been patrolling just out of his line of sight ran toward the far end of the Promenade.

The first guard put an arm around the second, who again shrugged him off. The second tried to stand, and nearly collapsed. The first guard supported him, and together they walked along the walls, keeping as far out of sight as possible.

He felt excitement flash through him, and he tamped it down. He couldn't let his emotions interfere with his observations. This might be nothing. It was a bit early to see results. He hadn't expected anything so soon.

The guards passed him. He had to press himself against the gray metal so that they wouldn't brush him. They weren't conversing, although he wished they would. He wanted to know exactly what had happened.

He needed to know.

He had moved to follow the guards, but the Promenade gave him no cover. So he remained in the shadows.

He would wait here, in the heat and the stench, just as he had done in his cell. He was good at waiting, especially when he knew it would end. And it would end.

Soon he would get his answer.

Chapter Two

"I TELL YOU, BARTENDER," the drunk Cardassian freighter pilot was saying, none too softly, "someone has been sniffing my Gamzian wine."

"You don't sniff Gamzian wine," Quark said for the eighteenth time. He loaded up another tray, carefully balancing the Saurian brandy bottle in the center so that Rom wouldn't drop the whole thing. As if training his brother weren't enough of a headache, Quark had a bar full of pilots and crew—mostly Cardassian, all of them drunk, and none of them more annoying than the pilot at the very edge of the bar, nearest the door. He had been complaining about hearing sniffing sounds, which, Quark had to admit, he had thought he had heard too. But they had been coming from an empty chair beside the pilot. They were probably an acoustical trick, caused by loud voices and even louder laughter, not to mention—

A crash echoed through the bar, and all the noise stopped as everyone looked at the table closest to the Dabo game. Quark couldn't see what was going on, but he knew. He knew even before his brother Rom pushed his way out of a group of Cardassians, looking like a misbehaving child trying to find his way past a group of annoyed grownups. Rom was bowing and apologizing and moving quicker than Quark had ever seen him move.

Rom darted behind the bar, just as a Cardassian stood, drenched in Romulan ale. The blue liquid coated his neck ridges, making him look as if some fanciful person had decided that he needed a spot of color.

"Ferengi!" he barked.

Rom was cringing behind the bar, clinging to Quark's legs. Quark kicked him off.

"It wasn't my fault, brother," Rom said.

"Sure looks like it to me," Quark said.

Rom peeked over the bar, then ducked quickly, narrowly missing the tray Quark had just filled. The Cardassian was heading toward them. He looked bigger than most Cardassians, if that was possible, and meaner too.

Quark shook his leg, but Rom wouldn't let go.

The Cardassian shoved two patrons aside as he reached the bar. "You!" he said, grabbing Quark's collar and lifting him against the bar itself. Rom was still clinging to his leg, and Quark felt as if he were being stretched so hard that he might actually snap.

"Me?" he asked, trying to sound innocent.

"You!" The Cardassian pulled harder. Quark shook his foot desperately. They were going to break something or worse—he'd be tall as a Bajoran when they were done.

"Me?" Quark said again, still shaking that foot. Rom was like a tube grub.

"You!" the Cardassian said, and yanked. Quark's foot slipped through Rom's grasp, and he overbalanced the Cardassian, who fell backwards, pulling Quark with him. Quark grabbed at the bar, then a customer, then a table to catch his balance. Instead, he bounced on the Cardassian's chest.

The man smelled so fiercely of Romulan ale that Quark nearly sneezed. He apologized and rolled off the Cardassian, resisting the urge to scramble behind the bar as Rom had done. Quark had learned, in his years on Terok Nor, that the best way to handle Cardassians—usually—was to act as if their most unreasonable behavior were normal.

He braced himself on a chair, got to his feet, and tugged his shirt in place. The Romulan ale smell had followed him, and he resisted the urge to glance down. Once that stuff was on someone's clothing, it never came off. He didn't want to add a ruined shirt to Rom's list of errors this night.

"Much as I enjoyed our game," Quark said to the Cardassian, "I must get back to work. Is there anything I can get you?"

The Cardassian held a hand to his head. Quark couldn't tell if that was because the man had hit it or because the liquor he had consumed was finally making itself felt.

"Get me the Ferengi weasel whom you use as a serving wench."

"Wench?" Quark heard Rom's voice from behind

the bar. This was the wrong time for Rom to take offense, at anything.

"You must mean my brother," Quark said, trying to think of a way to placate the Cardassian. "He's filling in tonight. He has never worked in a bar before—"

"That's obvious," someone said from behind Quark.

"—so if he's offended you in some way, let me make it up to you. I could refill your ale, or give you a half hour in one of my holosuites, or find someone to clean and press your uniform—"

"I want the Ferengi," the Cardassian said. He was sitting up on one elbow, his face grayer than Quark had ever seen Cardassian skin look.

Quark glanced at the bar. Rom would pay for this. All of it. The entire day. The entire *week*.

"I'm a Ferengi," Quark said.

"I'm not blind," the Cardassian said. "I want the other one!"

Quark closed his eyes for a moment. He would never get into the Divine Treasury. Never. Certainly not with Rom on Terok Nor.

"He's behind the bar," Quark whispered.

"What?" the Cardassian said.

"Behind. The. Bar." Quark opened his eyes. His eleven-year-old nephew Nog was watching him from the stairs, the boy's round face filled with a mixture of sadness and anger.

The Cardassian got to his feet. "You, you, and you," he said pointing to three other Cardassians. He certainly wasn't big on names. "Get that little maggot out here."

Quark held up his hands. "I really don't approve of bloodshed in my bar."

8

"I am not interested in blood," the Cardassian said.

The three Cardassian crewmen pulled Rom out from behind the bar. He was kicking, shaking his head, and apologizing all at the same time.

"Hold him there." The Cardassian pointed at the chair Quark was standing near. Quark took a few steps back, sneaking another glance at Nog.

The bar was silent except for Rom's protests. Nog mouthed, *Help him,* to Quark, who promptly turned away.

The Cardassians did as they were bid, placing Rom on the chair. Their ale-covered leader grabbed the Saurian brandy off the tray.

"Wait! Wait!" Quark said. "That's rare and precious and—"

The Cardassian was staring at him, the stench of Romulan ale coming off him in waves. "And?"

Quark bowed slightly so the Cardassian couldn't see his expression. "And I hope you enjoy it very much."

"I will." The Cardassian uncorked the brandy and poured it slowly, lovingly, over Rom's head. A roar of laughter went up in the bar, and then all the other Cardassians piled forward to pour their drinks on Rom.

Quark scuttled through the crowd and made it back to the relative safety behind the bar. He used a napkin to mop the ale off his shirt, and winced as another roar of laughter filled the place. The mixed drinks were turning purple on Rom's skull. He was spluttering, using his free hand to wipe at his nose and mouth.

"Stop them." Somehow Nog had found his way behind the bar. If Quark had thought his brother annoying, he had been mistaken. Annoying was this

9

kid who seemed to think he knew everything, even though he believed his father was worthy of respect.

"After all the glasses Rom has broken today," Quark said, "I think I owe him one."

"*You* owe him one," Nog said. "They do not. They're making a fool of him."

"He made a fool of himself," Quark said, and moved to the edge of the bar.

The lone Cardassian pilot still sat there, staring at his Gamzian wine. He was muttering. Quark hurried away.

Laughter again rose from the group.

"Why aren't you doing anything?" Nog asked.

"I am doing something," Quark said. "I'm making more drinks. Everyone will be out in a moment."

"How can you?" Nog said. "He's your brother."

"Don't I know it," Quark said. Rom was still standing on that chair. No one was holding him anymore. His head was covered with a sickly yellow liquid; his clothing was drenched; and it looked like his shoes were melting, even though they couldn't be. The drinks, even mixed together, weren't toxic enough.

But the shoes could be cheap enough.

The Cardassians were standing around him, shouting and laughing each time someone poured a drink on Rom, but more and more the Cardassians were noticing that they were running out of liquor. A few were already bellying up to the bar to order more. Then a few more came.

And a few more.

Suddenly, he was swamped. "Nog?"

He turned. The boy was gone. Nog was as bad as his father and as worthless, too.

Quark moved faster than he had in a long time, mixing drinks, trying to keep the drunken Cardassians from tearing up his bar further. Rom would have to clean up those drinks before anyone fell. Quark didn't want to think about the damage that a falling Cardassian could cause. He didn't want to think about money at all. Right now, all it would do was make him mad.

Even though he was raking it in at the moment. Maybe he should hold a "Drench the Ferengi" contest once a month. The only catch would be that the customers would have to buy the drinks that they poured on Rom. And it would have to be on Rom. He wasn't good for anything else.

He had been that way since he was a boy. Useless. No business sense. Quark had sold Rom's birthday presents, swindled him in his school ventures, even made Rom pay a toll to get into his own room, and still Rom had not learned.

Not even by example.

Not even when he was young.

Quark shivered. And now he was stuck with his brother. His brother *and* his nephew, both of whom managed to inherit Quark's father's business sense, or rather his lack of it.

The traffic at the bar was slowing down. Quark looked up. Nog was helping Rom off the chair. Rom was shaking himself like a wet dog, drenching customers on either side. Fortunately, they were still too pleased with themselves to care.

With Nog's assistance, Rom squished his way to the bar. Quark slid a pile of towels across the bar. "Go clean up your mess," he said to his brother.

"*My* mess? Brother, they assaulted me and you did nothing."

Quark set his lower lip. He had had enough of Rom's whining. If this new relationship were to work—and part of him truly wished it wouldn't—then Rom would have to learn a few things.

"Nog," Quark said. "Clean up the spill before someone slips."

"No," Nog said. "My father—"

"Nog," Quark said with some force.

Nog glared at him, then picked up the towels and headed back to the sodden chair.

"Come back here," Quark said to Rom.

Rom squished his way around the bar, leaving prints. A few Cardassians watched, still chuckling. The rest had gone back to their drinks and their Dabo game.

When Rom made it to the side of the bar, Quark grabbed him by the ear and dragged him toward the stairs leading to the holosuites. The tables were empty, and no one was looking at them.

"Ow!" Rom said. "What was that for?"

"For being stupid enough to dump Romulan ale on a Cardassian pilot. I'm lucky you didn't dump it on Gul Dukat. He'd close us down."

"It was a simple mistake, brother. I—"

"If I had a strip of latinum for each stupid mistake you've made since you arrived on the station, I'd be a rich man," Quark said. He had been quiet as long as he could. "You brought this on yourself, and you're lucky it wasn't worse."

"Worse? Didn't you see what they did? The Visscus vodka and the Itharian molé turned into a fizzing powder that—"

"I saw what they did," Quark said, lowering his voice so that Rom had to lean forward to hear. "And if you had dumped that ale on Gul Dukat, you'd be in the brig now. Or worse."

"Worse?"

"Worse." Quark crossed his arms. "I let them pick on you for your own good. Maybe you'll learn to be more careful. This is a dangerous place. You can't go around being your happy-go-lucky self. You have to watch everything you do."

"Yes, brother," Rom said, meekly. Then he added, "And here I thought you were just mad at all the glasses I broke."

"That too," Quark said. "I'm going to start deducting the price of everything you break from your salary."

"But brother—"

Quark held up a hand. "I'm doing you a lot of favors, Rom. I didn't have to give you a home and a job when Prindora's father swindled you out of all your money."

"You weren't going to bring that up again," Rom said, glancing over his shoulder for Nog. The boy was still wiping the floor. Those Cardassians had poured a lot of liquid on Rom.

"It's kind of hard to forget, Rom. What kind of idiot fails to read the fine print in a contract?"

"It was a marriage contract," Rom said.

"So?" Quark asked. "How is that different from a regular contract?"

"It was even an extension of the marriage contract. I read the first one."

"Twelve years ago," Quark said. "And I'll bet you forgot the terms, didn't you?"

Rom swallowed and looked down.

"You loved Prindora, so you trusted her."

Rom nodded.

"She's a female, Rom."

"She was my wife," Rom said miserably.

"At least she remembered the Sixth Rule of Acquisition."

"That's not fair," Rom said.

"What is it?" Quark asked. "Do you even know?"

Rom straightened his shoulders. "'Never allow family to stand in the way of opportunity.'"

"Good," Quark said. "Then you should understand why I let the Cardassians pour drinks on you. I made money, and that's more than I've done since you showed up."

"I'm sorry, brother," Rom said.

"You should be. Now go put on some clean clothes and get back out here. There's a lot of work to do." Quark glanced over at Nog. "And your son isn't a very good substitute."

"He's just a boy," Rom said.

"Go," Quark said, and Rom ran for their quarters. Quark shook his head and returned to the bar. Sometimes even he forgot the Sixth Rule of Acquisition. If he had remembered it, he wouldn't have allowed Rom here in the first place. But Rom had looked so pathetic when he arrived, dragging Nog behind him. Quark had actually felt sorry for them, although that emotion was quickly fading now. Every time he heard the sound of shattering glass.

"Nog!" he yelled. "When you finish that, I have some other things for you to clean."

The boy looked at him for a long moment. There was something in Nog's eyes, something a bit too rebellious for Quark, but then it disappeared as if it had never been.

"Yes, uncle," Nog said.

Quark nodded curtly, then leaned back and surveyed the bar. The Cardassian freighter crews were thinning. Drink had forced some of them to leave. The remaining ones weren't as rowdy as they had been earlier. The muttering pilot at the far end of the bar was still staring at his Gamzian wine. The glass was as full as it had been before the trouble started, but the Cardassian was an odd shade of green.

"And I thought the gray looked bad," Quark murmured. He frowned. A few of the Cardassians around the Dabo table were also faintly greenish. He had seen a lot of drunk Cardassians in his day, but he had never seen them turn vaguely green before. He had always thought that a hu-man trait.

Maybe they were all from the same ship. Or maybe the greenish tinge was being caused by something they'd eaten. Or maybe they were from a part of Cardassia Prime that made them look that way naturally.

"Or maybe that's how Cardassians look when they tan."

"What, uncle?"

Quark jumped. He hadn't realized Nog was beside him. "Do those Cardassians look strange to you?"

Nog peered at them. "They all look strange to me."

Quark nodded. Nog had a point. Maybe Quark had been here so long that everything abnormal was beginning to look normal.

What a frightening thought. He shuddered one more time, and then went back to work.

Chapter Three

THE LIGHTS IN THE MEDICAL LAB seemed dimmer than usual. Gul Dukat stepped inside, hands clasped behind his back. He was used to being here when colleagues and subordinates were wounded, but he felt uncomfortable here in cases like this. Illness. Especially unrecognized illness. The very idea made his skin crawl.

The displays were flashing, the monitors constantly recording various bits of information. In the main section, the physician assigned to Terok Nor, Narat, sat at his desk studying a screen before him. On beds hooked up to the monitors were two of Dukat's guards. Their skin was an odd greenish color, almost the color of a body shortly after it begins to decay.

Dukat raised his head slightly. Through the door of the second, smaller room, he could see the blanket-covered feet of the two Bajoran patients. Their doctor, Kellec Ton, stood beside them studying a Cardassian padd as if it were in a strange language. It looked odd to Dukat to see Bajorans here. They belonged in the medical part of the Bajoran area. It wasn't as well appointed as this, but then, they were workers. They didn't need all of this equipment.

He wouldn't have allowed them up here if Narat didn't believe that the disease the Bajoran workers had was related to the disease these two guards seemed to have.

Dukat took another step into the medical lab. Narat turned. He was slight, and his neck scales were hardly prominent. His eyes almost disappeared into his thin face. They were always bloodshot, but they seemed worse now. His thinning hair was cut short, almost too short, and stood straight up. He wore a lab coat over his uniform, and it gave him a scholarly air.

"Ah, Gul Dukat. I appreciate you coming here so quickly."

Dukat glanced at the patients on the bed. He felt uncomfortable, so he wasn't going to give any leeway to Narat. "I don't like to have Bajorans up here."

"We have a forcefield at the doors, just as you recommended," Narat said. "But they're not going anywhere. They will die here, probably within a few hours."

He sounded certain.

"I'd like you to see them."

Dukat frowned, glancing again at the guards. One of them moaned and thrashed, clutching at his stomach. Narat uttered a small curse, then found a hypospray and shut off the quarantine field around the bed. He stepped inside, restarted the quarantine field, and administered hypo to the man's neck. The guard calmed slightly.

"What about them?" Dukat asked.

"In a moment," Narat said, as he let himself out of the quarantine field. "Let me tell you this in my own way."

He led Dukat to the second room. They stopped at the door. The forcefield Dukat had insisted on was more for the Bajoran doctor than it was for the patients, but Dukat didn't tell Narat that. Dukat wanted Narat and Kellec Ton to work together as best a Cardassian and a Bajoran could. He just wasn't going to take any chances.

As if he knew that Dukat was thinking of him, Kellec Ton looked up from his padd. He had the wide dark eyes that Dukat found so compelling in Bajorans. His nose ridge set them off. His face was long, but didn't give an impression of weakness like Narat's did. On Kellec, the length accented his bone structure and gave him a suggestion of power.

Dukat had been careful around this Bajoran doctor, and had limited his access to the Cardassians. Women found him attractive, and Dukat didn't like that. Kellec Ton had the kind of charisma that could be dangerous if allowed to run free.

Dukat couldn't study him any longer. He had to look at the patients.

The Bajorans on the table were not a strange shade of green. In fact, their color was normal. Better than normal. If he hadn't known better, Dukat would have thought them the picture of perfect health.

It was the stench that made their illness clear. The pervasive odor of rot clung to everything, as if there were food spoiling along the floors and walls of the room—food and unburied bodies decaying in a powerful sun.

He resisted the urge to bring his hand over his face. Kellec Ton was watching him, as if measuring Dukat's response. "Disgusting, isn't it?" Kellec said. "You should go into the Bajoran section. The smell is so overpowering there I have no idea how anyone can eat." Then he tilted his head slightly. "Not that there's much to eat in the first place."

Dukat would not get into political discussions with this man. He was on Terok Nor because Dukat cared for his Bajoran workers. He was here because a healthy worker was a strong worker. The more uridium the Bajorans processed, the better for all concerned.

"What is this disease?" Dukat asked.

"If I knew, I might be able to help them." There was a controlled frustration in Kellec's voice. "So far, we've lost twenty Bajorans, and these two aren't far behind. They look good, don't they?"

Dukat nodded, then asked, "What is the odor?"

Kellec glanced at Narat, who nodded that he should continue. Kellec set the padd down on the instrument table. "Exactly what you think it is. Their bodies are decaying internally. I keep them sedated, but this disease, whatever it is, is incredibly painful. Some of the others broke through the sedatives before they died—I couldn't give them enough medication to ease the suffering."

Somehow, he made that sound like Dukat's fault. But Dukat had done nothing to cause this disease. Some Bajoran had brought it onto the station. He had left it to the Bajorans to cure. They handled their own health. That was why he allowed them Kellec Ton. If they needed specific supplies, Kellec Ton was supposed to act as liaison with the Cardassians.

"You should have notified us sooner. Perhaps Narat has something that will—"

"No, I don't," Narat said.

"Well," Dukat said, "I don't like diseases that destroy my workers. You should have brought this to me before it got out of control."

"The disease first showed up a day and a half ago," Kellec said. "I've been a bit busy since then."

"And it will only get worse," Narat said.

Dukat turned to him. Narat's face looked even more pinched than it had moments ago. "Why is that?"

He took Dukat's arm and led him to the edge of the nearest guard's bed. Up close, the greenish color was mottled. The ridges around the guard's eyes and down his neck were flaking, and a pale gray liquid lined his mouth and nostrils.

Dukat kept his distance, even though he knew the guard was surrounded by a quarantine field.

"This does not look like the same disease to me," Dukat said. Narat had told him earlier, when asking permission to have Kellec and two Bajorans brought to the medical lab, that the Cardassians were now infected with the disease that was killing the Bajorans.

"It doesn't look like the same disease," Narat said, "because you are looking at the symptoms. If you were looking at the disease itself on microscopic level, you would see that it is the same virus—even though it attacks Cardassians differently than it attacks Bajorans."

"So you'll be able to cure them," Dukat said.

Narat shook his head. "Not unless we discover something quickly."

"But if you know its cause," Dukat said, "then you should be able to find a counteragent."

"Should," Narat said, "and probably will." He glanced at Kellec Ton, who was standing near the door. Neither of them seemed as certain as doctors usually did.

"But?" Dukat asked.

"But we don't have the time," Kellec said.

"The disease progresses rapidly," Narat said. "That's a trait it shares in both Barjorans and in Cardassians. These guards came in complaining of dizziness and lack of coordination. Now they cannot sit on their own. The mucus that you see—" and he pointed to the grayish fluid leaking out of their eyes, noses, and mouths. Dukat grimaced in spite of himself "—is filling their lungs. They will drown by tomorrow if we do not find a way to stop this."

"Drown?" Dukat repeated. He couldn't imagine anyone drowning on Terok Nor. If he had to predict a way his people might die here, it would not be by drowning.

"That's the net effect," Narat said.

"This is not possible," Dukat said. "Bajorans and Cardassians cannot contract the same diseases. We have known that—" he caught himself. Kellec Ton looked at him, eyes sharp. The Bajoran doctor did not need to know how much information the Cardassians had gathered on the Bajorans. "We have known that for a long time."

"We have," Narat said. "But this is something new."

"Brand new," Kellec said.

21

There was something in his voice that annoyed Dukat, a faint accusation. Dukat approached the door. The stench seemed to have grown.

"What are you suggesting?" Dukat asked.

"I'm not suggesting anything." Kellec's expression was mild, but his eyes were not. They were intense, filled with something that Dukat recognized.

Hatred.

Good. Let the Bajoran hate him. He wasn't competing in any popularity contests.

"But," Kellec continued, "I have heard rumors that this disease is the result of a Cardassian experiment, designed to rid the universe of Bajorans. What better way to get our planet than to destroy us all?"

Dukat felt rage rush through him, but he did not move. He waited until the first wave of anger had passed before responding. He didn't want the Bajoran to know that his comment had hit the mark.

"If that were the case," Dukat said, making certain he sounded calm, "then this disease would not be killing Cardassians."

"It would if someone made a mistake," Kellec said.

Their gazes met for a moment. They both knew the Cardassians were capable of this. Then Dukat said, "Your job is to find a cure for this disease—both versions, Cardassian and Bajoran."

"You're feeling compassion for Bajorans?" Kellec asked, with great sarcasm.

"I prefer to have my Bajorans alive and working," Dukat said. "Not straining the medical resources of Terok Nor."

He turned away from Kellec, no longer willing to look at the man. "If this disease progresses as rapidly as you say," he said to Narat, "then we have to isolate it. We don't want it spreading through the station."

"I'll do what I can," Narat said. "But we have a problem here. We are, essentially, in a floating tin can, sharing the same air. I can have the computers filter for an air-borne version of this virus in the life-support system and neutralize it, but the disease might not be spread that way. We don't know enough about it."

"Isolate anyone who comes in contact with it," Dukat said. "I don't want this spreading."

"I won't be able to do that, treat these patients, and find a cure," Narat said. "You'll have to issue the order."

He had a point. "All right," Dukat said.

"It's probably too late," Kellec Ton said.

They turned to him.

Kellec shrugged. "If this disease has a long incubation period, then it could have been spreading all over the station long before any symptoms appeared."

"Then we'd all have it," Narat said softly.

Dukat felt his skin crawl again. He couldn't help himself; he shot another look at the ill guards. He would do anything not to end up like that.

Then the door to medical lab swished open. Two Cardassians Dukat didn't recognize entered. They were wearing the uniform of the uridium freighter crews. The woman was hanging on the man, barely able to walk. Her skin was green.

"You the doctor?" the man asked.

Dukat took a step backwards even though they hadn't come near him yet. He was standing near the second door.

23

"No," he said, and he sounded alarmed, even to his own ears. "I'm not the doctor."

"I am," Narat said, walking toward them as if this thing didn't bother him at all. "Quarantine protocol."

The quarantine field went up around the newcomers. Dukat let out a small sigh.

"Don't relax yet," Kellec said to him softly. "All it takes is a moment to get infected. One small breath of air. A touch."

Dukat whirled.

The Bajoran was watching him, that maddeningly calm expression on his face.

"Then find the cure," Dukat said.

"I plan to," Kellec said. "For my own people."

"I command you to find it for both." Dukat raised his voice. The new patient and his companion were looking at him, along with Narat.

"Why should I help your people?" Kellec asked.

"Why should I help yours?" Dukat asked.

They stared at each other for a moment. Then Kellec said, "You want our services and our planet."

"You cannot survive without us," Dukat said. "Not anymore."

"We could survive just fine," Kellec said.

There was a crash behind them. Dukat turned. The woman had collapsed. The man who had brought her was clutching the wall as if it gave him strength.

"I need some help over here," Narat said.

Dukat remained where he was.

"Open the force field," Kellec said.

Dukat looked at him.

"Open it, and I will help them," Kellec said.

Dukat brought the force field down. Kellec hurried to the others, demanding that Narat drop the quarantine field on that end as well. Both doctors picked up the female patient, helping her to a bed. Then they helped the male patient. They bent over the patients, lost in their work.

Dukat watched them for a moment, feeling itchy and cold. He glanced at his hand. The skin was its normal grayish color. Healthy. He was healthy.

For the moment.

Kellec wasn't looking at him, and Dukat didn't want to go any closer to taunt him. But Dukat knew Kellec, knew his kind. The man was a doctor first. He would heal a patient and then look to see the patient's race. That was why Dukat had Kellec brought to Terok Nor. For all his Bajoran patriotism, Kellec would save Cardassians if he had to.

In fact, he had just demanded to be allowed to. They would work together to solve this, Cardassian and Bajoran, because they had no other choice.

Chapter Four

DOCTOR KATHERINE PULASKI stood in the sickbay of the *Enterprise*. She was alone. The four medical staff members who were supposed to be in the area had honored her request and granted her the last few moments here alone.

She sighed. The instruments were on their trays, just as she liked them. The monitors were in their off positions. The desk was neat, but all of her personal experiments were gone. Sickbay was tidied up and ready for the new doctor.

Or the old doctor, as it were. Pulaski was being replaced by the doctor she'd replaced, Beverly Crusher. Which was as it should be. Dr. Crusher's presence had never entirely left this sickbay. No matter what Pulaski did, she had a sense of Beverly Crusher's presence. Part of it was the very layout of the bay. Of course, much was standard on each starship—and

Pulaski had served on a number. But there were items left to each doctor's discretion—where to put the experiments, for example, or the way the desk was situated in the office. Pulaski had always meant to move the pieces around, to make the sickbay more efficient for her type of medicine. But the demands of being the chief medical officer on a starship—particularly an active starship like the *Enterprise,* a ship with a demanding captain—had never allowed her enough free time to reorganize.

That wasn't entirely true. There had been down periods where she had had some free time—once she had even helped Data in his Sherlock Holmes holodeck program—but she had generally used those times for resting. Making big changes like rearranging sickbay would have required a lot of effort, not just in moving of furniture but in retraining the staff. Effort she was now relieved she hadn't expended.

She tugged at her blue shirt and glanced at her travel bags. She had already removed personal items from her quarters, and all of her experiments and notes were already on the shuttle that would take her to Deep Space Five. She wasn't sure what her new assignment would be—Starfleet was being cagey about it, as always, which usually meant they were considering her for several missions and that she would get the one that rose to the top.

Still, she would miss the *Enterprise.* She loved starships and the challenges they presented. On starships she saw diseases no one else had seen; injuries whose treatment required a knowledge of the most current techniques or the most primitive, depending on whether she was aboard ship or on a hostile planet; aliens whose physiology was so strange that she didn't know what they looked like well, let alone if anything was wrong with them.

She hoped she would get reassigned to a starship, but she doubted that she would. If Starfleet Medical had its way, she would be heading to some starbase where she would squire newly minted doctors through their residencies.

If the truth be told, she'd rather stay on Deep Space Five than do that.

Her combadge chirruped.

She sighed. She would have to leave now. She wasn't ready. But she pressed the badge anyway.

"Pulaski."

"Doctor, sorry to bother you before you leave, but we have an emergency." Geordi La Forge sounded all business. "One of the crewmen got caught in an explosion in Jefferies Tube Three. There was a localized fire. We put it out, but he's severely burned."

Burns. She hated them. The trauma to the skin could continue long after the fire was actually put out.

"Beam him directly to sickbay," she said. She hated the transporter, thought it an infernal device, but it had its uses. Right now, she needed speed more than she needed caution.

The crewman shimmered into place on one of the biobeds. His blue shirt was in charred ruins around his badly burned skin. He was human, which made her task just a bit harder. Vulcans and Klingons handled burns—indeed all pain—better than humans.

He wasn't conscious, for which she was grateful, but he was moaning. Burn pain was excruciating. She hurried to the biobed, with the fleeting thought that the sickbay wouldn't be in order for Dr. Crusher. Ah, well. Reorganization simply wasn't Pulaski's strong suit. Dr. Crusher would understand.

The smell of burned skin filled the sickbay. The biobed was giving his vitals, but she wanted more information. She picked up her medical tricorder and ran it over him, watching the readouts confirm the information she was already receiving.

No deep trauma, no internal injuries. Just burns. The crewman would live. But she didn't slow down. First she eased his pain and put him into a deep, restful sleep. Then, for the next five minutes she carefully repaired the burned skin, one area at a time.

Skin repair was delicate work, but something she had done all of her career. She was quicker at it than most, but that was partly because she disliked it so much. Burns, she often thought, were the worst injury of all.

After she had finished, she stood, brushing a strand of hair from her face, and checked his readings again. Still resting comfortably. She'd keep him that way for a few hours to give that new skin time to heal. And to give his mind time to deal with the memory of the pain. Sometimes in cases like this, the memories were the hardest to heal. Much harder than the skin. She'd have to let Counselor Troi know before she left.

"Nice work, Doctor."

Pulaski started. No one was supposed to be here, and she didn't recognize the voice. Had someone beamed in with the crewman? She had been too preoccupied to notice.

She turned.

Beverly Crusher stood in the center of the bay,

where Pulaski had been just minutes earlier. Her long red hair cascaded around her face. She looked thinner than Pulaski remembered.

"Very nice work," Dr. Crusher repeated.

"Thank you, Doctor." Pulaski smiled. The compliment meant a lot. Dr. Crusher was one of the best doctors in the fleet. Picard had told her she would always have a berth on the *Enterprise,* so when she decided that heading Starfleet Medical wasn't for her, she requested her old job back. Picard gave it to her without hesitation, even though—as he had solemnly told Pulaski—their current chief medical officer was one of the most talented physicians he had worked with. Picard was a diplomat, so Pulaski knew he might be exaggerating slightly, but he was also the captain of a starship, and he didn't give out idle praise.

Dr. Crusher looked around the main area of the sickbay as if she were a blind woman just recovering her sight. "You know, there were days at Starfleet Medical when I never thought I would ever see the inside of one of these again."

Pulaski smoothed her hair with one hand.

"I missed it a great deal."

"I imagine you did," Pulaski said. She felt her shoulders stiffen. She would miss it too.

"I'm sorry, Katherine," Dr. Crusher said. "You were doing an exceptional job here. I wouldn't have asked to come back to the *Enterprise* if it weren't for Wesley."

Pulaski nodded. "I had a feeling from the first that I was merely keeping this place warm for you."

"It looks like you did more than that." Dr. Crusher

nodded at the crewman. His vitals were closer to normal than they had been just a few moments before. "I've never seen such quick work on a burn patient. I doubt I could have done as well."

"I've studied your logs," Pulaski said. "You've done as well or better."

Their gazes met, and an awkwardness that had been reflected in their words seemed to grow. Finally Dr. Crusher tossed her long hair back—such a girlish move from such an accomplished woman—and laughed.

"I'm sorry about this," she said. "I didn't realize it would be so uncomfortable."

Pulaski frowned just slightly. If Dr. Crusher was referring to their meeting, she should have known. It was an unwritten rule among chief medical officers that they never share a sickbay—at least not on a starship. The new officer replacing the old officer would wait until his or her predecessor was off the ship before entering sickbay.

But Pulaski said nothing. An unwritten rule was a tradition, yes, but it wasn't as if Dr. Crusher had done much more than been slightly impolite. It was something easily overlooked.

Apparently Pulaski's silence went on too long. Dr. Crusher's smile faded.

"There is a reason that I'm here early," she said.

Pulaski felt some of the tension leave her. The breach of etiquette had bothered her, even though she had just been trying to convince herself that it hadn't. She felt Dr. Crusher's returning as a slight rebuke, almost as if she weren't important enough to remain on the ship. She had known that the feeling was irrational and, in her better moments, had forgotten all about it. But it had been a thread, an undercurrent, during the whole last month, since she'd finally learned that she would be leaving.

"I hope it's not too serious," Pulaski said.

Dr. Crusher's mouth formed a thin line. "Starfleet Medical wanted me to tell you there's a problem on Bajor."

Whatever Pulaski had expected, it wasn't that. She fought to keep her face impassive, not to let her emotions show. Dr. Kellec Ton, after all, was her ex-husband, and as much as she cared about him, she had known that this moment could come. She had urged him to leave Bajor, knowing that with his temperament, he couldn't be safe under the Cardassian occupation. But he had refused, just as he had always refused to do the sensible thing during their marriage, citing his loyalty to his homeland and its great need for him in time of crisis.

"Why did Starfleet Medical believe they needed to inform me of this?"

Dr. Crusher's gaze held hers. "There are rumors that a plague on Bajor is killing both Cardassians and Bajorans."

Pulaski threaded her fingers together and held her hands over her stomach, as if the pressure would keep her nerves from getting worse.

"That's not possible," Pulaski said. "Their systems are too different. Viruses cannot be spread from Bajoran to Cardassian and back again."

"I thought the same thing," Dr. Crusher said softly. "But Starfleet Medical is taking the rumors seriously."

Rumors. If they only had rumors, they wouldn't

know who died. For all they knew, Kellec was just fine.

Suddenly Pulaski knew why Dr. Crusher was telling her this. "They want me to contact Kellec for them, don't they?"

Dr. Crusher nodded. "A message from Starfleet might put him in jeopardy. A message from you—"

"Would seem normal. Or somewhat normal." Pulaski let her hands drop to her sides. She was on good terms with Kellec, as she was with her other two ex-husbands. But she didn't like talking with him. She had loved him a great deal, but his stubbornness had frustrated her—and it continued to frustrate her, even now.

"Starfleet Medical believes that Dr. Kellec Ton can confirm or deny the rumors."

Pulaski nodded. "As long as I present my questions in a way that won't put him in any danger."

"From what I understand of Kellec Ton," Dr. Crusher said, "he's probably already in danger, at least the political kind."

"He never could remain quiet about things that bothered him," Pulaski said.

"When was the last time you spoke with him?"

"A month ago." They had fought, as they often did. Kellec had agreed to go to a Cardassian space station to take care of their Bajoran workers. He hadn't explained his motives—he didn't dare on the unscrambled channels he could get out of Bajor—but he didn't have to. He would take care of the workers' ill health, document the atrocities he saw, and do what he could to promote the resistance movement from the inside—maybe even destroy the station, if it were within his power.

She had argued against the assignment, attempting to use medical arguments that couched her larger objections. But they had both known what she was talking about. And the argument had ended, as they all had, with Kellec shaking his head.

Katherine, my love, he had said. *Our fundamental problem is, and has always been, your unwillingness to let me make my own mistakes.*

She was letting him make his own mistakes. But she'd had to divorce him to do so.

"Can you contact him again?" Dr. Crusher asked.

Pulaski nodded. "I believe I know where to find him."

"Good," Dr. Crusher said. "I'm sorry to bother you with this, especially now. But it is the best way for us to handle this potential crisis."

There was something that Dr. Crusher wasn't telling her, something that Starfleet Medical was very interested in, something that they were willing to risk a high-profile contact with Bajor over. But Pulaski had been military for a long time. She knew better than to ask for information that she had not been given. If it had been something she needed to know, Dr. Crusher would have told her.

"Well," Pulaski said, "I guess it's time."

She glanced at her last patient on the *Enterprise*. The crewman's readings were mostly normal, his new skin looking pink and healthy. She went over to him and drew a blanket across him. He was sleeping peacefully. He wouldn't even remember his treatment. He would think Dr. Crusher had taken care of him, and even though she would probably correct him, he would never really know what had happened here.

But Pulaski would.

"I'm sorry it's such a mess. I had planned to leave it tidy for you."

Dr. Crusher smiled. "Medicine is rarely tidy."

Pulaski nodded. That was a fact she knew all too well.

Chapter Five

A MIST HAD FORMED at the base of the mountains. Gel Kynled felt the chill, even though he stood in the shadow of what had once been an excellent restaurant. It was Cardassian now, with the former restaurant owner working as a waiter and forced to suffer daily humiliation from the occupying army. Gel hated watching that. He hated so many things about Bajor these days. So many Bajorans simply took the Occupation as their lot in life. They looked away when their friends disappeared, mourned when their families died, but did nothing.

He couldn't stand doing nothing.

He had his arm wrapped around the waist of Cadema Hyle. She was too thin for him. Her clothing was baggy and barely hid the signs of starvation that had been so prominent a few months ago. Cadema had managed to escape from one of the camps—

probably because the Cardassian guards had left her for dead. She had climbed out of the mountains, surviving on roots and berries before she made it back to their resistance cell. She never spoke of the experience, not after that first day, but it had changed her.

Like him, she was willing to do anything to get rid of the Cardassians. Anything at all.

It was nearly curfew. Most of the Bajorans who were on the streets were hurrying toward their homes. The people left in this area had nominal freedom, all of them knowing they could lose it with a single error. Staying out past curfew could be that error.

The Cardassians passing him were no longer on duty, but they weren't in a hurry either. Gel resisted the urge to check the time. He and Cadema were standing casually, looking younger than they were—because they had always looked younger than they were—and pretending to be in love. Idle youth, not caring about deadlines or curfews or Cardassian soldiers. But it was getting late, and Gel didn't dare call attention to himself. He needed his freedom, and so did Cadema. In fact, Cadema said she would do anything she could, anything, to prevent being captured by the Cardassians again.

He felt her shift ever so slightly. Her movement wasn't noticeable to anyone watching, but it was a sign that she was getting nervous too.

"A few more moments," he said softly.

She smiled at him, tilting her head upward, a lovesick look that didn't make it to her eyes. He smiled back, so fond. Lovers, taking the last few minutes of precious daylight to be together.

Someone coughed a few meters away, a loud, honking cough. It was their signal. Cadema tensed. Gel slid his left hand behind his back. His fingers rested lightly on a stolen Cardassian phaser tucked into a belt, holding it against his spine. He could draw and fire the pistol faster than a Cardassian could raise his arm. Gel had killed at least ten Cardassian guards with that pistol over the last few months. He planned on killing a lot more.

A Jibetian trader walked past, still coughing. He was long and lean, like most of his people, and his ridged cheeks were very pronounced. Gel had never seen him before.

"You need to do something for that cough," Cadema said, her voice gentle, as if giving advice to a friend.

The trader stopped, his cloak flowing around him. The movement was fluid and powerful. It also revealed the weapons at his waist. A pistol like Gel's and something Gel didn't recognize.

The trader's pale green eyes took both of them in. Nothing in his expression changed, but he seemed to recognize them as a team.

He stepped closer, so close that his words were audible only to Gel and Cadema. "My boss does not like being summoned."

Gel didn't move. He kept one hand on his weapon, the other casually draped over Cadema. As he spoke, he smiled, so that anyone watching would think they were still discussing cold remedies.

"Bajorans are dying," he said.

The trader shrugged. "You were warned there might be some casualties."

"Some," Cadema said. "We thought that meant only those initially involved. Your boss misled us."

The trader's gaze flickered toward the street and then back to them. They were the last Bajorans out, and there were no more Cardassians. Curfew had started. In a few moments, they all would be in trouble.

"People in your business," the trader said, "should not be soft."

Gel's grip on the pistol tightened. He knew he was being goaded, and he would not let the trader get to him. All of the people he had dealt with, everyone who worked for the person—or persons—who had theoretically developed this perfect biological weapon to fight the Cardassians had been as cold and unfeeling and cruel as this trader. All of them. They were only in it for the money. Gel's resistance cell had spent the last of its reserves getting this weapon, and now it was backfiring on them.

"Soft, weak," Gel said, "those are all subjective terms. We're not talking about our ability to fight, or our own willingness to die for our beliefs. But this disease has spread beyond our cell, to the innocents. Our children have been dying. It's not a pretty death."

"You didn't buy a pretty death," the trader said. "You bought something a bit more destructive than that."

"My people are getting sicker faster than the Cardassians." Gel had to struggle to keep his voice down. Cadema was looking to make sure they were still alone on the street. They were.

So far.

"The disease incubates longer in Cardassians."

"Not good enough," Gel said. "You owe us more than that."

"We owe you nothing."

"You lied."

"What are you going to do? Turn us in? Which government will prosecute us for violating the local commerce laws? What remains of the Bajoran government? Or the Cardassian warlords?"

Cadema put a hand on Gel's chest. She knew how close he was to killing this bug.

"We have done what we promised," the trader said. "You wanted to get rid of the Cardassians. We offered you a way, and now they are dying. What more do you want?"

"The Bajoran antidote for the plague," Gel said.

The trader smiled. It was a cruel, empty smile.

"What if we turn you in to the Cardassians and tell them you're working for the person who started this plague?" Gel asked.

"And who's going to tell them? You, the great rebel leader killing his own people?" The trader laughed again, this time louder, his voice echoing down the empty street.

"We have kept complete documentation of all of our dealings with you, including surveillance of all of our meetings."

"You have never dealt with the same person."

"It doesn't matter. We have the conversations and the promises. We have it all."

"All except the names of the people you've really been dealing with," the trader said.

"That's not hard to find," Gel said. He was bluffing, but it was getting dark. He was getting desperate. He had thought this meeting would go better. "Give me the Bajoran antidote."

The trader smiled. "You think you are so courageous." He crossed his arms. "You believe you are so powerful, so smart. You don't like the idea that you've been tricked."

Cadema glanced at Gel. He knew what she was thinking, and he shook his head slightly, but she spoke anyway. "We will pay for it," she said.

The trader's ridged cheeks puffed out. Gel had worked with enough Jibetians to know that to be an expression of surprise. "Really?" he asked.

She nodded.

"You have no money. You used it all to pay us."

Gel felt cold. Perhaps they had been dealing out of their league.

Cadema let go of him and grabbed the trader by his long cloak. She pulled him close. She had surprising strength in those thin hands.

"We are losing our children, our families, the very reasons we are fighting the Cardassian dogs."

The trader stared at her for a moment. Cadema had let the veneer of civility drop. She had let him see their desperation. Gel thought he saw pity in the Jibetian's eyes.

"There is no antidote," the trader said.

"What?" Cadema let him go. "There has to be."

It hadn't been pity Gel had seen. It had been disgust. The look intensified. The Jibetian straightened his lapels. "My boss hates weakness. If you couldn't stomach the deaths, you should not have bought our services."

Gel brought out his laser pistol, aiming and firing as he moved. But he didn't get to see whether or not his shot hit its target. The Jibetian already had his pistol out. A shot caught Gel in the chest, smashing him back against the wall. His own pistol fell out of his grasp.

He didn't feel any pain, not yet anyway. He knew, somehow, that wasn't good.

Cadema dove out of the way, but the Jibetian turned toward her. The street was still empty. Why wasn't there anyone on the street? Why didn't anyone see this?

He tried to reach for the pistol, but he couldn't move his arms.

A second shot hit Cadema. She twitched once, and then didn't move, arms splayed, legs at an unnatural angle. The Jibetian pushed at her with his booted foot. She didn't respond.

Gel couldn't. His body wasn't obeying his commands. It had slumped down the wall until he was lying on his back, his neck shoved uncomfortably against the brick. Odd that the only discomfort he felt was in his neck. But he really couldn't feel much at all. And he seemed to have control of nothing more than his face. His breathing was short and uneven. He couldn't really take a deep breath at all. The pistol the Jibetian had used had scrambled Gel's systems. If he didn't get help soon, he would die here, on this street, just like Cadema.

Without the antidote. Without being able to tell his resistance cell there was no antidote.

All those deaths, on his shoulders.

The Jibetian leaned over him. That look of disgust was in his eyes again. He nudged Gel with his booted foot, and like Cadema, Gel didn't move.

"Trust me," the Jibetian said softly. "I've done you a favor."

"No," Gel whispered.

"Ah, but I did," the Jibetian said. "I gave you the only antidote to the plague."

And then he laughed. Gel closed his eyes, and the laugh followed him as he felt himself slip away into final blackness.

"No," Gul whispered.

"Ah, but I did," the Jin rasped. "I gave you the only antidote to the plague . . ."

And then he laughed. Gul closed his eyes, and the laugh followed him as he ran through icy, black corridors.

Chapter Six

THE BAJORAN MEDICAL SECTION of Terok Nor lacked everything the Cardassian medical section had. No quarantine fields, no biobeds, nothing except field medicine kits set up in corners, half a dozen of them, many of them without the most important equipment. Kellec Ton had been negotiating with Gul Dukat for more equipment when this plague hit, and then it became a minor consideration. Ton could barely keep up with the patients, finding them beds, making them comfortable. He couldn't worry about the lack of equipment.

He didn't have time.

The stench in this area was so foul he could almost touch it. The uncomfortable Cardassian heat, combined with the poor environmental systems, made the smell even worse. He tried to do an old-fashioned quarantine field: separate the sick from the healthy by placing the sick in a large room away from everything, but he had a hunch he was doing too little too late.

He bent over a teenage girl in the last stages of the disease. She lay on a cot he had found in one of the sleeping sections. She was moaning and clutching her stomach. All he could do was ease the pain, but even with the highest doses the pain slipped through. It was all he could do not to overdose these victims. He had to cling to some kind of hope that he would find a way to cure the disease before they all died.

His medical assistants, also people he'd had to fight for with Gul Dukat, had all been exposed. Kellec Ton had a hunch it was only a matter of time before they fell prey to this thing too. Before he did.

He had no idea what the incubation period was for this virus, but he knew it was longer than he had initially suspected. What research he had been able to do—mostly by word of mouth with the people who had fallen ill—revealed that they had felt fine for the last few weeks, and the illness had caught them by surprise. It was the secondary wave he was looking for, the people who had been infected by the earlier carriers. He had only spoken to a few—too many of them hadn't come in when they first noticed they weren't feeling well.

All of his training in the psychology of serious illness had prepared him for that, but he hadn't really expected it. If he knew something serious was happening on the station, and he felt poorly, he would have gone to get help immediately. Most people, however, entered a serious denial phase based on fear. *Yes,* the reasoning went, *my best friend has this disease, and I took care of her, but I'm strong. I never get sick. I am just out of sorts, making things up. I really can't be ill.*

By the time most of the second wave had come to him, they were so ill they couldn't talk. In fact, someone usually carried them in. All he could do now was watch them die.

He hated this.

He hated it as much as he hated the thick metal walls and the dim lighting, as much as he hated the way the Cardassians penned the Bajorans into these sections as if they were animals instead of people. Most of the Bajorans on Terok Nor already had weakened immune systems. They had been worked so hard that they were half dead on their feet. Their rations were meager, their hygiene poor. The close quarters made the spread of easily curable disease rampant. He knew that a virulent virus, like this one, would probably have found its way through the entire population already.

Now it was only a matter of time.

What he wanted was all that equipment in the Cardassian medical bay. The bright lights, the quarantine fields, the *chance* for his people to survive. Instead of working down here in the worst possible conditions, on the worst possible disease.

At least he had access to the station's computer system. Not all of it, of course, not even most of it, but Narat had made the medical files—the official medical files—available to him. What Kellec wanted was the unofficial files. He had heard that the Obsidian Order had done experiments on Bajorans, and it seemed likely to him that this was one of those experiments gone awry. Not in its treatment of Bajorans, but in the fact that it had somehow spread to the Cardassians.

Gul Dukat hadn't eased Kellec's mind on that, even though he had tried to. The fleeting look that had crossed his face when Kellec had accused the Cardassians of this acknowledged the possibility. If this were a Cardassian experiment to destroy the Bajorans that had gotten out of control, then Kellec needed to know. He was better at solving puzzles when he had all of the relevant information.

He pulled a blanket across the poor girl. The disease accented her natural beauty, flushed her thin cheeks. Her hands were permanently dirt-stained and callused, but with them covered, she looked as she should have looked at this age, a young girl who had just finished flirting with a young man, a girl with no cares at all.

Just by looking at her no one would be able to guess that she would probably be dead before the day was out.

The comm link that Narat had given him beeped. That was the third time in less than an hour. Kellec supposed he should answer it. He had been trying to ignore it. The Cardassians believed that Kellec should be using his considerable brain power to help them, not his own people.

He hit the comm link so hard that he hoped he'd shattered it. But no such luck. Instead Narat said, "Why haven't you been answering my hails?"

"Because I've been treating dying patients down here," he snapped. "I got fifteen new patients in the last hour. Thirteen in the hour before that. I've forgotten how many came in the hour before that. So my hands are a bit full. What do you want?"

"Gul Dukat wants you to come up here. He believes you can't get work done down below."

Kellec clenched a fist, and then glanced around the room. People everywhere, holding their stomachs, rolled in fetal positions. The moans were so soft and so prevalent that he had to focus on them to hear them. And the smell. . . .

Kellec shook his head. His assistants were doing what they could. A handful of others, brave volunteers, were sitting at bedsides, holding hands, comforting, even though they knew they were staring in the face of death.

"Work?" Kellec asked. "What kind of work?"

"Finding a solution to this thing. We need—"

"We need some understanding. My people are dying. Or has Gul Dukat forgotten how sympathetic he believes he is toward the Bajorans?"

Narat was silent for a moment. A long moment. Then he said, "I presented this wrong. I know you're working below. But you and I must solve this thing together, and that takes research, I'm afraid. I have patients too, and they're dying—"

"Are they?" Kellec said. "Well, they're dying in better rooms than my people are, and so far they're dying in fewer numbers. I don't see what I'll gain from working with you."

"Then you're not the man I thought you were," Narat said.

Kellec took a deep breath. He did know what he'd gain. He had lied. It was precisely what he had been hoping for a few minutes ago. Better equipment. More access. Hope.

His assistants couldn't do the research. Only he could do that. And he was essentially useless here.

"You're wasting time, man," Narat said. "And we both know how precious time is."

"Yes, we do," Kellec said. He sighed. It wasn't that he hated the Cardassians. He did, in theory, although Dukat had been right when he said that Kellec would save a life before he'd take one. Any life, even a Cardassian life. No. His hesitation was more complex than that. He feared that his work with Narat would help the Cardassians at the expense of his own people.

"Kellec," Narat said into his silence. "You are the better researcher."

How much that must have cost the proud Cardassian doctor. To admit that he was less talented at medicine—*at his job*—than a Bajoran. To admit he needed a Bajoran's help.

"I tell you what," Kellec said. "If Gul Dukat is so set on needing my services then he must pay for them."

"I don't have the ability to authorize payment," Narat said, just as Kellec expected him to. But Kellec didn't give him time to say anything more.

"I want to move all of my people, both the sick and those who were exposed, to your medical area. I don't want them held in place like prisoners, although I do want quarantine fields so that we can do proper work. I want them to die with dignity if they're going to die, Narat, and if we find a way to save them, I want to make sure my people get treatment as fast as your people do. I also want my assistants up there, at my side, helping with all the work."

"Done," Narat said. His answer was too fast. He apparently had been going to promise that anyway.

Kellec paused. He wanted more. Some other concession, something that would make him feel like he wasn't being pulled by the Cardassians.

"If Gul Dukat wants to keep his prisoners alive and working in uridium processing," Kellec said, "he needs to increase the food rations. And he can't keep up production at its current rate. We have too many sick down here, and if he pushes the remaining people, the illness will just get worse. I want a mandatory eight-hour sleep period for all Bajorans, and a decrease in production."

"You know I'm not authorized—"

"Yes," Kellec said. "I know you're not authorized. But Gul Dukat is. He's the one who makes the rules. Have him make this one. If he does, I'll come up."

"I'll do what I can," Narat said. "But you're wasting time."

Narat signed off.

Perhaps Kellec was wasting time, but he didn't think so. He needed to take care of his people first. It would only take Narat a few moments to get Dukat to agree to the concessions.

In the meantime, he stood and stretched. He needed some nourishment himself. He had some food and vitamin supplies in the tiny room the Cardassians had allotted him. It would do his people no good if he succumbed to this disease too. He had to do what he could to fend it off, and part of that was remembering to eat.

He slipped out of the medical area, and hurried down the corridor to his room. He suspected his room had once been some kind of storage closet. There was barely space for his bed. There was no replicator, no real bathroom—only a makeshift one with an old and malfunctioning sonic shower—and no porthole. Still, it was personal space, which was greatly lacking for Bajorans on Terok Nor.

He reached into his kit for a supplement, and saw instead that his personal link was blinking. He felt cold. He had brought the system up from Bajor, and so far the Cardassians hadn't tampered with it. Or if they had, they hadn't said anything. On it, he kept all his medical notes, and an open line to Bajor itself, since he theoretically was not a prisoner here.

His people on the surface were not to send him messages unless it was urgent. He had received several messages in the last few days about the plague, messages he had forwarded to Narat, partly as information, partly to prove he wasn't hiding anything from the Cardassians. Most of the messages requested that he return home. The plague had struck there, too, and was running through areas of Bajor the way it was running through Terok Nor.

He had sent carefully worded messages back, saying that he would remain on Terok Nor. Gul Dukat might see that as a twisted form of loyalty when, in fact, it was prudence. Kellec had not received word that the Cardassians on the surface had been affected. They had been here. That, plus the promise of using the Cardassian medical files, was enough to keep him here, for the moment. He had a better chance of finding the solution on Terok Nor.

With a shaking hand, he reached for the message button. It was a notification transmission. Once he responded, the person on the other end would be alerted, and they could have a conversation. He sat down and waited.

To his surprise, Katherine's face appeared on the small viewscreen. Her brown hair was tangled about her face, and her blue eyes were filled with compassion.

She looked very, very good.

And very far away.

"Ton," she said.

"Katherine."

"I was worried about you."

He smiled tiredly. "You always worry about me."

She nodded. "I'm hearing very bad things about your part of the quadrant."

"We're at war, Katherine," he said.

"No," she said. "I'm hearing more than that."

He frowned. She was asking about the plague. Had word reached the Federation then? He didn't dare ask her directly.

"Why are you calling me now, Katherine?"

"I'm surprised to find you still on Terok Nor. I would have thought they needed you on Bajor."

"They've been requesting my services on Bajor," he said. "But I'm too busy here. I haven't slept in two days, Katherine. I'm sorry, but I don't have time for small talk. Otherwise I'd ask about you and the *Enterprise* and all your various adventures. But I'm needed desperately elsewhere. Gul Dukat has demanded that I work in the Cardassian sickbay as well. It seems that my expertise is now considered to extend to Cardassians."

"It sounds serious," she said.

"It is." Then he paused and looked at her. They had always been attracted, and incompatible. He missed that soft, calm manner of hers. She had never been as intense as he was, but she was as driven, perhaps more so. She simply believed in conserving her energy for important things.

"Are you all right?" she asked softly.

"Tired," he said, "and distracted. There's too much I don't know, Katherine, and I have no time to learn it."

"Well," she said in that slow way of hers. "I wanted to tell you that I am no longer on the *Enterprise*. If you need to reach me, I'll be on Deep Space Five for a short time. I'll let you know when I go elsewhere. I haven't gotten my new duty assignment yet."

So that was her ostensible reason for this contact. Brilliant, Katherine. "Thank you," he said. "I always appreciate knowing what's happening with you."

She smiled. He loved that smile still, and missed it more than he wanted to admit. "Please," she said. "Take care of yourself."

And then she signed off. He sat in front of his system for a moment and forced himself to breathe. The Cardassians would find nothing amiss with that message, and yet he heard an entirely different conversation than the one they had in words. That was the benefit of having once been married; he and Katherine had a language all their own.

What she had really done was ask him about the plague. She had heard it was on Bajor, and was surprised he wasn't there treating it. He told her that it was bad, and that it wasn't just affecting Bajorans. The Cardassians had it too, which was why he was on Terok Nor. He also told her, as best he could in that limited conversation, that he had no solutions. Katherine was an excellent physician. She would know what that meant.

He sighed and ran a hand through his hair. That might be the last time he talked with her. Ever. If he got this thing.

But he couldn't think that way.

He didn't dare.

He stood. What he wouldn't give to have her here, now. She was the best researcher he knew, and she was up on all the current information. Her position at Starfleet gave her access to medical information from almost everywhere. He knew that the Federation had dealt with this sort of cross-species contamination, but he didn't remember where, and he didn't have the resources to find out. Katherine would.

She had one other asset that he couldn't discount. The most important one. She was one of the most creative physicians in the quadrant. She had discovered and neutralized all sorts of alien viruses, and she had a knack for discovering the right solution at the right time. If Katherine were here, she would look at that virus and the way it affected Cardassians versus the way it affected Bajorans, and she would know the detail he was missing. She would know, or she would do everything she could to find out.

Just as he was doing.

He sighed. Even if Narat wouldn't meet his terms, he would go to the Cardassian medical section. He had to. Discovering how to neutralize this virus was the only chance they had.

And maybe the only chance his people had.

Chapter Seven

DUKAT CONSTANTLY LOOKED at his skin. It was still gray. But he was rubbing it all the time. It had been crawling since the last time he had been in the medical area. He wasn't sick yet, but he had a hunch he was infected. He had a hunch they all were.

He didn't want to return to the medical area, but he had to. Narat hadn't reported since Kellec Ton had made his demands. Lower production. Eight-hour sleep schedules for Bajorans. Kellec's people were strong. They didn't need such precautions. Kellec Ton was taking advantage of Dukat, and Dukat was letting him.

It wouldn't last long. When this disease was cured he would make the Bajorans work double and triple shifts to make up for the lost production. He had to. He had quotas to fill. If he fell behind, he would lose his position here on Terok Nor. And that was the last thing he wanted.

The second-to-last thing. The last thing he wanted was to be the gul who watched an entire space station succumb to an incurable plague.

He stepped inside the medical area. It was jammed with patients. All the biobeds were full. Cardassians and Bajorans lay side by side, apparently not noticing each other. Bajoran and Cardassian medical workers examined the sick, carrying pads, studying readouts, administering pain medication.

The stench in the area was worse than before. Dukat put a hand over his mouth and nose. He couldn't help himself. The smell was so powerful, he doubted it would ever leave him. He would have to destroy his clothes.

If the odor was that strong, did that mean the quarantine fields weren't working? The crawling sensation in his skin grew worse.

He was a soldier. He had seen death countless times. He could handle this as well.

But he knew, deep down, that this was different. This was the kind of death every soldier feared. Impossible to resolve. Death by weakness, by illness, not in the course of battle, not for some important cause, but because something microscopic managed to defeat the body because the body wasn't strong enough to handle it.

Dukat made his way through the rows of moaning people to the office. He stopped at the door. Narat sat at one terminal, Kellec Ton at another. Above them, holographic images of the virus spun in slow circles. Computer readouts scrolled on each side, one readout in Cardassian, the other in Bajoran. The office was dark except for the light near the terminals themselves and whatever light was given off by the holographic image.

Dukat stared at it for a moment. Enlarged, the virus looked like an alien species, vibrant and alive. He didn't know much about biology—he didn't know the terminology for the prongs, or the fat center of the thing, or the ladder-like connectors on the sides. All he knew was that he would see the thing in his dreams. If he ever had time to sleep again.

"Are you finding anything?" he asked.

Both men jumped. Neither had heard him arrive. At least they were working hard. Narat turned to him. Kellec took another sample vial and placed it in the scope. He didn't bother to turn at all.

"Not enough," Narat said.

"We have found several things," Kellec said.

"We're just not finding out what we need quick enough," Narat said.

Kellec still hadn't turned. Dukat closed the door. "What things?"

"Well," Narat said, even though Dukat had directed the question at Kellec. "We have been able to confirm that this virus was created."

"Created?"

"By someone," Kellec said. "It doesn't occur in nature."

"We had suspected as much when we knew that it affected both Bajorans and Cardassians, but the virus's structure confirms it," Narat said. "See the—"

"I trust your opinion," Dukat said. "What does this mean?"

"Someone created it," Kellec snapped. "Someone targeted us intentionally, either both of our peoples or one of them."

Dukat suppressed a sigh. He had sent word to Central Command and to his contacts in the Obsidian Order. No one knew the cause of this virus, or if they did they weren't admitting it.

"If we could find who did this," Narat said, "we'd probably find a solution."

"But we don't have any time," Kellec said.

"I know," Dukat said. The casualties throughout the station were growing.

"No, you don't know," Kellec said.

Narat put a hand on Kellec's arm, but Kellec shook it away. He faced Dukat.

"This virus is extremely lethal." Kellec slid his chair back and pointed to the image above him. This time it showed small round blobs that appeared to be floating in something. "These are normal Bajoran cells. Now watch what happens when I introduce just one virus."

The virus was darker and flatter than the cells. It had a nonsymmetrical shape, accentuated by the precision of the cells themselves. It looked like a scout for an invading army.

Dukat stepped farther into the office, fascinated in spite of himself. The virus latched on to the nearest cell. Then the virus destroyed the cell and moved to another. If a cell happened to divide, the virus did too. The process was repeated cell by cell.

"The incubation period, at least in Bajorans, is fairly long for a virus of this type," Kellec said. "We don't know how it's introduced to the body, but we do know that once the virus has infiltrated the system, the disease progresses very rapidly."

Very rapidly. As Dukat watched, the virus destroyed the last remaining healthy cell.

He shuddered.

"I don't know if we can reverse the virus's path," Kellec said. "It completely destroys any cells it touches. But I suspect that we could stop it in the incubation phase—if we could only find it."

"This is the Bajoran version," Dukat said. "What about the Cardassian?"

"The virus seems to be the same, with slight differences; but it reacts the same way to Cardassian cells," Narat said. "It's as I told you before. Only the symptoms are different. But I am having no more luck than Kellec in discovering the way the virus is spread."

Kellec turned in his chair. His face seemed thinner than it had before, and he had deep shadows under his eyes. The disease was taking something from him as well, and he wasn't even sick.

"Actually," he said. "We're not being entirely accurate. You saw what happened in my sample. If I were to take the virus and touch you with it, either through fluid or saliva, you would get sick and die within the day. That is happening to some of our people. But they are not the ones who hold the secret. The ones who hold the secret are the ones who have incubated the disease for days or weeks. We do not know how many people are incubating it now. I'm testing my own blood to see if I am, but so far I have found nothing."

"We do know," Narat said, "that the virus itself can

be spread by touch and through bodily fluids, but not through the air. But it has moved into too many people to be spread simply that way, so something else is spreading it. We just don't know what."

Dukat tensed.

"We have been cautioning everyone, but I suspect it's too late. We must not allow anyone to leave Terok Nor, and no one should come here." Narat bowed his head. "We have to remain completely isolated until the disease has passed."

Dukat straightened his shoulders. He had stopped all departures from Terok Nor already, and he wasn't allowing most arrivals. But the ore shipments continued, and he had been planning to allow the ore ships that were docked, waiting for processed material, to leave when they reached their quotas. To fail at this would mean admitting to Central Command that Terok Nor was crippled.

But it *was* crippled—perhaps dying.

"You haven't done that already?" Kellec sounded shocked. "We explained how important quarantine was."

"I've done what was needed," Dukat said. He wasn't about to admit that he hadn't done a full quarantine on Terok Nor.

"Do more," Kellec snapped.

"You're out of line, Bajoran," Dukat said.

Kellec tilted his head. "What are you going to do to me? Kill me?"

Dukat froze, then forced himself to breathe, hoping Kellec hadn't seen the expression on his face. Kellec had hit something Dukat hadn't realized: If the surviving Bajorans believed they had nothing left to lose, if they believed they would die anyway, they might rebel in ways that the Cardassians couldn't stop, particularly if his people were ill. He would become the gul not just of a station that succumbed to a plague, but a station in which all the Cardassians were overthrown before the plague took everyone out.

"I wouldn't be so smug, Kellec," Dukat said. "You blame my people for this disease, but yours could just as easily be responsible. Your rebels are sometimes willing to die for what they believe in. They might think: If a few Bajorans die to rid the universe of the Cardassians, that is not such a great price."

"My people aren't the ones attempting genocide," Kellec said. "Yours are."

"If we were attempting genocide," Dukat said, "your people would all be dead by now. Don't you see that Cardassian rule is better for you than leaving you to your own devices?"

"I'm sure it is," Kellec said. "My people are so happy processing your precious uridium."

"Please," Narat said. "Please. Both our peoples are dying. Can't we stop recriminations for a few moments and just concentrate on saving lives?"

"It is not in Gul Dukat's nature to save lives," Kellec said.

"That's right," Dukat said sarcastically. "That's why you're on the station. Because I have not a thread of compassion in my system."

"Stop this!" Narat shouted. "Now!"

Both Dukat and Kellec turned to him. Dukat had never seen Narat so flustered. Not even when his medical section was filled with casualties all needing his attention did Narat look this distressed.

"We have to find a way to destroy this disease," Narat said, "or we will all die. Bajoran, Cardassian, it doesn't matter. The virus doesn't seem to care. And neither can we. We have to work together."

He stood. He was of the same height as Dukat, but his back was hunched after years of studying and researching, bending over computers and lab specimens. Narat had served as a field medic, but he had never been a soldier. His body lacked the rigid discipline that Dukat's had.

"I know you realize how serious this is," Narat said to Dukat, "but I don't think you realize the scale. People are dying on Bajor as well. It will only be a matter of time before this spreads to Cardassia Prime. *We* may have spread it there in our ore freighters. Kellec and I do not know, and we can't even hazard a guess. We don't know how long this thing incubates. We may have contracted this disease from Bajor months ago, and may have been spreading it to Cardassia Prime all this time. Or even farther. We don't know."

Dukat took a deep breath. He hadn't thought of that. "I can't do anything about that," he said. "Central Command knows we have sick Bajorans here, and that the disease has spread to our people. They know the extent of the disease on Bajor. They will have to work out the rest of it themselves."

"I'm not telling you this so that you do anything about Cardassia Prime," Narat said, "although if I knew of something you could do, I would tell you. No. I'm telling you this because Kellec and I need help. We have been treating sick patients and trying to find a cure for this disease. We are making progress, but it's not enough, and it's not fast enough. The more minds we have working on this, the better."

"You can link with doctors and researchers all over Cardassia," Dukat said.

"It's not enough," Kellec said. "We've contacted Bajor as well, and the physicians there are as tired and as stumped as we are."

Dukat sensed they already had a solution. They were simply preparing him to hear it. Which meant he wouldn't like it.

"I have heard rumors," Kellec said, "that the Federation dealt with a virulent cross-species disease recently, and found a way to contain it."

"You heard this—what, a few hours ago, when you received that wonderfully sweet message from your ex-wife?"

Kellec flushed. Good, Dukat thought. The doctor had gotten a bit too arrogant for Dukat's tastes. It was good to give him a bit of his own medicine.

"No." Kellec was obviously struggling to maintain his composure. "I knew of this before."

"So why didn't you ask her about it?"

"Because I thought someone might be listening in," Kellec snapped.

"But," Narat said quickly, "the contact did give us an idea."

So, Narat was going to present this idea. And he was going to present it as his own as well as Kellec's.

"I'm waiting," Dukat said.

"Kellec's ex-wife, Dr. Katherine Pulaski, is one of the Federation's best doctors. She is currently not assigned anywhere."

"If she's one of the best, why doesn't she have an assignment?"

"She will," Kellec said. "The Federation is arguing

within itself. There's too much demand for her services."

"So how does this apply to us?" Dukat asked.

"We'd like to bring her here. Have her work with us, and focus on the research itself," Narat said.

"No," Dukat said. "I will not have the Federation here."

"She wouldn't come as part of the Federation," Kellec said. "I could ask her to come for a family emergency."

"No," Dukat said again. "She's Federation. And I will not have them here." How many times did he have to repeat himself?

"Don't say no yet, Dukat," Narat said. "There's another, quite compelling, reason I think we should go with this plan."

Dukat crossed his arms. All he needed was the Federation to get its hooks into this place. They'd been looking for ways for years to discredit the Cardassians. This would be a first step. "What's your compelling reason?"

"She's human," Narat said.

Dukat shrugged.

"Chances are, she will not get this plague."

"So?" Dukat asked.

Narat put a hand on Dukat's arm. "Think of it. Right now, you have Kellec and me working on a cure for this disease. We can't keep up with both the research and caring for the patients. If one of us succumbs or, even worse, if both of us do, that's effectively signing a death warrant for you, Terok Nor, and all of Bajor."

Dukat stared at Narat's hand until Narat moved it.

"We'll send for someone from Cardassia Prime, then," Dukat said.

"But would they come?"

Narat's question hung between them for a moment. Dukat didn't have an answer. Or maybe he did and didn't want to face it. What would he do, if he were on Cardassia Prime and making decisions from there? He wouldn't see the death, wouldn't smell it. The lives here would be statistics, except for the handful of people he knew, and even then, he would have to evaluate their importance to Cardassia. Coldly.

He closed his eyes. In that situation, he would ask himself: Is it worth sending a needed doctor or medical researcher off Cardassia Prime on a mission that may or may not succeed? Or would he be better off letting everyone die and letting the plague die with them? Then, after some time had elapsed and someone had discovered a cure, sending in a cleaning crew and beginning all over again?

He knew the answer to that. He knew it. He would do the most efficient job he could, the one that would bring the best results. If Central Command saw what this disease did, they would do anything they could to keep it from coming to Cardassia Prime. They would help from the surface, but they would not send help. It would be too dangerous to send help.

Dukat sighed and opened his eyes. "All right," he said. "Send for the woman. But do it unofficially, as a family emergency, just as you suggested."

"Can she bring assistants?" Kellec asked.

Dukat glared at him. Kellec was never satisfied, always wanting more. Always wanting too much.

"Assistants would be a doctor's first request," Narat said. "It would be yet another guarantee."

Dukat was being manipulated and he knew it. But he couldn't see any way out of this. He couldn't see any way at all. At least, not a way he liked. Not a way that ended in success. This felt like one of his only chances.

"I want no more than five Federation people here, less if possible," he said.

"Good," Narat said.

"You may not say 'good' after a moment," Dukat said, "because I have conditions."

Kellec tilted his head back. Narat held his position, waiting, like the good Cardassian that he was.

"First," Dukat said, "they will have access only to our medical files. Second, they shall be restricted to the medical areas of Terok Nor only. Third——"

"That's not possible," Kellec said. "What if the illness spreads so fast that we can't get the patients here?"

"We'll deal with it then," Narat said.

"Third," Dukat said as if he hadn't been interrupted, "they shall have no contact with the outside while they're here."

"But what if they need information they didn't bring?" Kellec asked.

Dukat glared at him. "I will not negotiate these terms."

"We can deal with special requests on a case-by-case basis, I assume," Narat said, more to Kellec than Dukat. "Am I right?"

Dukat wasn't even willing to make that promise, although he knew it was probably sensible. "Fourth, if I suspect even one of them is spying for the Federation, none of them will leave here alive. Is that clear?"

"Very," Kellec said.

"If your ex-wife is willing to come here under those conditions, then we will be happy to have her," Dukat said. "But I do not want a Federation ship docking at Terok Nor. I do not want one in Cardassian space."

"Then how will she get here?" Kellec asked. "You've just quarantined the station, so no ships can come here."

Good question. The man was always thinking.

"I'll have one of the freighter pilots trapped here on Terok Nor take his ship to meet the Federation vessel at the border. I'll send a few of my men along to make sure nothing untoward happens."

"Make sure they're all pilots," Narat said softly.

Dukat felt himself go cold. Narat was right. There was no guarantee the pilot would live long enough to ferry their Federation passengers back to Terok Nor.

"Tell your ex-wife to get here as quickly as possible," Dukat said. "I'll handle the travel arrangements personally. And Kellec?"

"Yes?" Kellec said.

"Don't see this as a victory for the Bajoran people. I meant what I said about spies. Your Federation help had better be on their best behavior. I will give no second chances."

Kellec had the good sense to only nod.

Chapter Eight

FOR THE SECOND TIME in a few days, Katherine Pulaski was packing her bags. She was in her quarters on Deep Space Five. All of her possessions were scattered about. She had just unpacked, and hadn't had time to hang her favorite paintings or to place her few sculptures. Her hardcopy books stood on a single shelf, including the first edition of Sir Arthur Conan Doyle's Sherlock Holmes stories that Data had given her upon her departure. It was a sentimental gift, and it had surprised her coming from Data. Apparently that surprise had shown on her face because he had tilted his head in that slightly robotic way he had, and asked, "Is the giving of parting gifts not a human custom, especially when the recipient will be missed?"

"It is, Data," she had said, and then hugged him, to his surprise and (she had to admit) to her own.

She stared at that book for a moment, but it would only add weight. Better to keep it here until she returned.

If she returned.

She had only a few more items to add to her bag, and very little time in which to do it. Her assistants would be reporting here before they went to the docking area to reboard the *Enterprise.* How strange it would be to be a guest on the very starship she had just served on.

Her hands were shaking, but it was not from fear. It was a release of tension. Her meeting with Starfleet Medical had been dicey. Thank heavens the *Enterprise* was still in dry dock. She had needed Beverly Crusher's help.

Kellec's request had come in a few hours before. It was less than Starfleet had hoped for. They wanted to send in a large team to study the problem, perhaps work on Bajor. They wanted to use it so that they could gather more information on both the Bajorans and the Cardassians, as well as find a solution to this plague.

But some Cardassian official had anticipated this. The restrictions were severe. Pulaski wasn't sure she could do the work with only a handful of assistants. At first Starfleet wanted her to wait until they could get four specialists in plagues and alien diseases to go with her, but it would take days for the specialists to arrive from their various posts. She didn't have days. That was the one thing Kellec had made very clear.

He wasn't sure he would survive this. The Cardassian doctor who was looking over his shoulder as Kellec contacted Pulaski didn't look very confident either. The information she had gotten from them, purposely sketchy, was awful. They did give her the death rate on their space station, and it was climbing by the hour.

She played the message for Starfleet Medical. Then she asked that Beverly Crusher accompany her, as well as the three other ranking medical officers currently on Deep Space Five.

Starfleet Medical turned her down. This was a risky mission, they said. They didn't dare send that many valued officers.

Meaning they could sacrifice researchers but military medical staff was in short supply.

Meaning there was a good chance Pulaski and her team might not come back.

Starfleet Medical was going to try to negotiate with the Cardassians—after all, they reasoned, this was a medical emergency, and working together could benefit everyone—but Pulaski knew that wouldn't work. She had asked Crusher to come with her to argue for the high-ranking personnel, which hadn't worked. But Crusher had argued against negotiation, and on this Starfleet Medical had listened to their former director. They decided—and the Federation representatives agreed—to let Pulaski go in with lower-ranking assistants.

The next argument was about whether to bring in sophisticated equipment that would help send information back—not medical information, but information on the Cardassians and the Bajorans. Crusher had proved her worth here too, arguing that such equipment would jeopardize the lives of those being sent it.

"This is a mission of mercy," she had said. "We need to treat it like one. If Dr. Pulaski and her colleagues gain information on the Cardassians and Bajorans as a result, they can be debriefed when they return."

If they return. The last sticking point had been travel arrangements. They were going to use the Cardassians' plans to get them to Terok Nor, the space station that Kellec was on, but Pulaski had no idea how they would be able to leave. She was supposed to contact the Federation from Terok Nor when she was ready to go, but she had a hunch that sounded too easy. And what if she wanted to leave and they didn't want her to? They had to have a fail-safe for this, and so far no one had suggested one that seemed workable.

Pulaski finished the last of her packing. Amazing how she could bring her life down to two little suitcases—one a sophisticated medical kit with everything she hoped she would need. The other contained basics like clothing and Kellec's favorite—hot chocolate. He couldn't get it anymore on Bajor.

She closed the case just as someone hit the chime outside her door. "Come in," she said.

The door slid open and a woman entered. She was human—all of the team was, a precaution that Kellec had mentioned and Starfleet Medical had agreed with. She had blondish brown hair and compassionate eyes. She wore street clothes, just as she had been ordered to do. They were flowing garments of a gauze-like material, in a pale blue that became her fair skin.

"You must be Crystal Marvig," Pulaski said. "Welcome."

"Thank you," Marvig said. She glanced around the quarters, her gaze falling on the books. "I didn't know you collected real books."

"I don't," Pulaski said. "But each of these is personal to me, in its own way."

"I love books," Marvig said. "Particularly twentieth-century literature—you know the kind. The stuff that predicts the future."

Pulaski laughed. "I've seen it. It's amazing what they believed would happen."

"And how right they could be," Marvig said. She clasped her hands behind her back. The military posture didn't go with her relaxed attire.

"You've been briefed on this mission, I assume," Pulaski said.

"They told me it was a need-to-know."

Pulaski cursed under her breath. She had wanted her assistants to know what they were getting into. "And what did Starfleet Medical believe you need to know?"

"That this is a highly sensitive mission, and that it's quite dangerous."

"Brief and vague," Pulaski said. "How like them." She sighed. "Let's wait until Ensign Governo gets here, and then I'll brief you both."

"Edgar Governo? He's been assigned to this as well?" Marvig asked.

Pulaski nodded. "Do you know him?"

"We've been serving together here on Deep Space Five. He's never been on an away mission."

"Well, this is more complicated than an away mission," Pulaski said. "I trust they told you to pack lightly."

"And to keep suspicious items from my single piece of luggage, whatever that means."

Pulaski recited a list of items she believed could cause them problems on Terok Nor. Marvig shook her head at each item. As Pulaski was finishing, the door chime rang again.

"Come in," she said.

Ensign Governo entered. He was a thin young man with dark hair and intense eyes. He wore his regulation boots beneath black pants, and over a cotton T-shirt he wore a leather jacket. The effect was retro, and more stylish than Pulaski had expected. Seeing Starfleet personnel out of uniform was always a surprise.

She had met Governo just after her conference with Starfleet Medical. He was younger than she had would have thought from his record. He had an amazing gift for understanding alien physiology; it had gained him awards and accolades at medical school, and he had graduated at about the same time as Marvig, who was older.

Governo had a small bag slung over his shoulder. "I'm ready when you are, Doctor." Then, before she could respond, he saw Marvig standing near the books. "Crystal!"

"Edgar." She smiled. It was a warm smile, just the kind a patient needed to see. Pulaski was glad to see it too. Compassion and empathy were probably lacking at Terok Nor. "It looks like we're going on an adventure."

"Yes," Pulaski said, "you are."

"Only the three of us?"

"No. Alyssa Ogawa will join us on the *Enterprise*. She's one of the best nurses in the fleet, and I'm pleased to have her. She'll outrank both of you, and I want you to listen to her."

The two of them nodded.

"Were you briefed at all?" Pulaski asked Governo.

"I was told that this mission would be difficult and dangerous," he said, "and that if I had any qualms about working with infectious disease, I could back out now without a black mark on my record."

"That's more than I was offered," Marvig said.

"Well, I'm offering you more," Pulaski said. "I want you to know exactly what you're getting into."

She explained the situation to them, including the rules the Cardassians placed on their visit. She also explained the danger, the difficulties they would have on a station owned by a people who were not affiliated with the Federation, and the Federation's conflicting motives in sending them there.

"I do not want you to spy," Pulaski said. "You will be debriefed when you return. Remember all you can. I'm not even sure you should record anything in your personal logs—aside from the things you did that day, or medical notes. We have to be very cautious. *Very* cautious."

"Why are the Cardassians even allowing us to come?" Governo asked.

"They didn't say," Pulaski said, "and neither did Kellec. But I have a guess."

They waited, staring at her.

She took a deep breath. "I think they think this disease is so contagious none of them will be able to avoid it. I think they're gambling on it not affecting us, that we'll have a chance of curing it before everyone dies."

"Wow," Marvig said. "That's a dark view."

Pulaski nodded. "They wouldn't have sent for us otherwise. The Bajorans have no power over the Cardassians, and the Cardassians have repeatedly rebuffed Federation overtures in the past. I think this request smacks of desperation."

"I thought we were in negotiations with the Cardassians," Marvig said.

"We are," Pulaski said, "but they're not going well, and there are rumors they will fail. For whatever reason, the Cardassians do not trust the Federation, and we are representatives of the Federation. That's why we're going in an unofficial capacity, and that's what makes this mission even more dangerous."

"How's that?" Governo asked.

"If we run into trouble," Pulaski said, "we're on our own. The *Enterprise* will be just outside of Cardassian space, but she cannot enter it without Cardassian permission, permission they did not give in this emergency to get us to Terok Nor. I can't imagine that they would give it to get us out."

Marvig's face grew pale. "But what if we need to escape?"

"We have to be creative," Pulaski said. She stared at both of them. They were so young. Alyssa Ogawa was young too, but more experienced. A starship did that for its crew. "But we have to understand the risks. The greatest risk for all of us here is that we will not come out alive."

"What do you think the chances are of that?" Governo asked.

"High," Pulaski said. "I won't lie to you about that. I think at best we have a fifty-fifty chance of survival."

"I don't understand," Marvig said. "If we're in negotiations with the Cardassians, then why would they kill us?"

"We don't know what this disease is," Pulaski said.

"And we've never seen the inside of one of their ore-processing stations. If one of us inadvertently comes across information that the Cardassians see as sensitive, we could all be punished for it."

They were staring at her as if it were her fault the mission was dangerous. Perhaps it was. Perhaps this wouldn't be happening at all if it weren't for her relationship with Kellec. But that didn't matter. What mattered were all those lives being lost.

"You may back out now," she said, "as long as you keep what I've told you confidential."

Governo seemed to be considering what she was saying, but Marvig jutted out her chin.

"I joined Starfleet so that I could do more than practice general medicine in some human colony. I joined it for the risks," she said. "It wouldn't do my oath any good to back out now, just when things get really difficult."

Governo looked at her as if he were surprised at what she said. "You're right." He nodded, a crisp, military move. "I'm a healer first."

"All right," Pulaski said. "Let's hope that all my warnings were merely an overreaction to the Cardassians' conditions."

But in her heart, she knew they weren't. And she wondered, as she gathered up her things, whether she had misrepresented the odds to the two before her.

If anything, she had overestimated their chances of survival. If all the stories Kellec had told her were to be believed, she would be surprised if they got off the station at all.

Chapter Nine

KIRA NERYS STOOD in the heat, sweat plastering her filthy shirt to her back, her feet swollen inside her boots. A blister rubbed against the inside of her heel. These boots were too small, even without the swelling. She had taken them—a gift really—from a dying friend. Amazing, that all they had to give each other anymore were items of clothing, bits of food, things that they had once taken for granted.

Her earring tinkled in the breeze. She had been wishing for a breeze not too long ago, but it only seemed to make things hotter. She was outside a rebel cell, and it wasn't even her cell. That's why they kept her here, waiting, until they made some decision about her.

She stared at the makeshift tents. Whoever ran this cell didn't plan things real well. They were in a hidden valley, one that was not on the maps but was pretty well known in this part of Bajor. The tents were pitched near a small creek, bone dry in the summer heat. If she had been in charge of this cell, she would have had them pitch their tents on the mountainside, where scraggly trees and boulders would have provided cover. As it was, if the Cardassians found this valley now, they would have found the cell.

Not that she was in any position to give advice.

She was here chasing rumors. She had heard of serious illness to the south, and had actually seen some of the bodies in a message sent to her by Shakaar. The problem was that neither she nor Shakaar had seen them die. There was talk of a disease, there was talk of a plague, but—so far—no one in her part of Bajor had seen evidence of it.

Not that she doubted that it existed.

She was told that Javi's cell knew more about it, and she had set up a meeting with one of her contacts. It had brought her here, a long trip through areas that weren't friendly to people like her. She was known as a member of the resistance, and even before last year's escapade on Terok Nor the Cardassians had been watching for her. They didn't know she had been to Terok Nor—the station's constable, Odo, had seen to that—but they suspected her. They suspected her of everything, but could never catch her.

Not for want of trying.

She sighed and ran a hand through her short hair. She could feel the sweat at the roots. She wished Javi would hurry. She didn't like waiting in this heat.

Finally, a woman slipped out of one of the tents. She wore a ripped dark dress, stained with sweat and dirt. The poverty here—even among the resistance— broke Kira's heart.

"Javi will see you now," the woman said.

Kira wasn't sure she wanted to go inside the tent. It had to be even hotter in there. But she climbed up the small incline to the creekside where the tent was, and slipped inside.

She had been right. It was hotter here. The heat felt old and oppressive, as if it had been accumulating for days instead of hours. Javi sat cross-legged near his portable computer system—the heart and soul of each resistance cell, Shakaar had once called those things. Javi was thinner than he had been the last time Kira saw him. His skin had the look of malnutrition, but his eyes were still bright.

Near him sat Corda, his second in command. She was taller than Kira and too thin as well. But on her it looked tough, as if the dry air and the heat and the lack of food had hardened her skin and made her more resilient.

"Sorry to keep you waiting, Nerys." Javi spoke slowly, as he always had. He had been part of Shakaar's cell for a brief time, and he had always irritated Kira with his cautious consideration of each decision. Apparently he had annoyed Shakaar too, because one day Kira heard that Javi had left with some of his own people to form a new cell. They were on speaking terms, though, and still had the same goals, unlike some of the resistance cells Kira had come into contact with. There were some that frightened even her, with their talk of noble suicide and total destruction.

"If I had known what it was like in here, Javi," Kira said, "I would have insisted you keep me waiting longer."

Javi shrugged. "You get used to the heat."

"Maybe you can get used to this heat. I certainly couldn't."

"Don't start, Kira," Corda said. "You're not here to criticize us."

"And it's a good thing, too, because I think your campsite is too exposed—you're putting your entire cell in jeopardy."

"But you're not here to tell us that," Corda said sarcastically.

"No," Kira said, "I'm not. I'm here because I'm supposed to confirm some rumors."

"About the plague," Javi said.

Kira went cold despite the heat. "They're calling it a plague now?"

"Hundreds dead, Nerys." Javi's voice was solemn. "Everyone who comes in contact with this thing gets ill."

"Everyone?" Kira asked.

"In time," Corda said.

"How have you gotten your information?"

"Do you mean were we exposed?" Corda asked. "No. We've been getting it the same as you have, in messages sent through sanitary computers."

Kira had never liked Corda. And the heat wasn't improving Kira's mood. "I'm not here to talk to you."

"You get to talk to me whether you like it or not," Corda said. "I'm the one who has been following this thing and reporting to Javi."

Kira glared at her for a moment. Corda glared back, not at all intimidated.

"This isn't helping us," Javi said. "We need to work together. Nerys has come to us for information, the kind, I believe, that isn't easily sent."

"But Corda just said that you haven't heard anything that we haven't heard," Kira said.

"I did not," Corda said. "We've gotten that, and we've gotten reports from other sources."

"Others?"

"Non-Bajorans. Some of the relief teams not tied to the Federation. They seem to be unaffected."

The relief teams were from charitable organizations that went to planets they considered not as developed to help with basics: food, medicine, clothing. Sometimes Kira appreciated their presence, sometimes she resented them more than she could say. What she wanted was Federation intervention, to stop this occupation by the Cardassians. But the Federation had rules and regulations, things she had never bothered to understand, and those rules and regulations didn't seem to apply to Bajor, although some people were telling her to be cautious with her tongue, that some day the Federation might come through.

She would believe that when she saw Bajorans move around unfettered on their own planet.

"What are they doing to stop this thing?" Kira asked.

"What they can," Corda said.

"Most of them are volunteers, Nerys, with no more medical training than we have." Javi sounded tired. Kira wondered how much power he had ceded in this cell to Corda, and how long it would be before she took the group too far. "They provide comfort where they can, but they can't do much."

"They are sure it's a disease, then?" Kira asked. "Shakaar wasn't. He thought maybe it was a Cardassian trick to get us focused in the wrong direction."

"It's a disease, all right," Javi said. "But it might also be a Cardassian trick."

Kira frowned. "What do you mean?"

"The disease is too virulent." Javi's words hung between them.

Kira's chill grew deeper. She wiped sweat off her forehead. "Not even the Cardassians would do something this monstrous," she said.

"Do you actually believe that?" Corda asked.

Kira wasn't sure. "If we're talking about a disease that infects everyone who comes in contact with it—"

"We are," Corda said.

"—then we're talking genocide." Kira swallowed. "The Cardassians have always made it plain that they see us as a lesser species, as people who 'benefit' from their rule, as slaves to work in their various mines and processing plants. But not as creatures to be wiped out of existence."

"They've always wanted Bajor," Corda said.

"Yes—but with its Bajoran population." Kira wiped the sweat off her face.

"Get her something to drink," Javi said to Corda.

"But—"

"Now," Javi said.

Corda sighed and got up, sliding past Kira.

"I'm sorry, Nerys," Javi said. "I know you don't much like Corda. But you must listen to her. She has run this cell, for the most part, since last fall."

Kira glanced over her shoulder. Corda was out of the tent. "I'm just worried, Javi," Kira said. "She didn't always understand the complexities of the Occupation."

Javi smiled. "Once I could have said that about you."

Kira looked at him. "Why is she running everything, Javi? What's going on?"

"The Cardassians had me for a while, Nerys. We're just beginning to bring me back to health. The tents are here not because Corda thinks it's a good spot, but because my body can hardly tolerate thin air at the higher elevations. Even this valley is difficult for me. We should really move on, now that the creek is dry, but the cell has opted to stay with me. I've tried to order them to leave, but they won't."

Kira threaded her hands together.

"Corda loves me," he said.

"And is making the wrong decisions for the cell because of it," Kira said.

Javi nodded. "We agree on that. But they're not life-threatening. Not yet, anyway. And I'm nearly mobile—I think we can get out of here soon. But do me a favor, Nerys. Listen to her. And don't fight her. This Cardassian threat is too great for us to be fighting amongst ourselves."

Kira let out the breath she hadn't realized she had been holding. Javi was right, of course, and she knew it. But she had disliked Corda for a very long time. It was hard to set aside that kind of antipathy, even now.

"All right," Kira said.

"Good." Javi placed his hands on the ground behind him and rested his weight on them. "I hope she brings me something as well. You're giving me an appetite again, Nerys. That's a good thing."

Kira laughed. "I've been accused of worse, I guess."

"What's he accusing you of?" Corda asked as she came in. She was carrying a tray with three mugs. She handed one to Kira. It was moba fruit juice, and somehow they had found a way to keep it cool in all this heat.

Kira took a sip, and relished the bittersweet coldness. Corda handed Javi his mug, and he sat forward, taking it in both hands as if it weighed too much for him. Kira wondered if his prediction was wrong, if he wasn't getting better at all.

"He's been yelling at me to listen to you," Kira said. "He says you've changed."

Corda glanced at Javi as if he had betrayed a confidence. He was looking at the mug he was drinking from and didn't seem to notice.

"Whether I've changed or not shouldn't matter," Corda said. "What does matter is what's happening. You don't believe the Cardassians can commit genocide. I do."

"I didn't say that," Kira said. "I said it's not in their best interest to kill us all."

Corda sat down, cradling her own mug in one hand. "But what if it is now? What if they no longer need us for all those jobs Cardassians refuse to do? What if they've finally found a way to automate the most dangerous tasks?"

Kira stared at her. It was possible. It was even probable.

"Now tell her the rest," Javi said.

Corda set her mug down. "We don't know for certain."

"Tell her," Javi said. "If you're going to do this right, tell her all you know. In every case."

Maybe Corda hadn't changed after all. Maybe Javi only believed she had. Maybe he had no other choice. Kira waited for whatever "the rest" was.

"We've heard," Corda said, "through less reputable sources, that Cardassians are dying of this also."

"That's not possible," Kira said. "They've always lorded their superior physiology over us, saying they're not vulnerable to Bajoran diseases. How could that change?"

"Do you believe all Cardassian lies?" Corda asked.

"That one I do," Kira said. "I've seen Bajorans die of horrible diseases, and never once have I seen a Cardassian get sick like that."

"Maybe they don't allow their people to get sick."

"And maybe it's the truth," Kira said. "If they got sick, we would have seen it. I've been in places where I know I would have seen it." She set her mug down as well, although she was reluctant to give up the last of the juice. "Maybe you're the one who is believing the lie. Maybe the Cardassians are the ones spreading the rumors that Cardassians are getting sick. That would make this illness look like an innocent virus instead of something the Obsidian Order dreamed up."

Javi smiled slightly. He was still the only one drinking. "See why we needed to hear from Kira?" he asked Corda. "Neither of us thought of that."

Corda's lips thinned. "We can't operate on supposition."

"I agree," Kira said.

"What we have heard is that a few Cardassians here have gotten ill, but they've been spirited away so fast that no one can confirm that it's the same disease. A few of the rumors say it's not. The Cardassians turn green and their scales flake off—or so they say. And Bajoran victims look even healthier than they did before they got sick, so maybe it's not related at all."

"But we don't know," Kira said.

"That's right," Corda said. "We don't know. And I have no idea how we could find out."

"Where were the Cardassians taken ill?" Kira asked.

"In the same regions where the Bajorans were sick," Corda said. "And a Ferengi said that he saw some green Cardassians on Terok Nor."

"Ferengi can't be trusted," Kira said. "They can be paid to give false information."

Corda nodded. "The problem is that, if my sources on Bajor are right, the sick Cardassians here have already been sent away."

"To Cardassia Prime?"

"I don't think so. But it doesn't matter. We have no idea where they've gone."

Kira frowned. "Just before I came here, I'd heard that Gul Dukat just gave an order that no outside ships were to arrive on or leave Terok Nor."

Corda's gaze met hers. Javi set down his mug. "Now we're getting somewhere."

"I didn't think much of it, until you mentioned the station."

"Dukat wouldn't care about his Bajoran prisoners," Corda said. "But he would care if Cardassians were getting ill."

"And even if he didn't, Central Command would order him to shut down operations if the Cardassians had a disease that spreads the way you described."

They stared at each other.

"What if it's a different disease?" Corda asked.

"What if it's not?" Javi asked.

"It doesn't matter," Kira said. "I'd been thinking of going to Terok Nor anyway."

"What? Nerys, what are you talking about?"

She turned to him and took his hand. It was cold from the mug, but the skin was dry and his bones felt thin beneath her fingers. He had lied to her. She had seen starvation victims before—the ones who survived but were never really healthy again. He wouldn't live long, and it wouldn't take a designer virus to kill him. A simple cold would do it.

"I've been to Terok Nor before, Javi," she said. "Just last year, I was there getting information for the resistance. It's dangerous, but it's possible to get around."

"Why would you go?"

"I was planning to go for a completely different reason," she said. "If the rumors of the disease among the Bajorans proved to be true, and now after talking with you I believe they are, I was going to Terok Nor to bring Dr. Kellec Ton home."

"What's Ton doing there?" Corda asked.

Kira glanced at her. She hadn't expected Corda to be familiar with Kellec Ton.

"Apparently, Gul Dukat sent for him a month ago. Dukat claimed his precious workers needed better health care, which I think is unlikely. Dukat has never cared for anyone. His production must have been down or something."

"Or perhaps this disease started on Terok Nor," Javi said, "and that's why he sent for Kellec."

"Maybe," Kira said. "But it didn't sound like that. I talked to Kellec before he went. He was going to see what he could do to further the resistance on Terok Nor. He was also going to use his free time to find weaknesses in the station, maybe a way for the resistance to get the Bajoran workers out of there."

"We don't have the ships for that," Corda said.

Kira shook her head. "You need to choose someone else to lead this cell after you, Javi."

"I don't appreciate all your insults, Kira," Corda said.

"I shouldn't have to tell you about the benefits of a quick and dirty surprise operation. We may not have big, powerful ships like the Cardassians, but we can slip in and out of any place, and with the right plan, we could get workers off Terok Nor."

Corda's smile was cruel. "Just don't pick Kira to relieve me, Javi," she said. "Kira has no idea about the realities of war."

"You don't know—"

"Ladies!" Javi said tiredly. "We fight Cardassians, not each other." He ran that thin hand along the side of his face, tugging at his earring. "Maybe that wouldn't be a bad mission, Nerys. Going to Terok Nor. You could find out if the Cardassians were ill, and if they were you could report back. But bring Kellec home."

"If he wants to come."

Javi nodded. "One more thing. I've been studying the information we've received. It's only a matter of time before everyone on Bajor gets ill if this is as bad as it seems. And so far, whoever has gotten ill has died."

Even in the heat, Kira couldn't suppress a shiver.

Chapter Ten

NOG WAS SITTING on the bar, his feet dangling over the edge. He was kicking the front with one heel, then the other, with no apparent rhythm at all. Quark didn't know what was worse, the boy's idleness, his disregard for the bar's rules, or the constant *bang, bang, bang* echoing in his ears.

"Do something useful," Quark said, shoving Nog as he passed. "And get off my bar."

"There's nothing useful to do, uncle," Nog said.

"There's always something useful." Quark picked up a dirty glass off one of the empty tables. Three groups of Cardassians sat at various tables, but they certainly didn't look as if they were celebrating. They were at least drinking—to excess, always a problem with Cardassians. Not that Quark could blame them. If there was really a disease going around that was going to make him turn green (which was only one

89

step down from that hideous Cardassian gray), he'd probably start drinking too.

Or leave. Sneak off. Find somewhere else where the threat of death wasn't hanging over everything. He might do that anyway. He'd hardly had any customers in the last few days.

"But *what*, uncle?" Nog asked, still on the bar.

"For one thing," Quark said, "you can get off my bar. Then you can polish it from top to bottom with an earbrush."

"You're not serious."

"I've never been more serious," Quark said. "And remember, you'll do that every time you sit on my bar."

"You could have told him that sitting on the bar wasn't allowed, brother." Rom had apparently come out of their quarters. He wore a hat the Volian dressmaker had made him. It was made of some stretchy black material and molded itself to Rom's skull. It made his head look smaller, but at least it hid his ears.

"I would have thought sitting on the bar would be an obvious mistake, wouldn't you?" Quark asked.

"Actually, no," Rom said. "Rules are easier to follow if they're clear."

"Like not spilling things on the customers?"

"Are you ever going to forget that?" Rom asked.

"Not as long as you wear that silly hat." Quark brought the glass around back and set it beside Nog. "And wash this too, while you're at it."

Nog jumped off the bar, picked up the glass and started for their quarters.

"I want that bar shiny within the hour!" Quark called after him.

Nog didn't respond. He disappeared into the darkness as if he hadn't heard.

"I mean it, Rom," Quark said. "I want that bar cleaned in the next hour—"

"I'll do it," Rom said.

"—by Nog. He has to learn too." Quark sighed and surveyed the bar. He hated this quiet. The Cardassians were panicked and Gul Dukat had ordered that no more ships of any type could dock on Terok Nor. So not only were the Cardassians dwindling, thanks to disease and general fear, but the others who came through here, the suppliers, traders, and shadier types weren't appearing either. Quark's supply of Saurian brandy was getting low, and so were some of his more popular but hard-to-find items.

Rom scratched the top of his head. "Brother, do I have to wear this hat? It itches."

"Yes, you have to wear the hat," Quark snapped. Then he lowered his voice. "I can't have you serving customers with that blister on your ear."

Rom's hand went involuntarily to his right ear and Quark turned away in disgust. Nothing, ever, would get the memory of that out of his brain. Rom said it didn't hurt, but it was the ugliest thing Quark had ever seen. It served Rom right for the mistakes he had made earlier—and for not telling Quark that he was allergic to Jibetian beer.

Who knew what that horrible mixture of fluids had done to Rom's ears, anyway? The ears of Ferengi were their most sensitive spot. If an allergic reaction was going to start, it would start there. And Rom's allergy to Jibetian beer was bad enough, apparently, to have put him in sickbay on a freighter when he was a young man. Of course, Quark had been long gone by then and hadn't known about it. And Rom, typically, hadn't bothered to tell him, even when he knew he'd be working around the stuff.

"There aren't that many customers, brother," Rom said. "Perhaps it would be better if you waited on them yourself."

"You're right," Quark said. "Perhaps it would be better. Then I wouldn't have to pay you."

"But brother, how will Nog and I live?"

"Good question," Quark said. "And the answer is not very well if you refuse to do the work you're assigned. Now, go see if those tables need refills."

Rom tugged the hat. Quark could see the blister as an added lump on Rom's ear. Quark grimaced in distaste. How the Volian had managed to make a hat while looking at that ear was beyond Quark. And of course, Quark had had to pay for it. Rom didn't have any latinum yet; Quark was keeping track of all of these expenses in his ledger, but he had no idea how expensive the whole proposition was going to be. Rom had arrived—with Nog—and then the bar's business had dropped off. Who knew how much an eleven-year-old would eat? And constantly. It was as if he was going to grow as tall as a Cardassian. Or more likely, as if Rom hadn't fed him well before.

Rom reached the first table. Three Cardassians sat there, bent over their glasses as if their posture would protect them from the virus floating around the station. One of the Cardassians shook his head as Rom spoke to him. Rom smiled and bobbed a little, then backed away.

He stopped at the second table. There the Cardassian, one of the pilots who had poured liquor on Rom, said in a loud voice, "If you're trying to protect your skull from getting drenched, you'd better make sure that hat is waterproof."

"No, actually," Rom said. "I'm allergic to Jibetian beer and—"

"Rom!" Quark shouted.

"—I break out—"

"Rom!"

"—so I'm wearing this hat—"

"Rom!"

Rom looked up. "Brother, I—"

"One more word," Quark said, "and I will fire you."

Rom put a hand to his mouth. The Cardassian laughed. Rom made his way through the tables and leaned across the bar.

"I'm sorry, brother," he whispered. "But if I can't talk, how can I take orders?"

"One more word about the ear," Quark said slowly, as if he were speaking to a child. "Make up a story about the stupid hat. A story that doesn't involve pus."

"Sorry, brother," Rom said.

Nog came out of the quarters, clutching an earbrush in his left hand. Quark's earbrush. His best earbrush, the one with the real scagsteeth bristles.

"Nice try," Quark said, "but you use your own brush."

"He doesn't have one, brother."

"Then he can use yours," Quark said.

"He does anyway."

That was it. That was all it took. Quark's stomach actually somersaulted.

"Or I did," Nog said, "until Dad got that—"

"Enough!" Quark shouted. "Enough! No one is ever going to mention that again. Do you hear me? No one!"

All of the Cardassians stared at him as if he had gone crazy. The second group, the one that included the pilot that had been harassing Rom, seemed a bit bleary-eyed, and Quark realized they were drunker than he had initially thought they were. Getting them out of the bar would be difficult. Not that it mattered. He hardly had anyone in the bar as it was.

"I heard you, brother," Rom said.

That brought Quark back to himself. He turned toward Nog. "You, young man, you put my earbrush back and never touch it again. I don't share earbrushes with anyone, and I don't let just anyone touch them." Then he glared at Rom. "How could you? Not buying your own son an earbrush."

"He had one," Rom said. "He forgot it when we left Ferenginar, and I—"

"Didn't have enough latinum to buy him a new one, I know," Quark said. "Believe me, I know."

He shook his head. How did it always end up that *he* was the one who paid for everything? He sighed.

"Get yourself an earbrush, Nog, but for now, use your Dad's." Then Quark thought of that blister, and all the germs it carried. "Never mind. Don't after all. Get a cleaning cloth. But I still want the bar spit-polished. You understand?"

"You want me to spit on it?" Nog asked.

"No," Quark said. "It's a military term. I just want it so polished that it shines. Is that clear?"

Nog nodded. Why did everything become an impossible task with these two? Running the bar was suddenly three times harder.

The first group of Cardassians got up and left their tables, mumbling something about sleep. The second group was still huddled over their drinks. He could barely see the third group, but they seemed to be deep in conversation.

Customers leaving and none entering. Things couldn't get any worse.

Quark took a padd. He would inventory his alcohol one last time, and hope it lasted—of course, with this drop in business, it would last easily. He glanced at Rom.

"Just go away," he said.

"But brother, I haven't asked the other table if they wanted more to drink."

"Ask them, and then go away."

"Where are the cleaning cloths, uncle?" Nog asked.

Five times more work, Quark thought. At least.

Rom walked over to the last table. The drunken Cardassians at the second table cat-called him in soft tones. Quark didn't pay attention to what they were saying. He told Nog where the cloths were and was about to get back to his inventory when a Cardassian at the third table stood up.

He was green, like so many others had been in the last few days. Quark knew now that that was the beginning of the disease. He had been denying service to anyone who was green, but apparently the Cardassian had changed shades while he was in here.

The Cardassian raised a hand, looked at Rom, and toppled over backwards. His companions didn't seem to notice. Neither did the drunks at the next table.

Quark walked over. The Cardassian was on his back, moaning, a hand on his stomach. The other three at his table had passed out but they, at least, were a normal gray.

"Brother," Rom said. "We need to call for help."

"Oh no we don't," Quark said.

"But, he's—"

Quark put a hand over Rom's mouth. "I'm going to ban you from ever speaking in this place again."

"Bashender?" One of the Cardassians at the other table said. "You got any blood wine?"

"Yes," Quark said, even though what he had probably wasn't any good. He just didn't want the Cardassian looking at him.

"Get me shome," the Cardassian said.

"Nog!" Quark shouted. "Blood wine?"

"What?" Nog asked.

"Blood—oh, never mind." Quark turned to Rom and said very softly, "Stay right here, and cover his face."

"With what?" Rom asked, but by then Quark was already gone. He got the blood wine, and brought it back to the drunks.

"You know," he said to them, "you gentlemen look like you could use a free hour in a holosuite. Why don't you come with me?"

"Free?" Rom asked. "Brother, have you lost your mind?"

"What did I say to you about talking?" Quark snapped. He helped the Cardassians up, and guided them away from the sick Cardassian. He was careful to keep their backs to him, by talking to them the whole way, expounding the virtues of the various programs, hoping that Nog wasn't listening too closely to some of the programs.

He got them up the stairs and into one of the suites, the door closed behind them. Then he came back down the stairs.

The Cardassian's companions had well and truthfully passed out.

"What should we do?" Rom asked.

"Take his feet," Quark said.

"We're carrying him to the medical section?"

"Are you nuts?" Quark asked. "That's what medical people do."

"Then why aren't you calling them?"

"Why are you still talking?" Quark asked. "Pick up his feet."

Rom walked to the Cardassian's booted feet. "Can we get this disease?"

"If anyone can, you can," Quark mumbled.

"What?" Rom asked.

"No, we can't," Quark said.

"How do you know?"

"Because we would have had it by now."

"They don't have it," Rom said, looking at the three passed out at the table.

"Ferengi don't get Cardassian diseases," Quark said, although he had no idea if that was true.

"Oh," Rom said. "Are you sure?"

"Positive."

"All right, then," Rom said, and crouched. He grabbed the Cardassian's feet and lifted them.

"Nog," Quark said. "Keep a lookout. Let me know if you see any Cardassians or Odo."

"Odo?" Nog asked.

"The obnoxious shape-shifter who has been harassing me"—then Quark realized that Odo hadn't been in the bar in almost a week. "Never mind. Just let me know if you see anyone."

"All right," Nog said, and bent over the bar, continuing his polishing.

"At the door, Nog," Quark said. "Go to the door. Like a lookout."

"Oh," Nog said. "You didn't say that."

"What do I have to do? Put it in writing?"

"That might help," Rom said.

"Shut up."

Nog scrambled to the door. He stood there like a small sentry, looking just like Rom had at that age. Sincere, honest, clueless. Quark sighed. He hoped Nog understood what he was looking for.

"Brother . . ." Rom said, still holding the Cardassian's feet.

Quark nodded. He picked up the Cardassian by the armpits, and nearly staggered under the weight. Who knew that Cardassians were so heavy? Or that they smelled like this? Up close, the Cardassian's green skin looked even more noxious. His scales were flaking. Quark's stomach, already queasy thanks to Rom's ear blister, threatened to revolt.

"I don't know how much longer my back can take this, brother," Rom said.

Quark didn't know how much longer his stomach could take it either. "All right," he said, "here goes."

He stumbled backward, kicking a chair as he went. The Cardassian's butt dragged on the ground, his uniform leaving a polished streak mark on the dirty floor.

"Everything I do creates more work," Quark mumbled.

"What?" Rom said.

"Nothing. Just lift him higher."

"I can't, brother."

"You could if you weren't holding his feet."

"What do you suggest?" Rom asked. "His knees?"

They were halfway to the door. Quark wanted this guy out of the bar as quickly as possible. If he made Rom switch positions, quickly might not happen.

"No," Quark said. "Let's just keep going."

At that moment he backed into another table. Pain ran along his spine and he bit back a curse.

"Are you all right, brother?" Rom asked.

"Fine," Quark said, and moved around the table. Why did he have so much furniture in here in the first place? What had he been thinking?

The strain on his arm muscles was almost too much. He felt sweat run down the side of his face, get caught on his lobe, and work its way into his ear. It was his own fault for thinking the day couldn't get any worse.

He glanced over his shoulder. Nog was still at the door, looking out into the Promenade. Apparently he didn't see anything, or he would have said so. Right?

"Nog," Quark whispered. "Is it clear?"

"What?"

"The Promenade. Is there anyone there?"

Nog took a step farther out, which did nothing to bolster Quark's confidence. Then he turned back to Quark. "Yes."

Quark nodded at Rom. "This is the last leg," Quark said.

"I hope so," Rom said. "Is it my imagination or is he beginning to smell worse?"

It wasn't Rom's imagination. The Cardassian was beginning to smell like a Klingon meal made by a bad cook. Quark moved as fast as he could. He was still looking over his shoulder as he went through the doors. It wasn't that he didn't trust Nog. Or maybe it was.

The Promenade was mostly empty. The doors to the restaurants and stores were open, but there were no clients. The Volian sat in the window of his tailor's shop, working on an outfit, but he didn't appear to be looking up. Quark thought he saw something shimmer near the door to the bar, but when he focused on it, he saw nothing at all.

"Clear," he whispered.

"What?" Rom asked.

"Is that blister making you deaf?" Quark snapped.

"I hope not." Rom brought a hand to his ear, and the Cardassian tipped sideways. The Cardassian's foot bounced loudly on the floor. Quark nearly collapsed under his weight.

"Will you do your job?" Quark snapped. "Pick up the foot. Pick it up."

"Where are we going with him?"

"Just behind that post," Quark said, nodding in the opposite direction from the Volian's store. They were getting close to the second floor balcony, but he didn't see anyone there either. And he would have to take the risk.

They also couldn't leave a polished streak running from the Cardassian to the interior of the bar.

"Wait!" Quark said. "Nog, grab the Cardassian."

"Me?"

"Do you see anyone else named Nog?"

Nog came over, rubbing his hands together. His small face was squinched in an expression of disgust. "Where do you want me to hold him?"

"Where do you think?" Quark asked. "He can't be touching the ground."

Nog gave him the most pitiful expression Quark had ever seen. "I can't."

"You will or I'll make you clean the bar with your head skirt every day this week."

"You can't do that!" Nog said. "It isn't sanitary."

"Then I'll make you sanitize it after you're done."

"Don't underestimate him, son," Rom said. "Remember the drinks." And he reached for his ear.

"No!" Quark said too late. The foot bounced again, but this time Nog had grabbed the Cardassian's midsection.

"I want to go back to Ferenginar," Nog said. "Maybe I can live with Moogie."

Rom struggled to reach the foot without dropping the other one. Quark thought his arms would break.

"Moogie wouldn't treat me like this."

"Moogie would hide you in a closet," Quark said. "She has dreams of finding a better mate, and the last thing she needs is a grandson hanging around so that people know her age."

Rom got the foot. He nodded. "I promise I won't drop it again."

"Good," Quark said. "Or Narat will think broken ankles are part of this disease."

"You think I broke his ankle?" Rom said. "I didn't mean to. I mean—"

"No, I don't think you broke his ankle," Quark said. "But I might break yours soon."

They carried the Cardassian into the Promenade. Their footsteps echoed on the floor. Quark had never heard the Promenade echo before.

It was only a few meters to the post Quark had seen, but it felt like they had to travel light-years. When they reached it, and Quark gave the okay, all three dropped him at the same time. It sounded as if something exploded on the Promenade.

"Come on!" Quark said and ran for the bar.

"But, brother, what about the medical staff?" Rom was keeping up with him. So was Nog.

"You call them," Quark said. "But you will not mention the bar, got that? Tell them—oh, never mind. I'll do it."

They got inside and Quark slipped behind the bar. Before he contacted anyone, he was going to wash his hands. They felt sticky with sweat, and something else. Germs, probably. Virus. Possible infection.

He grimaced. He had a hunch things were going to continue to get worse. Much, much worse. And he doubted they would ever get better again.

Chapter Eleven

THE CARDASSIAN CREW piloting the freighter didn't mix with its passengers. Pulaski, Governo, Marvig, and Ogawa were confined to a small area that had once served as the crew's mess. The tables were bolted to the floor. The walls were a gunmetal gray, undecorated, and the room smelled of stale food Pulaski couldn't identify. There were no portholes, so she couldn't see the stars, but the freighter ran relatively smoothly, so she also couldn't feel the hum of the engines. It felt as if she were in a room on Cardassia Prime instead of in a freighter heading toward Terok Nor.

Her team was already working. Governo was bent over his research padd, reading about infectious diseases. Marvig was studying Cardassian physiology. Ogawa was supposed to be looking in the files to see if there was any previous history of cross-contamination between these two species, but she wasn't. She was staring at the walls, much as Pulaski was doing.

Alyssa Ogawa was slender, with dark hair and dark eyes, as human as the rest of them. Pulaski hadn't planned on putting together a completely human team, but Starfleet Medical thought it for the best. The less the Cardassians had to object to—and they would probably object to every species that arrived on Terok Nor—the better.

Pulaski was glad to have Ogawa for several reasons. The first and most important was that they had worked well together on the *Enterprise*. The second was that Ogawa was familiar with Bajoran physiology. The third was that she was the best nurse Pulaski had served with in her entire time in Starfleet.

Ogawa was also fairly level emotionally, and Pulaski would need that. Kellec wasn't, and even though Pulaski usually was, one of the things that had caused their marriage to dissolve was that Kellec could pull her into his moods. Ogawa would help Pulaski keep her own sense of self. She wasn't sure about the other two; since she had never worked with them before, she didn't know if they would be calm or highly volatile. Nothing in their personnel histories suggested any problems along those lines, so the best Pulaski could do was hope.

The group had managed the trip well so far. Captain Picard had strained the *Enterprise*'s engines getting her to the border of Cardassian space within sixteen hours of Pulaski's appointment. He would continue to patrol the area, waiting for her signal, for the next two weeks. If she didn't come out by then, another starship would take its place. The area would be patrolled indefinitely—or so Pulaski had been told. She doubted that Starfleet would continue to expend such resources for four officers, albeit good and valuable ones, much longer than a month. She had mentioned that to Captain Picard and he had looked away from her ever so briefly, as he had done when he told her that Beverly Crusher was returning to the *Enterprise.*

I am afraid I have been told the plan for the next two weeks. The other starship will wait at least as long, but you know as well as I do, Doctor, that things change within our universe in an instant. Should something happen and the Enterprise *must leave ahead of schedule, I shall get a message to you, and we shall make certain you have a way off Terok Nor.*

She had thanked him, of course, but they both knew that she was taking a great personal risk. Starfleet could only support that risk so far, and then she was on her own.

She sighed and stood up. She had forgotten how warm Cardassians liked their ships. She had forgotten a lot about them. How big they were, on average, and how disconcerting it was to see that gray skin—a color she associated with illness. Governo mentioned how reptilian he thought they were; she had forgotten that he had never seen a Cardassian before. That was why she gave him the assignment to study their physiology.

The room they placed the group in was getting smaller by the minute. Pulaski hated waiting. The Cardassian pilot had told her the trip would only take a few hours. She took that to mean three. It had been four, and she felt that was too long. She did know the freighter was operating at its highest speed, trying to get her to Terok Nor.

The Cardassians on board, the pilot and the handful of others, whom she could only think of as guards, had obviously been instructed not to talk to the group. The pilot had looked uncomfortable just telling Pulaski their arrival time. When she had asked for information on the plague, he had stared at her. When she pushed, he had said, "I'm sorry, ma'am. I'm a pilot, not a doctor."

She had let the topic drop after that. She would find out all the pertinent information soon enough.

The door to the mess opened. She turned. One of the Cardassian guards stood in the doorway.

"We're about to dock on Terok Nor. Gather your things."

As he spoke, the entire freighter rumbled ever so slightly. Ogawa glanced over at Pulaski. They were the two used to being on board ship, and they both recognized the sensation. The freighter wasn't about to dock. It had docked.

Governo put his padd in his duffel. Marvig closed her research. Ogawa's was already put away. The three of them stood. Pulaski grabbed her two bags and walked to the Cardassian. "I guess it's time," she said.

He nodded.

He led them down a dark and dirty corridor, with dim lighting that made the gunmetal-gray walls seem black. Even the air here seemed thick and oily. Pulaski had to walk swiftly to keep up with him.

"Have you been to Terok Nor since the plague started?" she asked.

"No one's calling it a plague," he said.

That was more than she got out of the pilot.

"Have you?" she asked.

"We were told we were quarantined on Terok Nor.

We were surprised to be assigned to pick you up." His voice was flat. He wasn't speaking softly, but the net effect, from his tone to his demeanor, was one of secrecy. For some reason he had decided to talk with her.

"How long have you been trapped on Terok Nor?"

"A week." He ducked into another dark corridor. It felt to Pulaski as if they were going in circles, but she knew they weren't.

"That's not very long."

"It is when most of your friends are dying."

Ah, so there it was. The reason he was speaking to her. "And you don't have the disease?"

"I probably do," he said. "I'm going to die like the rest of them."

"Surely you can't believe that," she said. "One must always have hope."

"Hope?" he said. "You'll forget the meaning of the word after you've spent a day on Terok Nor."

He opened one last door, and pointed. Through the airlock, she saw a series of huge, round doors, shaped like giant gears in an ancient machine. The Cardassian pressed a button and the doors rolled back, clanging as they did so, one at a time.

Her door opened first. She stepped through the airlock onto the docking platform, and then another door rolled back, and she was in Terok Nor.

The heat didn't surprise her, but a faint odor of rot did. Space-station filtration systems should take care of smells, unless the odor was so pervasive nothing could be done about it.

She resisted the urge to glance over her shoulder at her Cardassian guide, but his warning rang in her ears like an old Earth curse: *Abandon hope all ye who enter here.*

She did look around her for her team. Governo was at her side, Ogawa and Marvig were behind her. They looked as serious as she felt.

Pulaski stepped out the final door into the corridor. The ceiling was higher here than on the freighter, and the place was clean. It was still decorated in Cardassian gray, however. Didn't they understand the value of a well-placed painting? Or even a nicely designed computer terminal?

The corridor did seem to extend forever, however, despite the branches off it. Another feature of Cardassian design, she assumed. At least poor lighting wasn't part of the design here. The lights were bright enough in this corridor to show that these walls were clean.

Behind her someone cleared his throat. She turned. Three Cardassians blocked the corridor. She had been so intent on her destination that she hadn't looked both ways when she came out the door, and she had turned in the wrong direction.

Two of the Cardassians stood a few steps behind the Cardassian in the middle. He was taller than the others, his shoulders broader, and his face thinner. His eyes had an intelligence that made her wary. With his strange ridges, that sickly gray color to his skin, and those bright eyes, he looked like a particularly charming reptile, the kind that smiled before inflicting its poisonous bite.

In fact, he was smiling now. "Doctor Katherine Pulaski?" he asked. He had a warm, seductive voice that seemed, to her, completely at odds with his appearance.

"Yes," she said.

"I'm Gul Dukat. I run Terok Nor. We're pleased you could come here on such short notice." As if she were coming for a dinner party or to give a speech.

"If you'll point the way, my assistants and I will get right to work."

"First," he said, "I thought we'd get you to your quarters and give you a short tour of our facility. Then we'll take you to the medical section."

She drew a sharp breath. No wonder the Bajorans hated the Cardassians. How insensitive was this man? And then she realized what he was doing. He saw her as a representative of the Federation first, a doctor second. He didn't want her first impression of his station to be one of illness and death.

Governo stepped up beside her, and was about to speak. She put a hand on his arm, and shoved him backwards. Out of the corner of her eye, she saw Marvig take him and hold him back. That answered one question. Governo would be her impulsive assistant.

"Mr. Dukat," she said, purposely making a mistake on his title. "I—"

"*Gul* Dukat," he said in those dulcet tones. "Gul is my title."

"I'm sorry," she said. "I didn't know." She took a step closer to him. The three Cardassians were so tall, it felt as if she were stepping toward a forest.

He watched her as if he had never seen a human before.

"I would love to see the station," she said, "but I was led to believe the medical situation here is urgent. Perhaps if we get this thing under control, you can give me a tour. Right now, though, my assistants and I

109

would like to put our things in our quarters and report for our duties."

Dukat inclined his head toward her. "What you will see in our medical section isn't normal for Terok Nor."

She smiled at him. It would be another part of her job, she realized, to charm the snake. "It isn't normal anywhere." She glanced up at him, making her look purposefully vulnerable. "Perhaps Kellec didn't tell you about me. I'm a doctor. I have no interest in politics. I'm here as a favor to Kellec."

"And your assistants?"

"Are here because they have leave and they volunteered."

His smile was just a bit jaded. "And that's why the *Starship Enterprise* brought you to the rendezvous, because you're a simple doctor, volunteering your time."

"No," she said. "Until a few days ago, I served on that ship. I am between assignments. Captain Picard gave my position to his former chief medical officer, so he owed me a favor."

Dukat clearly wasn't buying that, so she sighed.

"And besides, having a starship escort me was the only way we could convince Starfleet to let us come. They worry about having valuable personnel so close to the Cardassian border."

"You're inside Cardassian space."

"I know," Pulaski said. "And with luck, we'll be able to make your people well. Please, let us work first."

"As you wish," he said.

"In fact," she said, "it would probably be best to show my assistants to their quarters and lead me to the medical area. I'm sure Kellec and your doctor could use the relief."

"All right." Dukat turned to his guards. "I'll take Dr. Pulaski to the medical section. You escort her assistants to their quarters, and when they're settled, bring them to the section as well."

"Forgive me, Doctor," Marvig said, "but perhaps one of us should come with you. We can both get right to work."

"Good suggestion, Crystal, but I'm used to field medicine. None of you are. Trust me, it's better for you to get your bearings and then come. It will prevent burnout later." Pulaski turned to Dukat. "Shall we go?"

He nodded and then, to her surprise, he took her hand and placed it on his arm. Such a courtly gesture, and one that would certainly rile Kellec if he saw it. Still, she let Dukat do it.

His uniform was softer than she expected from its design, and his skin was cooler. She wondered if the heat in the Cardassian ship and now here, on Terok Nor, was because Cardassians had cold blood, just like the Earthly creatures they resembled. She was surprised she didn't remember, and made a mental note to brush up on her own Cardassian physiology when she had a free moment. Every detail was important, and things she had studied years ago that were now lost to the sands of time might be more crucial than she had initially thought.

Dukat led her through the maze of corridors. "What have they told you of Terok Nor?" he asked as they walked.

"Only that it's an ore-processing plant," she said.

"Ah, such an oversimplification," he said. "Terok

Nor is more than a simple factory. We are a very large station, and many ships come through here on their way to Cardassia Prime. Did you see the station as you came in?"

"No," she said. "We were restricted to the crew's mess."

A dark, troubled look crossed his face, and that hint of danger she had felt from the beginning returned. This was not a man to be trifled with. "They should have treated you better. After all, you've come here as a favor to us."

"I assumed that they made room for us where they could," she said.

He nodded. "Well, if you had seen us as you came in, you would have noted the difference in design from your space stations. We have a docking ring, and a habitat ring, and we are at the cutting edge of Cardassian technology—perhaps of technology all through the sector."

She didn't know if he wanted her to ask questions or not.

"We've put your quarters in the best section of our habitat ring. If there's anything you need, you come directly to me."

"I'll do that," she said.

"I wanted to show you the heart of the station," he said. "It's our Promenade. We have restaurants, stores, even a Ferengi-run bar, if your tastes run to alcohol, Dabo, and questionable holosuite programs."

"I hope I will get a chance to sample all three," she said. "I'm sure I'll need them when we have everything under control."

"You sound confident that you can cure this disease," Dukat said. "Is there something you know that my people don't?"

"Perhaps it's ignorance on my part," she said, thankful that her year with Picard had helped her brush up on her diplomacy. "I do not know as much as Kellec or your doctor about this disease, and they refused to send me the specs before I arrived. But it's my nature to be optimistic. If I weren't, I wouldn't be a doctor. We're all a bit egotistical, you know."

"I hadn't realized that," he said with all the smoothness of a lie.

These corridors seemed to go on forever. She wanted to remove her hand from his arm, but felt she didn't dare, not yet.

"Yes," she said. "We are. I think it a necessary skill. It leads us to places that aren't safe, to try things others wouldn't think of, and never to accept failure."

"Have you ever accepted failure?" Dukat said.

"Accepted it?" she asked. "No. Experienced it? Yes."

"Ah, yes, your marriage to Kellec." He didn't miss much. Her sense of him was correct.

"I wasn't thinking of that," she said. "I was thinking of death. We all lose patients, and we're never happy about it."

"You're bringing that attitude to my station," he said.

"I am, and so are my assistants. We'll do everything we can to stop this thing."

He paused. The corridor opened onto a larger area. It must have been the area he had called the Promenade. Ahead she saw lights and advertisements in

Cardassian. A group of Cardassian guards were crowded around a post. She saw that catch Dukat's attention, and then saw him pretend that it didn't matter.

"I believe you will do everything you can to stop this disease," he said, and he sounded a bit surprised. She frowned. Was this the real Dukat? Beneath that reptilian coolness, was there a worried leader beneath? He would have to be stupid not to be. If the disease were half as bad as she had heard, he had to be worried about dying himself.

"Just be careful, Doctor," he said. "Kellec Ton is a bitter man. Do not believe everything he says."

She smiled, even though she had never felt less like doing so. "I know," she said. "I was married to him, remember?"

Dukat laughed. The sound echoed in the wide-open space and the huddle of guards near the post all turned in his direction. He led her into the Promenade. There were shops with windows opening onto the walk area. In one window, a Volian sat at a table, hand-stitching a shirt. Another door opened and a strange-looking man slipped through it. He wore a brown uniform, and he crossed his arms over his chest as she walked by. His face seemed half-formed, or imperfectly formed. She had never seen anyone from a species like that before.

Dukat was explaining what all the places were, but she wasn't really listening. The guards had lifted a man from the floor and were carrying him without a gurney in the direction she and Dukat were walking.

"And this is Quark's," he said, sweeping a hand toward a nearly empty bar.

She peered inside. There was a lot of light and

color, but no customers. A Ferengi stood behind the bar. He looked nervous, but then they all did to her.

This would probably be her only opportunity to let go of Dukat. She slipped her hand from his arm, and went inside the bar. The Ferengi looked at her in surprise.

"Care for a drink?" he asked.

Three Cardassians were passed out at a back table, and another Ferengi was trying in vain to wake them up. She frowned at them.

"A bit of hot water on the back of the neck usually wakes up a Cardassian," she said to the bartender.

"Really?" he asked.

Dukat came inside. "I thought you were in a hurry to get to the infirmary."

"I am," she said. "I just thought—well, I had the impression that this would be the hub of the station."

"It is," the Ferengi said. "When no one's dying."

"Quark." That menacing tone was buried in Dukat's voice again. He sounded so threatening and yet so nice. How did he manage that?

"Have we far to go?" Pulaski asked, walking out of the bar ahead of him.

"Um, no," Dukat said.

"And I take it the infirmary is this way?" She headed in the direction the guards had walked.

"Yes," Dukat said.

She couldn't look too knowledgeable or he would get suspicious, so she slowed down just enough for him to catch up to her.

"What I've seen of the station," she said, "is already impressive."

He smiled at her, and then turned a small corner. "Here is the medical section." A door to her right slid open, and instantly the stench of rot overwhelmed her. She gagged involuntarily and put a hand to her mouth.

"She's turning green!" Dukat said, a hand on her shoulder, trying to push her further inside.

She shook him off. "It's a normal human reaction," she said, barely keeping control of her voice, "when faced with a smell like that."

His call, though, had brought a Cardassian to the front, and behind him, Kellec.

Kellec. Too slim by half. He hadn't been eating again. His hair was messy and his earring was caught on the top of his ear. He had deep circles under both eyes, and lines around his mouth she had never seen before.

And he looked dear. Very dear.

"Katherine?" he asked. "Are you all right?"

"I just don't care for the local perfume," she said, and wrapped him in a great hug. He was thin, so thin he felt fragile in her arms.

He returned the hug, but she could feel him looking over her shoulder at Dukat. So she had been right. They were in a pissing match, and Dukat had tried—and failed—to turn her into an issue.

She stepped back and surveyed the room. There were cots everywhere, and makeshift beds, all filled with green Cardassians, many of them holding their stomachs and moaning despite obvious sedation. The green color was startling. No wonder Dukat had panicked when he saw her get nauseous from the smell. It showed that he was a lot more panicked than his let-me-give-you-a-tour-of-the-station demeanor let on.

She made herself turn to him, even though she didn't want to. "Thank you for your kindness, Gul Dukat," she said. "I do hope we'll be able to finish our tour later."

He bowed his head slightly. "It would be my pleasure, Doctor. And remember, if you need anything, anything at all, come to me."

"I will."

Dukat glanced at the Cardassian who stood to the side, and then his gaze met Kellec's. There was pride in that look, and measuring, and something else, some sort of challenge. And then Dukat left.

"Tour?" Kellec asked. "He took you on a tour of the station instead of bringing you here?"

"He's afraid I'm going to send a bad report to Starfleet," Pulaski said. "But I made him bring me here directly."

"No one makes Dukat do anything," Kellec said.

"Oh, I don't know," Pulaski said. "You managed to get him to bring me here." She put a hand through her hair, wishing now that she had had a chance, a very brief one, to stop in her quarters. Kellec always made her feel like that.

"Dr. Pulaski," the Cardassian who had rushed to the door said. "I'm Dr. Narat."

He was hunched over more by the demands of his profession than with age. His dark eyes were sharp as well, but his face wasn't as reptilian as Dukat's. There was a softness to Narat, a compassion that seemed built into him. Even though she had never met him before, she got a sense from him that he, too, was exhausted.

"Thank you for coming," he said. "You are alone?"

"I brought three assistants. I sent them to their quarters to drop off their things before coming here. I wanted to assess the situation alone."

Narat nodded. He swept a hand toward the beds. "This is just one area, only the Cardassians. We have two other rooms full in the medical section and we've had to take over an empty business space right next door."

"My heavens," Pulaski said.

Kellec nodded. "If it weren't for all the deaths," he said, "we would need even more room."

She glanced at him. She wasn't used to him being so blunt. At least not about losing patients. So things were awful here. Only doctors who had seen a lot of death in a short period of time had that flat affect, that way of speaking about terrible things as if they were commonplace.

And apparently they were.

"How many have died?" she asked.

"Everyone who has been sick for longer than two days," Narat said.

Her gaze met Kellec's. It wasn't just exhaustion she saw in his eyes. It was deep, overwhelming sadness, and more—a frustration and anger so strong that he had to fight to keep it held back. He knew as well as she, as well as any doctor, that anger only blinded. He needed to remain level.

"How many is that?" she asked gently. "How many have died?"

Kellec shook his head. "We've been too busy to keep track of the numbers, and we have no real assistants. It's not a relevant statistic at the moment."

"But how have you notified the families?"

"Niceties are gone, Katherine," he said. "We

haven't done anything except triage, palliative mea-sures, and research. We haven't had time."

"Maybe now," Narat said. "Now that you're here, we can do some of those things again."

Pulaski nodded. It wasn't like Kellec to let go of the small details. For any reason. "You said everyone who contracts the disease dies?"

"Everyone," Kellec said. "Within two days."

She glanced around the room. If something weren't done, a solution wasn't found, all of these people would be dead soon. And all of the patients in the next room, and the next.

"Cardassian and Bajoran?" she asked. "No one has survived?"

"No one."

She shook her head. "I've never heard of a plague like that," she said. "The black plague on Earth, in the days when medicine consisted of trickery and leeches, left one-quarter of the population alive. The Triferian flu on Vulcan only killed half. The worst plague I've ever heard of, the Nausicaan wort virus, which struck a thousand years ago, killed 95 percent of the Nausicaan population. No plague kills one hundred per-cent. Someone always survives."

Kellec shook his head. "If you contract this thing," he said, "you die."

"And that's why you believe this is a designer virus?" she asked.

"That, and several other factors. Its precision, for one thing. And the way it works. Let us show you what we've found so far. It would be nice to have a fresh eye on things." He took her arm and started to lead her toward the office.

She stopped though, and gazed at all the moaning

patients. One hundred percent death rate. No wonder Kellec didn't want to talk about it. That made their job a thousand times harder. The best way to beat a viral infection was to discover what was different within those patients who were exposed and didn't get sick. Or those who got sick and survived. Often their systems produced antibodies that worked against the virus, and those antibodies could be replicated and placed in those patients who didn't manufacture them naturally.

But a 100-percent death rate completely cut the traditional options out. The solution had to be a lab-devised one, just like the virus itself. And that required researchers, not medical doctors. She did research, yes, but her main focus had always been her patients. Maybe Starfleet had been right in trying to send the viral experts here.

Maybe. But to do so would have meant at least a hundred more deaths in the time it took those experts to arrive. At least she was here now. Her assistants could look after the patients, and she could work with Kellec and Narat to find a cure.

The confidence she had spoken of to Dukat had vanished. In her entire career, she had never faced odds like this. Terok Nor had a small population. In order to save any of it, she and her colleagues had to find a solution fast.

The problem was that all the shortcuts had been blocked off. They had to do the impossible, and she wasn't even sure how to begin.

Chapter Twelve

HE STOOD IN THE SHADOWS next to Quark's bar, marveling at the difference a few days had made. Before there had been laughter and shouting, games and relaxation, but now there was silence. The Ferengi, Quark, was complaining about the silence, still worrying about his business, not realizing that soon, everything on Terok Nor would come to an end.

He had found it amusing when Quark had carried the ill Cardassian outside the bar before allowing his brother to report the illness. Quark still believed everything would turn around, things would get better, his bar would come back to life, and he would continue to earn his precious latinum.

Soon latinum wouldn't be important at all.

He had had a bad moment, though, as Quark, his brother, and his nephew had passed, carrying the Cardassian. For an instant, his shield had fizzled. He

121

had caught it in time, but Quark had turned his head, almost as if he had seen the shimmer the malfunction caused. Fortunately, the Ferengi was so self-involved that he apparently thought nothing of it.

Ever since, though, he had kept close watch on the shield. It was his only protection here, allowing him to go undiscovered. Not that there were many left to discover him. The sick Cardassians had made their way, one by one, to the medical section. The well ones were staying away from populated areas, keeping themselves in their rooms unless they had duties— and sometimes even then.

Humanoids all shared an attitude toward disease. No matter how sophisticated the society, humanoids still feared tiny little microbes that attacked the body unseen. From Cardassians and Bajorans to Trills and Klingons, the fear of illness was uniform. And all the more amusing in societies like Cardassia's. Soldiers seemed to fear disease most of all.

He had enjoyed watching Terok Nor's leader, Dukat, when he felt he was alone. The constant washing of the hands. His reluctance to touch other Cardassians or Bajorans. His nervous movements every time he was about to enter the medical section. All of them were tiny gestures, but they were oh, so telling. And if Dukat felt that way, so did all the other Cardassians. He almost wished the symptomatic part of the disease lasted longer. It brought out the fear in the unaffected—or the not-yet-symptomatic, to be more accurate—so much better.

He made a mental note about that, not certain if he were going to use it or not.

But he was here to observe, and since he had arrived, he had observed a lot. The way the Cardassians simply kept going until they lost control; the resigned futility among the Bajorans; the added calls to the Prophets who, of course, were not listening: All of this intrigued him. And pleased him, if he had to be honest. Things were progressing better than he had expected.

Although that could change. Dukat's mood seemed lighter since he escorted the human woman across the Promenade and into the medical section. She looked vaguely familiar, with her brown hair and calm demeanor. He had a moment of panic when she excused herself from Dukat and walked into Quark's. For a moment, he thought she was going to walk over to him. It was as if she saw him, as if she knew he was there.

Instead, she had asked the Ferengi a question or two, and then had gone on.

He hadn't expected humans on Terok Nor. He hadn't expected anyone associated with the Federation. He had purposely chosen Cardassians and Bajorans because they had no official ties with the Federation and so wouldn't request Federation help.

What this woman was doing here baffled him, but she had obviously been brought in to help find a cure. Fortunately, a cure would prove extremely difficult. If not impossible. Diseases did not act the way this one did. Most doctors weren't creative enough to understand something so different, so fundamentally *alien*.

A single human woman would make no difference in this laboratory. He would worry only when teams of scientists came in. Federation scientists.

And by the time they arrived, it would be too late. No matter how light Gul Dukat's mood, the fact was that Terok Nor was doomed.

He had done the projections before he came, a timetable assuming everything went according to plan—which it had, much to his surprise. It was now time for him to leave. His cloaked ship would pick him up shortly.

And probably just in time. According to his projections, Terok Nor had very little time left.

Chapter Thirteen

SHE WAS CRAZY to have come back to Terok Nor. What had she been thinking when she offered to come here? Certainly she hadn't been thinking very clearly.

It no longer seemed like the risks that she took getting here in her small rebel ship, keeping it hidden from Cardassian scans, and then beaming aboard, were going to be worth it. It had been harder this time, because Terok Nor was closed to almost all ships. She wasn't sure if the beam-in had been detected; she doubted anyone was scouting for security breaches in the middle of this internal crisis.

Kira stood in the center of the Bajoran section. It looked nothing like it had a few months ago, when she had come here to get a list of Bajoran collaborators from a chemist's shop. She didn't like to think about that visit, and how close she had come to becoming a true prisoner of the Cardassians.

She ran her hands over her arms. She had goose-bumps despite the warmth. This place smelled like rot, and if she hadn't known better, she would have thought it like one of the prisoner-of-war camps on Cardassia. Dukat had always prided himself on keeping a clean, well-run station, where he treated the Bajorans "fairly."

There was nothing fair about this place any longer. Not even the most delusional could miss that.

Ill Bajorans lay on the floor, their cheeks rosy, their eyes too bright. They held their stomachs and moaned, while family members tried to take care of them. Others were on blankets or coats that someone had given up. There were no Cardassian guards in sight—it was as if the guards had forgotten the Bajorans were here.

Not that it mattered. The Bajorans were too busy dying to think of revolution.

She had had no idea the disease was this bad. If she had to guess, she would estimate that half of the Bajorans she saw were in some stage of illness.

And she saw no sign of Kellec Ton at all. No sign of any doctors, no sign of any help. How could Dukat allow this? How could anyone?

There had to be someone that the Bajorans looked to for leadership, someone who took control of various situations. But she didn't even know where to look. The fine web of corridors and large rooms that had served as the Bajoran section no longer had any order to it at all. The sick lay everywhere, even in the eating areas, and there were a few bodies stacked near the entrance to the processing plants.

Bodies. Stacked. She had never expected to see this.

She didn't even know where to begin.

She wanted to roll up her sleeves and help, but she knew nothing about medicine, at least this kind of medicine. Give her a patient with a phaser burn and she could treat it, or a broken arm and she could set it, but to die like this, moaning in excruciating agony while everyone around was busy with their own deaths, was something completely beyond her.

Two Cardassian guards walked through the corridor. They stepped over the ill and dying Bajorans as if they were simply rocks lying in their path. They were talking in low tones, their conversation impossible to hear.

Kira tensed. If they saw her, they might bring her to Dukat. And that was the last thing she needed.

She slid down the wall, and buried her face in her knees. She couldn't bring herself to moan, to feign the illness so many others were dying of. But she kept herself immobile.

As the Cardassians passed, their conversation became clearer.

". . . so desperate that he's allowing the Bajoran doctor to work on Cardassian patients."

"That's not what I've heard. I've heard the illnesses are related, and if they find a cure for one, they find a cure for both."

"It's a Bajoran trick."

"What makes you think that?"

"They designed this virus to kill us, but it backfired. It makes them sick as well."

"Surely if that were true, Dukat wouldn't let that Bajoran anywhere near the medical section."

"Dukat is smarter than you think. Perhaps he wants Narat to catch the Bajoran infecting Cardassians . . ."

Their voices faded. Kira raised her head just enough to be able to watch them leave out of the corner of one eye. So the rumor about the Cardassians was true; they were dying of this disease as well.

And of course, the lower-level guards believed that the Bajorans were behind the illness, not realizing that the Bajorans no longer had the capability to do anything like this. Bajorans were struggling just to stay alive.

She hadn't expected it to be so easy to discover where Kellec Ton was, though. He was in the Cardassian medical section, helping save Cardassians. She would never have believed it of him. He had to have some other plan in mind. But she wasn't sure what that would be, nor was she certain how to reach him. It would mean leaving the Bajoran section. Some Bajorans did, she knew, but very few. And they were usually collaborating somehow.

She had been outside the Bajoran section last year, when she went to the chemist's to steal that list of collaborators, but everything had gone wrong. She had had to kill the chemist, and she had gotten caught. She managed to lie her way out of it, though, and escape with her life.

She wasn't sure she'd be that lucky this time.

But if the Cardassians were sick too, and the guard levels down here were any indication, she might have an easier time of it. The entire station seemed to be preoccupied with itself, turned inward, not outward. Maybe no one cared any longer about collaborators and the resistance. Maybe all anyone on Terok Nor cared about was surviving from moment to moment.

She waited until she was certain the guards were long gone. Then she rose ever so slowly, looking both ways. As she did, the wall at her back moved.

She gasped and turned. What she had thought to be a small beam attached to the wall turned into a liquid, then formed itself into a man.

The security chief. Odo.

She swallowed. He had caught her the last time, and nearly tried her for murder. But she had convinced him that she hadn't killed that Cardassian chemist and he had helped her escape. She hadn't expected to see him again.

"Kira Nerys, isn't it?" Odo said, as his shape solidified.

She didn't answer him, just watched him.

"I wondered who would be foolish enough to beam aboard a quarantine station."

She swallowed hard, but lifted her chin in a defiant movement.

"Or didn't you know that everyone is dying here?" He tilted his head. He was such a strange creature. His features weren't completely formed, and yet she could see something in those eyes. A sadness, perhaps.

"You're not dying," she said.

"I'm not Bajoran or Cardassian." Odo crossed his arms. "You do realize that I should tell Gul Dukat of your arrival."

"I thought you said everyone is dying."

"It was only a slight exaggeration. Dukat, so far, seems fine."

"That's no surprise," Kira said.

"What does that mean?"

"It means those guards had this whole thing backwards. The Cardassians designed this plague to kill Bajorans, and now it's backfired on them."

"Do you actually believe that?" Odo asked. "You always struck me as such an intelligent woman before."

She felt herself flush. "So you believe the Cardassian version?"

"Actually, I have a feeling that there's something else going on entirely. Your people and the Cardassians are so focused on your hatred for each other that you can't see beyond yourselves."

She frowned. "What do you know?"

"Nothing, really. It's just a hunch." He tilted his head toward her. "Just like my hunch says it's no coincidence that you're here, now. What are you coming to do? Start a rebellion now that the Cardassians are weak?"

She swept her hand across the floor, indicating all the ill people. "As if that would do any good. Why isn't anyone taking care of them?"

"Believe it or not," Odo said, "someone is. It's just there is so much sickness on the station that each patient can only expect a moment or two of personal attention a day."

It was sadness she saw in his eyes. He was as helpless as she was. "Kellec Ton?" she asked. "He has been coming down here?"

"Is that why you're here? To check up on him?"

She couldn't answer that. Much as this shapeshifter's demeanor made her feel like trusting him, she had been in this situation too many times to trust anyone in authority. "Is he still alive?"

"I thought you overheard those guards," Odo said.

"He's in the Cardassian section, trying to find a cure."

"Is he having any luck?"

"I'm not privy to the medical discussions, but from what I've seen, no. If anything, the plague has gotten worse."

She shivered ever so slightly. Kellec hadn't gone crazy, had he? He hadn't started the plague, as those guards accused him of doing?

Of course not. What was she thinking? Kellec Ton wasn't that kind of man. No matter what circumstances drove him to, he would never voluntarily take a life, let alone hundreds of lives.

"Is it as bad as they say?" she asked, not able to help herself.

"What do they say?"

"That anyone who catches this disease dies."

He looked away from her, at the moaning people around them. He seemed smaller than the last time she saw him, as if the suffering had diminished him somehow. Or perhaps everyone seemed smaller in the face of this kind of anguish.

"From what I have observed," he said slowly, "any Cardassian or Bajoran who is exposed to this disease eventually gets the disease. And anyone who gets it, dies."

"So I'm at risk," Kira said.

"I'm afraid so," Odo said.

They stared at each other for a moment. Then he said, "I'm going to have to locate your ship and warn its crew away from here."

She almost told him that she was in a scout ship, and that she had come alone, but he didn't need that information.

"They left anyway," she lied, "just after they brought me here."

"I'm going to check anyway," he said. "Because you made the biggest mistake of your life coming here."

"Are you threatening me?" she asked.

He shook his head. "I wish it were that easy. But this station is under quarantine. Anyone who comes here cannot leave, not until the quarantine is lifted, and I doubt it will be lifted anytime soon."

She look at him.

"I will keep an eye out for any illegal transportation devices, and in fact, I think I'll recommend to Gul Dukat to raise the station's shield so that no one can leave via transporter."

"Then I will die here," she said.

"You chose to come," he said. "It was a bad decision." Then he gave her a compassionate look. "If you stay in the Bajoran section, you'll be all right."

"And if I choose not to?"

"I can't vouch for what happens to you."

"Why should I care what happens to me?" she asked. "From what you say, I'm dead anyway."

He sighed. "I have hope," he said, although his tone belied his words, "that someone will find a way to end this thing."

"You don't seem like an optimistic man."

He inclined his head toward her as a sort of acknowledgement. "I'm usually not. But your friend has brought his ex-wife aboard, and it took some doing. I have to believe she has the skills to help with all of us."

Kellec Ton's ex-wife? What had Kira heard about her? Not much, except—she was Starfleet. The Federation. That had to take some doing.

"What makes you think one person will make a difference?" Kira asked.

"I'm looking at it from a practical standpoint," he said. "She's not Bajoran or Cardassian."

"And so has no stake in developing the disease further?"

"Actually, no," he said. "She has a chance of staying alive long enough to develop a cure."

Chapter Fourteen

"And so has no stake in developing the disease further."

Chapter Fourteen

PULASKI'S EYES ACHED from the strain of staring at the Cardassian computer monitors. The LTDs here were set on a different frequency than the Federation mandated. These settings were not designed for human eyes, and were creating a serious version of eye strain. She leaned back in her chair and with her thumb and forefinger massaged the bridge of her nose.

Ten hours of work, and it felt like only a moment. Ten hours. She thought she might have something, but she wanted to rest for just a second, to allow the hope to diminish.

The mood on Terok Nor, the hopelessness, had infected her more than she wanted to admit. She had tried to get Kellec to leave the medical section, but he refused to go. She thought of actually giving him a sedative so that he could sleep, but she couldn't do that. They might need his clear thinking.

At least she had convinced Narat to rest. What she wanted to do was to place the three main doctors on a rotating schedule, two on and one off at all times. This might continue for days, and it would do no good for Narat and Kellec to court illness by shorting themselves on sleep.

When Narat returned, she would convince Kellec to go. No matter what it took.

She would be doing the same in their shoes, though. One of the reasons she wanted to set up the new system was so that she ensured she would get some rest. Right now, she was the fresh one, seeing things with a new perspective, but over time that would change. She wanted all of them to have an advantage.

She sighed and stood, stretching. Even the chairs were poorly designed, at least for her human form. Apparently Cardassians had the assumption of height working for them. She had to rest her feet on the base of the chair instead of the floor, and that was playing havoc with her back. She turned and looked out the office door at the medical section's patient areas.

Ogawa was taking care of the Bajorans in the medical section, offering kind words and comfort. Marvig was below, in the Bajoran section, working in the corridors with the people too sick to make it here. Eventually, they would switch places. Pulaski had seen the Bajoran section on one of her short breaks, and it had been the worst thing yet on Terok Nor. Dozens of sick and dying people, with no one to care for them except their own families—if they had any families left.

Some of them were already weakened from years spent as Cardassian prisoners or as workers in the ore-processing area. Pulaski had no idea what working with uridium did to the immune system, but if uridium was like any other ore, it weakened everything it came into contact with.

Governo was ministering to the Cardassians. His bedside manner was gruffer and blunter than either Ogawa's or Marvig's, and the Cardassians seemed to appreciate that. They were the kind of patients who wanted the unvarnished truth—rather like Klingons in that respect—so that they could make decisions from there. Only the Cardassians were too sick to attempt to die with honor, as a Klingon would have done. Or perhaps it wasn't part of their culture. She didn't know. She had never really made a point of studying Cardassian social habits.

"Are you all right?" Kellec was behind her, his voice soft in her ear.

She nodded. "I needed to think."

"Staring out there helps you think?"

"There's nowhere else to look," she said.

"Up on the Promenade, there are windows that look out to the stars," Kellec said. "I go there if I need a moment alone."

"I'll remember that," Pulaski said. "But that wasn't the kind of thinking I needed to do."

"You've found something," Kellec said. He knew her so well. They had spent years apart, and it felt as if they had only been away from each other for a few hours.

"I think so." She turned away from the door and came back to her chair. She put her hands on it instead of sitting in it, more out of courtesy to her back than any other reason. "Let me show you."

She ran her fingers across the flat control board, punching up two holographic images. They were of the virus, its perfect form sinister to her, as if it had already imprinted itself in her subconscious as something evil.

Kellec stood beside her, staring at the images. "You see something here that I've missed."

"Yes," she said. She lowered her voice. "These are not the same virus."

"Katherine," Ton said. "I've been studying them for days. They're exactly the same."

"No," she said. "I double-checked your work and Narat's. You examined the viruses at first and thought they were the same. The computer reported that they were as well. From that point on, you've only been working with one form of the virus, pulled from the same culture."

He frowned at her, then peered at the images. He touched the control pad, making the images larger. "I don't see the difference."

"It's subtle," she said, "and this system, sophisticated as it is, isn't calibrated for such tiny differences. Apparently, Cardassian medicine is a lot more straightforward than the types we practice in the Federation."

He glanced at her, obviously not following.

"These systems," she said, "are designed for Cardassian physiology only. And why shouldn't they be? Even though several species come through Terok Nor, most everything here is geared toward Cardassians. On starships, and throughout the Federation, we're dealing with a wide variety of species all the time. Small things—infinitesimal things—can sometimes mean the difference between life and death."

"All right," he said. "What infinitesimal thing have I missed?"

She pointed to the image on the left. "This is Virus B, the virus that's killing the Bajorans." She punched in a label that ran across the bottom. Then she pointed to the image on the right. "This is Virus C, the one that's killing the Cardassians."

Kellec peered at both screens. Then he made them larger. "I must be tired," he said. "I can't see the difference."

"You are tired," she said. "This is why I want us all to have a few hours of sleep a day. But that's beside the point. Look here."

She pointed to a single strand on Virus B's DNA.

"Now," she said, "compare it to the same strand on Virus C's DNA."

He closed his eyes and brought the heel of his hand to his forehead. "How could I have missed that?"

"You weren't looking for it," she said. "They look so much alike—'"

"Don't make excuses for me, Katherine. I should have caught it."

"Why? You thought the viruses were the same."

"But they manifested differently."

"Yes," she said, "and that's completely logical given the differences between Cardassian and Bajoran physiology."

"But Cardassians and Bajorans don't get the same diseases. We all know that."

It wasn't like Kellec to go into recriminations. He was exhausted. She had to get him focused on something else. "You brought me in here for a new perspective."

"Yes," he said. "I did."

"Well, I have more."

He frowned. "This is the part you were reluctant to tell me."

She nodded. "And frankly, I'm relieved Narat isn't here. Are you sure we can talk here without being overheard?"

"No one out there is listening," Ton said.

"And Dukat?"

Kellec shrugged. "I don't know. I don't think he would be. It's not the way he usually does things."

"Good," she said.

"Why?"

She took a deep breath. "Because Virus B, found in the Bajorans, is mutating into Virus C and killing Cardassians."

Instantly Kellec's face went white; then he did the same thing she had been doing. He quickly checked around him to make sure no Cardassians had heard. If this information got out, Pulaski didn't know what Dukat would do with the news. But from the reports she had heard, she doubted he would stop short at wiping out most of the Bajoran people to stop this.

"How can you be sure it's not the other way around?" Kellec asked.

She punched up a different image. "Watch," she said.

She had a time-lapsed image of the Bajoran cultures that Kellec and Narat had been using. Over a period of a few days, the Bajoran virus mutated. She highlighted the new viruses in red.

"What made you look for that?" he asked.

"I saw how closely they were related. I knew we weren't dealing with a coincidence. Kellec, you and Narat are right. This is an artificially created virus."

"You mean it's designed to go from Bajoran to Cardassian?"

She nodded.

He gripped the back of the nearest chair. "If the Cardassians find out about this—"

"They'll wipe out every Bajoran they can find," she said. "And it will kill the Cardassian source of infection."

"You can't condone that!" he said.

"Of course not. But the Cardassians strike me as the kind of people who can justify such a thing."

Kellec sank into his chair. "I don't know what we do now, Katherine. We need this information to find a cure. But I want to wipe it all off the system."

"I already have," she said. "These are my files, coded to me only."

"That's precisely the thing that will get you in trouble with Dukat."

"I know." She touched the screen and the images disappeared. "But since I destroyed the material, he can't accuse me of spying, now can he?"

"Katherine, we needed that."

She shook her head. "It's enough to know it. The comparisons are gone, that's all. We have the knowledge. Now we have to use it."

"Swear to me you won't tell Narat."

"I wish we could," she said. "He has a keen mind."

"It's also a Cardassian mind."

"I know that too. And for that reason, I won't say a word."

Kellec squeezed her arm. "Thank you, Katherine."

"Don't thank me yet," she said. "We haven't found a cure."

"But we're one step closer than we were before you arrived. Narat and I never would have found that."

"You would have," she said.

"Just not in time." Kellec pushed his chair closer to the console. "At least now I have a bit of hope."

She prayed that that was enough to sustain him. Because the mutation of the virus worried her. She would have expected it to go the other way. She had actually been looking to see if the Cardassian form mutated into the Bajoran form when she found that she had the process exactly reversed.

She wasn't sure what that meant yet, besides the obvious results that Kellec envisioned, should the Cardassians discover how the virus traveled. But she didn't like what she was thinking, and she didn't know how to clear the suspicions from her brain.

Were an oppressed people wrong in doing anything they could to get rid of their oppressors?

She turned back toward the patients in the outer rooms, and got her answer.

Yes, they were. Some prices were too high, no matter what the cause.

Chapter Fifteen

QUARK RUBBED HIS LEFT EAR with the back of his left hand. It felt as if something were tickling the edge of his lobe, and not in a pleasant way. He leaned across the bar and surveyed his business.

His empty business.

He hadn't had a customer in hours. At this rate, he would be broke within the month, faster if Nog and Rom continued to spend all his latinum. No wonder Prindora left Rom. He could go through money faster than anyone Quark had ever seen.

Quark peered into the Promenade. There was no one there either. The Volian's shop was still open, but he hadn't had a customer since Rom needed his new hat. Several of the restaurants had closed, and most of the stores were closed as well. No one even wandered the Promenade, as if just moving around the station made a person vulnerable to disease.

Quark rubbed his ear again. All of this worry was making him break out. And of course, it would happen on the most sensitive spot on his body.

He heard a clang above him and he glanced up. Nog came out of the first holosuite, a bucket in his left hand. He set the bucket down, scratched his ear, and then picked up the bucket.

Quark felt cold.

He turned and leaned toward the mirror behind the bar. It wasn't a pimple that he was scratching. He hadn't broken out since he was a young Ferengi just hitting puberty. He leaned closer. The reddened area on his left ear looked more like . . . a blister.

"Nog!" he shouted.

"Coming, uncle," Nog said. He clanged all the way down the stairs. Quark had had to look all over his quarters to find a bucket, but when he had found one, he gave it to Nog with the instruction that the boy scrub the entire bar, including the holosuites. It was just a way to keep him out of the way for a while, so that Quark could think. Quark had hoped he would come up with ways to save the business, but that hope had been in vain.

Nog reached the bottom of the stairs. He set the bucket down, and absently scratched his ear again.

Quark's eyes narrowed. "Come here, Nog."

Nog looked up. He came toward the bar, and smiled at Quark. When he reached the edge of the bar, Quark grabbed him and pulled him close. Nog's smile faded.

"Turn your head," Quark said.

Nog did.

"Not that way. The other way."

Nog looked in the other direction. Sure enough,

there was a reddish spot on Nog's right ear. A reddish spot that was swollen and had a pus-filled tip. A blister.

"You little grubworm!" Quark said. "I should have known better than to use my earbrush after you touched it."

"What?" Nog asked. "What did I do?"

"Your filthy hands had germs on them from your father's ear infection, and you touched my brush and you spread those germs to me. And now I'm in agony. Look!" He turned his ear toward Nog and leaned toward Nog's face. Nog grimaced and strained backwards, but didn't get very far because Quark was holding him.

"I'm sorry, uncle. I didn't mean to—"

"You didn't mean to. Your father didn't mean to. You're an entire family of Ferengi who have no idea how to take responsibility for anything. Well, I do." Quark shoved Nog backwards. "Get your father."

"What for?"

"Just get him."

"Don't fire him, uncle. You're all we have."

"Yes," Quark said. "I am reminded of that sad fact daily. Now get him."

Nog backed out of the bar, bumping into a chair, then turned and ran for their quarters. Quark leaned across the polished surface and stared at all the empty tables. No customers. No latinum. And an ear infection spread by his careless brother. And that hunch of Quark's was still playing.

Things were going to get worse.

Nog came out of the quarters, dragging Rom by the hand. Rom was trying to shove his hat over his head.

Quark came out from behind the bar, plucked off the hat and threw it over his shoulder.

"But brother," Rom said. "The customers!"

"Are you seeing customers?" Quark asked. "Because if you are, then there's more wrong with you than that ear infection."

Rom glanced around, his movements jerkier than usual, like they always were when he was nervous. "If there are no customers, then why did you have Nog come to get me?"

"Because," Quark said, "you've managed to infect all three of us through your carelessness."

"I thought you said it was my carelessness," Nog said.

"It was both of you!" Quark snapped. "Now come with me."

He took them both by the hands and dragged them out of the bar.

"Where are we going?" Rom asked.

"To the medical lab," Quark said. "We're going to get this solved."

"But they have dying patients," Rom said. "Why would they help us?"

"Because we have latinum," Quark said.

"Dr. Narat doesn't take latinum," Rom said.

"And you know this how?" Quark asked.

"When we first arrived, I wasn't sleeping. I went to him for—"

"For what?" Quark stopped in the middle of the Promenade. It was empty.

"For—for a sleeping draught."

"A sleeping draught. And you offered Dr. Narat latinum."

"Of course," Rom said. "That's how business is done."

He seemed so proud of himself.

"And he didn't charge you anything?"

"No," Rom said. "He gave me something to help me sleep and then he laughed when I offered him latinum, and said that Cardassians don't take payments from Ferengi."

"Well, that's a blatant lie," Quark said.

"Is there a point to this, uncle?" Nog asked. He stared down at Quark's hand, which was wrapped around his wrist.

"A point to what?" Quark asked.

"This conversation about latinum?"

"Not really," Quark said. "Except that I was wondering where my brother was going to get the latinum to pay the good doctor."

"Well, you said that we should make ourselves at home. I figured you wouldn't mind that I was going to take care of myself."

"You figured. You figured. Just like you figured this boil on your ear would go away?"

"It's just an infection, brother, caused by the drinks."

"It's an infection that your carelessness has spread. And we're going to stop it." Quark dragged them down the hall. The stench coming from the medical area was stronger than he had expected. He had been smelling the rot for a week now and ignoring it, like he did in butcher shops on Ferenginar, but here it was nearly impossible to ignore.

"I don't think I'm going in there," Rom said.

"Yeah," Nog said. "They probably won't have time for us."

"They'll probably be happy to have something they can solve," Quark said with more bravado than he felt. If his ear didn't itch so badly that he wanted to scratch it off the side of his head, he wouldn't go into that place either. But he couldn't stand itching, especially on as sensitive a place as his ear.

He shoved Rom and Nog ahead of him, and the door to the medical lab opened. The smell was even worse. A hundred voices moaned.

Rom shook his head. "Brother, I—"

And Quark pushed him forward. Nog followed him in, and then Quark brought up the rear.

"Whatever it is," Dr. Narat said as he passed, "it will have to wait."

"It can't wait," Quark said.

"Are you dying?"

"No."

"Then it can wait." And Narat disappeared through a door.

"See?" Rom said. "We have to wait. Which means we should leave."

Quark caught him by the sleeve. Quark wasn't too happy about being here either—he'd never been in a room filled with green Cardassians before—but he wasn't about to leave now. For one thing, he might never make it back. And then he'd have to scratch until his ear bled, and the infection would grow worse, and his lobes would—

He couldn't allow himself to follow that train of thought. He shuddered and headed toward the office.

"I wouldn't go in there," a human woman said. She had long dark hair and beautiful eyes.

"Who are you?" Quark asked.

"Alyssa Ogawa," she said. "I'm helping here."

"We have a problem, and it needs some attention."

"Let me see what I can do," she said.

She slipped through the office door, and Rom turned to Quark. "She's beautiful, brother."

"She's hu-man, Brother," Quark said. "You can't trust a hu-man."

"Ah, but you can look at them," Rom said.

"Women are not your strong suit," Quark said. "Stop thinking about her."

She came out the door with Kellec Ton. He looked exhausted. "I don't have much time," he said. "What do you need?"

Quark leaned forward, pointing to his ear. "Look at this. *Look* at this. My brother got—"

"Couldn't this have waited?" Kellec Ton asked. "We have a real crisis here."

"We know and we're sorry," Rom said. "We'll leave now."

Quark pulled him closer. "No, we won't." He glanced around the room. "I admit, our problem is nothing like theirs—" and he shuddered a little at the very thought "—but it is uncomfortable."

"You can live with discomfort," Kellec Ton said. "Now, if you'll excuse me."

"No," Quark said. "I won't. Don't you understand? This itches."

"And I'm very sorry," Kellec said. He was holding the door like it was a lifeline. "But I don't have time—"

"These are our *ears,*" Quark said, his voice going up. "It would be like you getting an infection on your—"

148

"Brother!" Rom said, breathless with shock. "Remember Nog."

"I know about their—" Nog started to say, but Rom clapped a hand over his mouth.

"I'm sure the good doctor will help us when he has time," Rom said. "Now let's go."

Kellec Ton let out a small laugh and shook his head. "All right," he said. "You made your point. Let me look at that."

He bent down and turned on a small, handheld light. "It's an infection all right," he said, looking at Quark's ear. Then he examined Nog's and then Rom's. "And it's clearly transmittable, probably through the pus. Let me give you some antibacterial cream that should ease the itching and clear this right up."

"Thank you," Quark said.

"Yes," Rom said. "Thank you very much."

The doctor went into the office, and rummaged through a drawer. Rom leaned over to Quark. "I still think we shouldn't have bothered him."

"Shut up," Quark said. "We're getting help, aren't we?"

"Yes," Rom said. "But he's right. There are people *dying* here."

Quark nodded. He had to admit that he did agree with Rom, but for entirely different reasons. He wished they hadn't come here. Before it had seemed entirely personal. The Cardassians got sick and no one came to the bar. But it wasn't personal. In fact, it was so impersonal that it hurt. No one came to the bar because everyone was afraid of this—turning green, scaly, and the stench! And then dying.

Quark shuddered. He would have to start planning his future, a future that didn't include Terok Nor. He wasn't sure what he'd do, because once the word got out that Terok Nor was the site of a plague, Quark wouldn't be able to work anywhere—at least not have a bar. Customers didn't like hearing about contagious diseases in their bartender's past.

"Here you go," Kellec said, placing a tube in Quark's hand. "Follow the instructions. Your problems should ease by the end of the day."

"Thank you," Quark said. "We didn't mean to interrupt. If we had known—"

"No," Kellec said. "It's all right. You did me a favor. You reminded me that there's an entire universe out there. Even if things on Terok Nor and Bajor . . ." He shook his head. "Anyway. I needed to remember that life does go on."

"Yes, it does," Rom said. "And—"

Quark kicked him. He shut up.

"We do appreciate it," Nog said. "We won't bother you again." He scurried for the door. Quark followed a bit more slowly, the tube cool against his right hand. He was staring at the Cardassians on the beds and makeshift cots. He recognized a number of them, had served them drinks, listened to their problems. And they would all be gone soon, if something didn't change.

He sighed and slipped outside, where Rom and Nog were waiting for him.

"Well, brother," Rom said. "You did the right thing. Now all we have to do is apply that cream to our ears—"

"No," Quark said. "I'll apply it to my ears, and I'll

give you your own dab of it. I'm not touching anything you touch ever again. Is that clear?"

"Perfectly," Rom said.

"Does this mean I get your earbrush?" Nog asked.

Quark stared at him for a moment, and then he sighed, unwilling to fight them anymore. "I guess it does," he said.

Chapter Sixteen

NEARLY TWENTY-FOUR HOURS without sleep. Pulaski
felt it in the grit of her eyes, the sluggishness in her
arms and legs. She had pulled all-nighters hundreds of
times from college on, and she'd hated each and every
one of them. Of course, she had to admit that this one
she didn't mind, because the work needed to be done.

She bent over the culture she had been working on.
She took a dropper and placed a small sample of
solution on it, then glanced at the screen. Narat stood
beside her. They watched as the solution moved
through the viral cells, destroying them. It left all the
other cells alone.

"I think we've got it," Narat said.

Part of it, anyway, Pulaski thought—but didn't
add. She and Kellec hadn't told Narat about Virus B
and Virus C and how that discovery had led them to
this formula, which might actually be a cure. Kellec

was testing a slightly different form of solution on Virus B, although what she and Kellec had told Narat was that Kellec was merely doing a double check.

Narat trusted them. He hadn't looked too closely at either experiment.

"The next step is to use test subjects," Pulaski said. She wiped a hand over her forehead. "But we don't have any."

"Just the patients," Narat said.

"I hate injecting an untried solution into someone," Pulaski said.

"I have to agree with Narat on this one, Katherine," Kellec said. "They're going to die anyway. We have to see if we can stop it."

She nodded. She knew. She had done the same several times in crisis situations, the last time on the *Enterprise.* But each time her scientist's brain warned that one day they would inject the wrong substance into the wrong patient, and that that patient would die too soon.

"Why don't you and Narat try the Cardassians?" Kellec said. "I'll try the Bajorans."

"It might not work on one group or the other," Narat said.

"We'll deal with that when it happens," Pulaski said. She took a deep breath. "Let's at least try a couple of patients before we inject everyone."

Narat nodded. "That much caution I can accept. Let's take three: one who is nearly gone, one in the middle of the disease, and one at the beginning."

"Get Edgar to help you find the patients," Pulaski said. "And Alyssa is among the Bajorans."

She sat down. Something was bothering her about

the cure, she wasn't sure what. But it would come to her. Eventually.

Kellec was working among the Bajorans, moving beds so that they were closer to the office, injecting hypospray on the three patients. In the cultures, the results had happened quickly. Pulaski wasn't sure what would happen in an actual body.

Narat was doing the same with the Cardassians.

Ogawa looked excited. A strand of hair had fallen from her neat bun, and she was smiling for the first time since they had reached Terok Nor.

Governo seemed solemn. He probably wasn't certain this would work. The entire trip had been hard on him—first-time away missions often were for medical personnel, and this one was particularly difficult. Failure here would be worse than anything any of them had ever faced before, except Pulaski, and right now even she would be hard-pressed to remember an occasion worse than this.

Kellec finished with his few patients and sat down beside her. "How long do you think this will take?"

"If we're lucky, twenty minutes," she said.

They both knew what would happen if they were unlucky. They watched Narat work with the Cardassians.

"If this works," Kellec said, "it's only going to work on the virus. People will still catch it."

"I know." He had put his finger on what had been bothering her. "Maybe, though, it'll be like catching a cold—not anything to worry about."

"Maybe," he said. "But it bothers me that we haven't found how this thing incubates. You know how pernicious viruses are."

She did. Viruses mutated, often after medicine was introduced. She shivered. "Don't even think it."

"I have to," he said. "I'm worried."

"Dr. Kellec?" Nurse Ogawa called from the Bajoran section. "You need to come here."

Kellec cursed. "It backfired. We should have known better than to try this untested—"

Pulaski put her hand on his arm. "Shhh. You're jumping to conclusions."

They both went into the next room. The patient nearest the door, a young Bajoran girl, looked tired, her skin sallow. She sat up, with a hand on her head. "I'm hungry," she said with a bit of surprise.

Pulaski opened her tricorder and ran it over the girl. There wasn't a trace of the virus in her system. Kellec was confirming the information on the biobed readouts.

"She's cured," Pulaski said.

He examined the readings another time.

"Which one was she?" Pulaski asked Ogawa.

"The least sick," Ogawa said. Her smile had grown bigger. "And look, the next is losing some of that healthy color."

How odd that they were celebrating the fact that their patients were looking less healthy, but it was part of the disease to look that way. And part of the cure to go back to the way they had looked before, when they were subjected to all the difficulties of Terok Nor.

"Katherine," Kellec said softly. "We did it." And then he flung his arms around her, pulling her close. "We did it!"

She hugged him back and let him dance her around

the room. Finally, she put a hand on his arm. "Kellec, we have a lot of people to inject with this cure."

"Yes," he said. "You make up a large batch, and I'll get going on injections."

"I'll take some down to Crystal in the Bajoran section," Ogawa said.

"Help her down there," Kellec said. "She'll need it."

Ogawa smiled and left. Pulaski went into the office. The Bajorans were cured, but she didn't know about the Cardassians. Her heart stopped when she saw Narat.

He was standing over a bed, his hands covering his face, his body so hunched that he looked as if he were in pain.

"My god," she whispered. What had saved the Bajorans had killed the Cardassians. And she had been so careful to make sure they had the slightly different injection.

She went to the other room and put a hand on Narat's shoulder. He was shaking.

"Narat?" she asked.

He raised his head. "I didn't think we'd—I didn't think—Look!" He pointed down. The Cardassian on the bed, whom Pulaski recognized as one of the guards, was his usual gray. His scales still flaked, but they didn't look as irritated as they had. And his eyes were bright.

She ran her tricorder over him as well. The virus was gone.

"Narat," she said. "You gave me quite a scare. I thought it hadn't worked."

"Oh, but it did, Dr. Pulaski. Thanks to you, we're all going to survive."

"I think we all had a part in it," she said. She put an arm around him and felt him lean against her. He wasn't a Cardassian to her anymore. He was simply a fellow doctor who had given up hope and didn't know what to do now that hope had been restored.

"Edgar," she said to Governo. "Start injecting our Cardassian patients. Dr. Narat will help you in a moment."

Governo nodded. He took the hypospray out of Narat's shaking hands. Pulaski led him into the office and helped him to a chair.

"I should be helping," he said. "I should—"

"You have enough to do," she said. "Edgar can handle things for the moment."

Narat looked at her. "What do you mean I have enough to do?"

"You need to reach Gul Dukat," she said. "We have to get this cure to Bajor." It was time to explain one thing to him. Otherwise nothing would work. She crouched. "Narat, I made a slightly different antidote for the Cardassians than for the Bajorans. It had to take into account the differences in physiology. I was afraid the Bajoran cure would make the Cardassians sick."

"It worked," he said, and she let out a small sigh of relief. He didn't ask any more questions.

"I'm going to continue to make up batches of the antidotes," she said. "The Cardassian version will be in the blue vials."

He nodded. Then he took a deep breath. "I didn't expect to react this way. I've never reacted like this—"

"Have you ever been faced with something like this before?"

He shook his head.

"Then give yourself a moment," she said. "Doctors have feelings too, even though we pretend not to."

She stood. Governo was injecting Cardassians all over the medical section. It was nice to see two of them back to their normal gray. The other test case wasn't bright green either. His skin color was a greenish gray that she assumed would become gray in a short period of time.

Kellec was smiling as he worked his way through the Bajorans. She had forgotten how good-looking he was when he smiled.

Out of the corner of her eye, she saw Narat stand. He went to the console and pressed a section with his palm. Dukat appeared on the small screen.

"I have good news," Narat said. "We found a cure."

Dukat closed his eyes and turned his head. Pulaski moved so that she could watch the entire interaction without being seen. Dukat let out a breath and then seemed to regain control of himself. He again faced the screen.

"If we move quickly," Narat said, ignoring Dukat's reaction, "we can save every life."

"Then what are you talking to me for?" Dukat said. "Do it."

"I don't just mean on the station," Narat said.

Dukat sucked in his breath. Pulaski threaded her fingers together. This was the key point.

"We need to get the information to Bajor, and Cardassia Prime, in case the plague gets there. The faster we do it, the better off we'll be."

"Can they manufacture this antidote themselves or must we make it for them?"

"Both," Narat said. "Some areas may not have

anyone with the skills. I figure we take care of Terok Nor first and then send supplies to the planet below. Before that, though, I'll need to send the information to both planets."

"All right," Dukat said. He looked visibly relieved. "Is there anything else?"

Narat shook his head, but Pulaski stepped forward, and put her hand on his arm. "If I might intrude, Gul," she said.

Dukat looked surprised to see her. So, in truth, did Narat. He had apparently forgotten she was there.

"Did you find the antidote?" Dukat asked.

"All three of us did," she said.

"We wouldn't have found it without her," Narat said. "She brought a fresh perspective to the work."

Dukat templed his fingers and rested the tips against his mouth. He was contemplating her through the screen. It made her as uncomfortable as he had when they first met.

"We have found the cure for the virus," she said, "but we don't know how long the virus incubates. People will still catch it, until we figure out a way to stop it before the symptoms appear."

"But they won't die?" Dukat asked.

She nodded. "They will no longer die."

"Good. Then what do you need?"

"This is a designer virus," she said. "Someone made it. If we could find out where it first appeared, then we might be able to find who created it. Or at least, figure out how it is transmitted in its nonviral state."

"I'm afraid I'm not a doctor," Dukat said. "I didn't follow that."

"You see," Pulaski started, but Narat put his hand on her arm.

"The virus has several stages," Narat said. "We've caught it in all but the first stage. We're looking for that one still. If we find that one, we can prevent this virus from ever infecting us again."

"So what do you need from me?" Dukat asked.

"Permission to search for the source of the virus," Pulaski said.

"And you believe that it's on Bajor?" Dukat asked.

"I believe nothing," she said. "It could easily be here. But we must cover all of our bases."

"*I* believe it is on Bajor," Dukat said. "*I* believe the Bajorans infected themselves so that they could pass the disease onto us. They just didn't realize how lethal it would be."

"In my experience of the Bajoran people," Pulaski said, "I have never seen such behavior. It violates all of their beliefs."

"Forgive me, Doctor," Dukat said, "but your experience of the Bajoran people is of one rather eccentric Bajoran doctor."

"It seems you haven't read my file as carefully as I thought you had," Pulaski said.

Dukat shrugged. "I will not give you or your assistants permission to go to Bajor."

"If we find the source—"

"I said, I will not give your people permission to go to Bajor. I'm bending the rules to allow you here."

She took a deep breath. "It's important—"

"I understand that," Dukat said. "Narat will send a Cardassian team to Bajor in the next day or two. That will suffice."

No, it wouldn't. It wouldn't suffice at all. They

would be looking for the wrong things. They would be looking for proof of Dukat's theory, that the Bajorans started this disease.

"I think an impartial observer would be best," she said.

"And we have none, as you have just indicated, Doctor. You and your people seem closer to the Bajorans than I'm comfortable with." He smiled at her. "I am very pleased with your work so far. Don't spoil it."

Narat's grip on her arm was firm. "We'll do what you say, Gul Dukat," Narat said. "I'll have a team ready."

"Good. Prepare my announcement. I want to send those messages to Bajor and Cardassia Prime within the hour," Dukat said.

Narat nodded.

"One more thing," Dukat said. "I don't mean to sound insensitive." He paused and as he did, Kellec entered the room, but remained outside of Dukat's sight range. "But I am getting pressure about the decreased ore production. When do you believe we can get our Bajorans back to work?"

The question was directed at Narat, but Pulaski felt herself start to answer. Narat's fingers dug so hard into her arm that she nearly cried out in pain.

"A few days," Narat said.

"A few days is a long time, Narat," Dukat said. "We're already disastrously far behind."

Narat smiled. "Look at it this way," he said. "Just an hour ago, you were worried about surviving. Now you're worried about your future. Things have improved."

Dukat laughed. "So they have," he said, and signed off.

"Cardassian dog!" Kellec said, closing the door behind him. "All they think about is how much slave labor they can get out of us."

Narat stiffened beside Pulaski.

"Not all of them, Kellec," Pulaski said gently. "Narat has a different perspective."

"If you had a different perspective," Kellec said, "you wouldn't have made that promise."

"And what would you have had me do?" Narat said. "Tell him nothing and let him make the decision?"

They stared at each other for a moment. Finally, Kellec looked away. "Katherine," he said, "I need more of the antidote. I'm going to help with the work below."

"You've finished here?"

"For now," he said.

She nodded. "I have a batch already made up. I'll have another by the time you get back."

He picked up the vials she indicated, and then shook his head. "If there weren't lives at stake, I wonder if I would be doing this. I certainly don't want to be the agent that forces our people back into slave labor." And then he left himself out the door.

"He talks a big game," Pulaski said. "But he'll do what's right."

Narat nodded. "He's a good doctor."

They were both silent for a moment and then Pulaski said, "I'm afraid I don't think a Cardassian team will do us any good."

"It's all you're going to get," Narat said. "We can be impartial, you know."

She didn't know that. She didn't believe it either. That comment Gul Dukat made had angered her as well. She hadn't realized that she was closer to Kellec's beliefs than Narat's. But she said nothing. She made herself smile at him. "Well, then," she said, "I guess we have work to do."

"Good work," Narat said. "We're back in the business of saving lives."

"Thank heavens," Pulaski said. She wasn't sure how much more death she could take.

Chapter Seventeen

THE STENCH IN THE BAJORAN SECTION seemed worse than it had just a few hours before. Kellec entered the main corridor. The nightmare he had alleviated above still existed down here, the sick people all over the floors, the awful moaning, the heightened skin color. He wished it all would end.

He was carrying his kit with him. In the mess area, Ogawa and Marvig were inoculating the sickest patients first. Bajorans who had no symptoms or who had very few were helping find the sickest patients and getting them treatment first. It looked like an efficient system and Kellec wasn't going to interfere with it.

Instead, he went as far from that area as he could, to a room he wasn't even supposed to know existed. The Cardassian guards never came here; they thought it was a supply closet, not knowing that the Bajorans had long ago taken over the closet and made it a base.

There were sick people lining the corridors here, too. He bent over the nearest person—a young man, barely into puberty, and gave him a hypospray. It didn't take long for an older man to crouch beside him.

"Kellec," the man said.

"Rashan," Kellec said. "Is Ficen Dobat still well?"

"Well enough," Rashan said.

"Could you find him for me?"

Rashan nodded and disappeared down the corridor. Kellec went from patient to patient, inoculating each one, working as fast as he could. Soon he would have to go back to the med lab to get more of the antidote. He wasn't sure how he could look at Narat.

Katherine was right, of course. Narat was a good man who did what he could within the system. But Kellec believed a man should do more than "what he could within the system." If the system was flawed, a man had to work outside it. But Kellec said nothing to Narat. It would do no good.

Katherine didn't know that yet. Kellec wished he had arrived at the office just moments earlier. He had been too far away when he saw her step near the monitor. He had hurried to the office and held the door open ever so slightly, hearing her every word.

If only she had spoken to him first, perhaps Dukat might not have noticed if she disappeared off the station for a while. Kellec might have been able to smuggle her to Bajor, for her and her crew to witness the horrible conditions on the planet. Dukat would never agree to that. And Kellec wished Katharine hadn't told him her suspicions—all of their suspicions actually—that the disease had originated on Bajor.

Dukat chose to look at that as a sign that the Bajorans were infecting themselves so that they could make the Cardassians ill. But Katherine was right; the majority of Bajorans would find such a practice abhorrent. Though there were deviants in every group—he'd met a few in the resistance—they were always dealt with by the group leader. The crazies never got the upper hand.

No. Kellec understood what had happened. It was subtle and it was scary. The Cardassians had planted the virus, just as he had always suspected, and had done it on Bajor to make sure it would look like the Bajorans had created the disease. He found it suspicious that the disease hadn't made its way to Cardassia Prime. It was just like the Cardassians—but not the Bajorans—to sacrifice a few of their people for the good of all of them. If only he could get to Bajor, or if he could get someone there he could trust, he would be able to prove this.

At least Katherine had seen Dukat's true colors. He wasn't worried about losing Bajorans. He was worried about the drop in production. If Terok Nor failed to meet its quotas, Dukat could lose his comfortable position. And once the threat of death was removed, that was all he cared about.

He had moved far from the corridor he had started in. He was almost out of the antidote. He would have to go back to the medical lab in a moment. He couldn't stall much longer. He didn't see any Cardassian guards, but he couldn't assume that there weren't any. The Cardassians would leave guards down here until they were all dead. There just weren't as many as usual, because the sickness had depleted the Cardassian ranks as well.

Kellec stood and put a hand against his back. The moaning had quieted, and a few of the patients were looking brighter-eyed than they had a short time before. He smiled. At least he had been able to do this. His work rarely gave him satisfaction anymore—he was always repairing wounds that would never happen if the Cardassians didn't occupy Bajor—but this did satisfy him. Just that morning, he had thought everyone on Terok Nor would die. Everyone but Katherine, her team, and those silly Ferengi.

Rashan reappeared, silently, a talent of his. He put his hand on Kellec's shoulder. "Is there anything I can do?" he asked.

"Check on the patients near the area where I started," Kellec said.

Rashan nodded. As he passed, he said under his breath, "There are three Cardassian guards at the mouth of the corridor. Have a care."

And then he was gone.

Kellec resisted looking in the direction Rashan had indicated. Instead, he examined his kit to see how much more antidote he had. Enough to stall for a few more minutes.

But he wouldn't have to. As he looked, he realized that someone was standing beside him. He turned, and found himself face to face with Ficen Dobat.

"I understand you need a bit of help," Ficen said. He was a small man, the kind who disappeared easily in a crowd. Even when he was noticed, most people couldn't describe him well—a Bajoran of average height, brown hair, brown eyes, not very remarkable.

But Ficen *was* remarkable. He currently led the resistance on Terok Nor, and he frequently accomplished the impossible.

Kellec smiled. "We found an antidote."

"Not a moment too soon," Ficen said. "We've already lost some good people."

They crouched near the kit. Kellec found a second hypospray and pretended to fill it. He didn't dare let Ficen use it—the man was untrained—but if those Cardassians poked their heads in this corridor, it would look as if he were helping Kellec.

"I have a favor to ask," Kellec said.

"Anything," Ficen said. "You've saved us, once again."

"Remember that when I make this request," Kellec said.

Ficen frowned.

"I need someone to go to Bajor for me. I need to find the source of this disease."

"The source?"

"Where it was first reported."

"And you think that was on Bajor?"

Kellec met Ficen's gaze. "I need to know, to clear this completely from all of us."

"Our people—" Ficen began, but Kellec held up a hand.

"I think the Cardassians started this and tried to make it look like we did it," Kellec said. "That probably means it started in a resistance cell somewhere, probably a place that's fairly centrally located."

"No resistance cell could be infiltrated by the Cardassians," Ficen said.

"Are you implying that we did this, just like the

Cardassians say? Do we have cells that desperate?" Kellec said.

Ficen frowned. "Desperate times call for desperate measures."

"But this?" Kellec said. "Surely we wouldn't do this." He swept his hand over the corridor.

Ficen shook his head. "Of course not," he said. "But we know what it's like here, and it's easy even for us to contemplate the idea. Imagine how easy it is for the Cardassians."

"The ones who aren't already in the know," Kellec said.

Ficen sighed. "I don't think sending one of our people there is a good idea."

"I don't see any other choice," Kellec said. "Dukat is sending a team of his own to Bajor to investigate this. You know what he'll find."

Ficen cursed. "If they believe we did this, they'll retaliate."

"That's why we need real information, gathered by our own people." Kellec glanced over his shoulder. No guards so far. "But it has to be people we can trust."

Ficen nodded. "I'll see what I can do."

"Not good enough," Kellec said.

Ficen stood and handed the hypospray back to Kellec. "All right then," he said. "I'll let you know as soon as our team leaves Terok Nor."

Kellec smiled. "That's better," he said.

Chapter Eighteen

KIRA WAS VIOLATING HER AGREEMENT with Odo, but she had to. Ever since she had heard that a representative of the Federation was on Terok Nor, she'd been trying to figure out a way to make contact. And if Odo's report was accurate, she had to do so quickly. She had been exposed to the virus, and didn't have a lot of time left before she would have to seek out medical attention. She had heard that Kellec and his team had found a cure to the disease, but only after someone already had symptoms.

She wasn't looking forward to that.

She was in the habitat ring, near the quarters assigned to newcomers. It had taken her most of the evening to find where their rooms were located; she couldn't ask anyone, and her computer skills, while good, weren't good enough to find all of the alarm triggers the Cardassians had built into the system.

The only thing she had working for her was that as many Cardassians were sick as Bajorans. There were very few guards, and the ones she had seen were more preoccupied with the state of their own good health than with keeping an eye on Bajorans. Kira made sure she was wearing tattered old clothes, and she kept her hair tousled, so that she looked as if she were struggling—either with ore production or keeping her family alive somewhere.

She *was* struggling; that much was true. All of her contacts here were either ill or dying. She still hadn't found Ficen and she didn't know how to ask for him. Most of the Bajorans in the Bajoran section were preoccupied with their own families; they couldn't keep track of anything else.

Since she had arrived, she had been uneasy, frightened. She wished she could see Kellec Ton, but that was clearly becoming impossible. She thought of approaching the Federation assistants who were working in the Bajoran section. She had even come close to them once, close enough to overhear their discussions and to realize they weren't in charge of this mission. They were all on their first assignment outside Federation space, and were as baffled by it all as new recruits always were when brought into their first resistance cell.

No. She was in this corridor because she had no other choice. She hoped no one had found her tracks yet in the computer system. She had looked up several things, just in case someone was trying to find her, and had buried her request among half a dozen others. She figured it would give her time.

It had also given her the access code to the visitors' quarters' door. She hoped the Federation doctor wasn't paranoid enough to change her locks when she arrived. This would be the test.

Kira moved away from the wall and turned to the door. She punched the access override code into the lock—and heard the door shush open. One more step completed.

The quarters were dark. Apparently the doctor liked to sleep in total blackness. Kira stood completely still for a moment, letting her eyes adjust.

They did.

She listened, and heard deep, even breathing from the next room.

This was her first opportunity with the Federation doctor. The woman hadn't come to her quarters until very late. As Kira's eyes got used to the light, she saw clothing scattered on a nearby chair. Kira had heard that the woman had been awake for thirty-five hours straight. When she got to the room, she probably couldn't wait to get to sleep.

Well, Kira had no choice but to interrupt that sleep. She knew the layout of the quarters. It was like all others in this side of the habitat ring: a large main room, with a sleeping room to the right, replicators and the bathroom to the left. Kira slipped into the bedroom, and said softly, "Computer, low-level ambient light."

She wasn't sure if that gambit would work, but it did. Apparently the computer was programmed in the guest quarters to accept commands from any voice. The lights came up just a little, relieving the complete darkness and adding a very faint golden glow to the room.

The bed was in the center of everything. The

woman who had been sleeping there was older than Kira had expected, and she wasn't particularly beautiful—which struck Kira as odd. With Kellec Ton's natural charm and good looks, she would have assumed he would have found a gorgeous mate. Apparently he was attracted to nice-looking women with a lot of brains.

"Who're you?" the woman—Pulaski, wasn't it?—asked. She was amazingly calm, given that she had just awakened to find a stranger in her bedchamber.

"My name doesn't matter," Kira said. "And I don't have a lot of time, so please listen to me."

Pulaski sat up in bed, adjusted the blankets around her, and pushed brown hair out of her eyes. "Computer," she said, as if Kira hadn't spoken, "how long have I been asleep?"

"One hour, three minutes, and forty-five seconds."

She sighed and leaned her head against the headboard. "One hour, three minutes, and forty-five seconds. I was hoping for at least two hours." She looked up at Kira. "This had better be good."

"I would like you to come with me to Bajor," Kira said.

Pulaski frowned, just a little. "I've already been through this with Gul Dukat. I'm afraid I can't leave the station."

"He doesn't have to know," Kira said. "I'll smuggle you down there and I'll bring you back."

"How is that possible?" Pulaski asked.

"I was on Bajor just two days ago. There are ways," Kira said. Her hands were damp. She was nervous. "I understand you've found a cure. They don't need you up here right now—"

"On the contrary," Pulaski said. "They do need me. The cure is only effective if someone is symptomatic. That means this disease can still spread all over the quadrant because we haven't found a way to take care of it in its incubation phases."

"But that's not urgent," Kira said. "Taking you to Bajor is."

"And why is that?" Pulaski asked. "We've already sent them the formula for the antidote, and we're sending some live cure down in shuttles. I'm not needed."

"You are," Kira said. "Not as a doctor. As an observer. We've been trying to get Federation representatives to Bajor for a long time, to see the conditions the Cardassians have imposed on us during the Occupation. Please. I'll take you to a few places, and we can do it quickly. No one will know you're gone. There are rumors of Federation negotiations with the Cardassians. We—"

Pulaski held up her hand. "I'm sorry," she said.

"No." Kira clenched her fists. "I won't take no for an answer. I won't. We need you."

Pulaski closed her eyes for a moment, then leaned her head back. It seemed as if she were making a decision. Finally she opened her eyes and looked at Kira.

"Now it's your turn to listen to me," Pulaski said softly. "The Cardassians didn't want us here. We had to agree to a lot of terms before we could arrive."

"One of them was turning your back on Bajoran suffering?" Kira asked.

"That's not fair," Pulaski said. "We're here because of Bajoran suffering."

"And Cardassian. I guess those rumors were correct. You are working with the Cardassians."

Pulaski shook her head. "I am here as a consultant on this disease only. I have strict orders to stay out of the political fights. In fact, I have to."

"Have to." Kira took a step forward. How many times had she heard that argument before? "Of course. You have to. So you won't see the atrocities being committed under your nose. So that you have deniability."

"I didn't say that." Somehow Pulaski's voice was still calm . . . what would it take to get this woman riled up? "What I did say was that in order to come here, we had to agree to terms. Or we wouldn't have been able to come at all."

"What does that have to do with me?" Kira said.

"Everything." Pulaski got out of bed. She was wearing a nightshirt, and her feet were bare. She grabbed a robe from her suitcase. She apparently hadn't even had time to unpack. "If the Cardassians find out that I was meeting with a Bajoran in my quarters, I would be reprimanded at best."

"You're afraid of a reprimand from Gul Dukat?" Kira couldn't keep the sarcasm from her voice.

Pulaski shook her head. "One of the terms we agreed to was that if one of my team got caught spying—or there was a suspicion of spying—we would all be killed."

"That's traditional Cardassian rhetoric," Kira said.

"You don't believe they'd do it?" Pulaski asked.

"Oh, they would if they caught you. But right now they're not going to catch anyone. So many of the Cardassians are sick, and those that aren't are concerned about staying well. It's a perfect scenario. Like I said, they won't miss you."

Pulaski's smile was small. "I wish I had your confidence in that. But I'm responsible for three other lives, and I'm not willing to risk them."

"How Starfleet of you," Kira said. "Your lives are so much more important than ours."

"You have quite a temper, don't you?" Pulaski asked.

Kira felt a flush build.

"It prevents you from seeing clearly." Pulaski took a step closer to Kira. They weren't that far apart now. Pulaski was slightly taller, but Kira was in better shape. She could kidnap the lady doctor and get her on that shuttle with no trouble at all.

"I see clearly enough," Kira said.

"Then you understand why I don't risk my team," Pulaski said.

"Because you are afraid of violating an agreement with the Cardassians." Kira spit out that last.

Pulaski shook her head. "We've had the privilege of coming to Terok Nor. As far as I know, no other Federation group—official or unofficial—has come here. I have spent most of my time in the medical lab, but my assistants have been all over the station, caring for Cardassians and Bajorans. The majority of the work two of my team members have done has been in the Bajoran section."

Pulaski stopped there. The words hung between them. Kira was beginning to understand where Pulaski was going, but wasn't sure she wanted to join her.

Pulaski's face was filled with compassion. "The Cardassians have worked hard to keep up their little fiction that everything is going well. But they've been having trouble doing so. As you said, there are very few guards and very little security right now. And my teams have had to venture into areas that I'm sure would have been off-limits otherwise."

"It's not the same as seeing Bajor," Kira said.

"No," Pulaski said. "It's not. But it will have to do. We'll be debriefed when we leave. And we'll be honest. We won't have to make anything up."

"You're trying to pretend that you sympathize with us when you make agreements with the Cardassians."

Pulaski's shoulders sagged. "If I were a Cardassian sympathizer, do you think I would have been married to Kellec Ton?"

"But you aren't any longer."

"That's right," Pulaski said. "Yet he's the one who asked for my help. There are many qualified doctors in Starfleet—and many unaffiliated ones all over the quadrant. Why do you think he asked for me?"

Kira crossed her arms and turned away. The woman had a point. A good point. Kira was letting her own disappointment blind her. She wanted the Federation group to come to Bajor so badly. She needed someone there. She felt if there were outside observers, things would change. They had to change—

She felt a hand on her shoulder. She looked back to see Pulaski's calm eyes measuring her.

"You could do us a favor, though."

"Us?" Kira said.

"Kellec and me."

Kira frowned. "How?"

"I tried to get permission to go to Bajor today. Gul Dukat refused, understandably. He's as afraid of letting me go down there as you are desirous of it. And probably for the same reason. He's worried about what information I'd take back to the Federation."

"I know," Kira said. "If you—"

"Please," Pulaski said. "Let me finish. We need to find the source of the virus."

"I thought you had a cure."

"We do, but it's not as effective as we'd like. We'd like a cure that destroys this virus completely. I don't know if you've been told, but this is a designer virus—"

"I know," Kira said.

"Then you understand that someone created it and someone planted it somewhere, we're not sure where. I wanted to go to Bajor to search for the source of the disease, but Dukat said no. He assigned a Cardassian team to conduct the search."

"Cardassians!" Kira pulled away. "You know what kind of search they'll do. They'll search until they have enough to prove that Bajorans did this thing, and then they'll use it as an excuse to slaughter hundreds of us."

"That's what I'm afraid of," Pulaski said. "So we need a pre-emptive strike. If you would go to Bajor and get this information on where the virus started *before* the Cardassians do, then we have two chances. The first is to find a solution that neutralizes this disease completely, and the second is to prevent the very scenario you're describing. If I can go to Dukat with proof that the virus started somewhere and it was brought in—or, even better, we can find the virus's designer—he'll have to call off his team. He wouldn't dare slaughter Bajorans in revenge. Not in front of a Federation observer."

"No," Kira said bitterly. "He'll wait until you're gone."

"And by then, the Bajorans at risk will have disappeared, won't they?" Pulaski asked.

Kira frowned. She had completely misjudged this woman. No wonder Kellec Ton had been attracted to her. Beneath that calm exterior, she had the courage of a Bajoran.

"Yes," Kira said slowly. "They could disappear."

"Good," Pulaski said.

"Before I go, I'd like to check with Kellec Ton, see if he agrees with the plan."

"Then do so," Pulaski said.

Kira shook her head. "It's not that easy. I can't move about freely in the Cardassian sections."

"Then I'll make certain he's in the Bajoran section in—what?—forty-five minutes?"

Kira should be able to make it back by then. "That'll do."

"Good," Pulaski said. She headed back toward the bed. "I understand your need to check up on me. But you'll find I'm on the level. I'm sure Kellec will have no objections to your trip to the surface."

"If you send Cardassian guards, I'll shoot them," Kira said.

"If I send Cardassian guards," Pulaski said, "you have every right to shoot me."

"Don't think I won't."

Pulaski smiled. "I know better than to double-cross a person like you," she said. "After all, I was once married to one. Now, if you'll excuse me, I'll contact Kellec, and then try to catch at least another hour of sleep."

Kira nodded. She couldn't quite bring herself to thank Pulaski—things hadn't gone as well as Kira had hoped. But they were still moving forward. And Kira felt as if she were being useful for the first time since this plague began.

And for her, being in the fight was always better than standing on the sidelines watching.

Chapter Nineteen

"I DON'T KNOW WHAT WENT WRONG," Kellec said. He was in the office staring through the door at the green Cardassians staggering in and the Bajorans brought up from below. Pulaski was at his side. She had never felt so discouraged in her life.

"Obviously something did," Narat said, and Pulaski could hear the blame in his voice. The two of them got along fine when things were moving well, but now they weren't getting along at all. They were taking the problems out on each other.

Reports of illness had started to come in only an hour ago. Now they had an official run on the med lab. Patients who had been cured ten hours ago were coming back, the sickness obviously in its early stages. A few had waited until the early stages were long past, and so, Pulaski believed, continued passing the disease on to others.

"Something did go wrong," she said without turning around. Governo was handling the Cardassians as he did before. She had instructed him to give them another dose of the antidote. Marvig was still in the Bajoran section, but Nurse Ogawa had come up with some of the sicker Bajorans to get them better treatment in the med lab.

"You know what it is?" Narat asked.

Pulaski nodded. Kellec was looking at her too. She let the door between the office and the main room close.

"If you think about it, you know just as well as I do," she said. "We haven't found how the virus starts. We have succeeded in preventing these patients from dying, but they're clearly reinfecting themselves."

"Or picking up the virus elsewhere," Narat said.

She shook her head. "I don't think so. Even when a patient caught the disease from the virus—and could prove that it wasn't incubating—that patient took at least two days to show signs of illness. These patients are coming back within ten to twelve hours."

"That means," Kellec said, "that the infecting agent isn't the virus."

Pulaski nodded. "Perhaps if we run some cultures, we can imitate the course of this reinfection in the lab."

"It should work," Kellec said.

"We should examine some of our older cultures as well," Narat said, his irritation with Kellec obviously forgotten.

"Good idea," Kellec said.

"It's not quite as hopeless," Pulaski said. "At least we have a point to work from."

The office door opened. Governo peeked in. "May I see you for a moment?" he asked Pulaski.

She walked over to him.

"I'm doing what you said," he said softly, "but I'm a little worried about reinjecting these Cardassians with the antidote. I mean, we don't know what this will do in high quantities in the body."

"The boy has a good point," Narat said.

"Yes, he does," Pulaski said. She put a hand on Governo's shoulder. "Just continue for now, Edgar. Whatever happens, it's better than dying for these poor people."

He nodded and went back into the main room. Pulaski closed the door again and leaned on it. The exhaustion she had been trying to fight was coming back, worse than before. "We're going to have to notify Bajor and Cardassia Prime."

"I suspect they already know," Ton said. "Let's not waste our time on that."

"No," she said. "We have to. What if they've sent patients away, thinking they were cured, and they can't get back to a medical facility?"

"They would have done it twelve hours ago, Katherine," Kellec said. "We have to focus our efforts here."

"Kellec is right," Narat said. "At this moment, everything we do should go toward finding the correct solution."

Pulaski nodded. But something was flitting around at the edge of her consciousness. Something she vaguely remembered—

"One of us should be doing as your assistant implied, Katherine." Kellec was standing near his console. "One of us should see if there are detrimental effects from too much antidote. We have to know where our limits are."

She looked at him. She knew he was going to suggest that Narat do it.

"You two found the cure in the first place," Narat said. "I'm not the researcher that you both are. You continue your search for the virus's origins. I'll investigate the effect of the antidote."

Pulaski let out a breath she hadn't even known she was holding. She made herself look away from Kellec, afraid that she would show her relief too clearly.

"All right." She walked over to the console. "Still, something more is bothering me. Something I feel I should know—"

"There were rumors," Kellec said, "that the Federation dealt with a similar plague, but I don't know the details."

"Of course," Pulaski said. "That's why this is bothering me."

"That was one of the reasons I asked permission to get you to come here. I figured you would know."

"I do know," she said. "The *Enterprise,* the ship I was on, dealt with it. But I never read the files. I always meant to—in fact, I was supposed to go through all of Crusher's logs, but I simply didn't have time. I looked at the overview and went on with my day-to-day work."

"That's not going to help us, Katherine," Kellec said. "You—"

"What is the meaning of this?" The office door crashed open and Dukat strode inside followed by three guards. One of them could barely stand. He was a light gray-green.

All three doctors glanced at each other. They had agreed moments ago to stall telling Dukat as long as possible.

"We told you, sir," Narat said, "that we can only treat a patient once the symptoms appear."

"Do I look like an idiot to you?" Dukat asked. His voice was lower than it had been a moment ago, and seemed a lot more menacing. "I have sent newly infected people back to the med lab for their shots. Those people are fine. But Linit here nearly died yesterday of this disease, and now he's got it again! You told me this was a cure."

"I know," Narat said. "But—"

Pulaski put a hand on his arm to quiet him. Narat seemed panicked by Dukat's anger, and panic would not do in this circumstance.

"When we told you about the cure," she said, "we also told you that it wasn't complete."

"You didn't tell me this would happen," Dukat said.

"We didn't know. We hoped the cure would hold once it killed the virus. But our patients seem to be reinfecting themselves."

"Themselves?"

"Yes," she said. "It's coming from within. That may sound bad to you—and I must admit, none of us are too happy about this turn of events—but it is good news in a way. It gives us something to base our new research on. It gives us hope."

"Hope! We had hope when we thought we'd gotten rid of this disease."

"We can get rid of it," Narat said. "For a few hours anyway."

"What good will that do?" Dukat asked.

"It'll prevent anyone from dying," Kellec said.

Dukat's lips thinned. He turned away from Kellec. "I'm very unhappy about this," Dukat said.

"We all are," Pulaski said.

"Yeah," Kellec said. "You would save us a lot of grief if you would just ask your people what the source of the virus was."

"Kellec!" Pulaski said.

"No," Dukat said. "That's fine. He can accuse us all he wants. It covers his Bajoran tracks. You're reinfecting everyone, aren't you, Kellec? That way no one gets off this station alive, and the Cardassians get the blame."

"You know better—" Kellec started forward, but Pulaski grabbed him.

"Both of you, stop it," she said. "You're acting like children."

She glanced at Narat for help but he hadn't moved. He was looking terrified.

"Fighting won't get us anywhere." She kept her hands on Kellec, but stepped between him and Dukat. "I've been with Kellec all day, and he hasn't done anything to reinfect your people. He hasn't had the opportunity. And you," she said, turning to Kellec, "can't you see how terrified he is? If he knew how this thing started, he wouldn't be this afraid."

"I am not afraid," Dukat said.

Kellec had the common sense to say nothing. Only grunt.

Dukat's eyes narrowed, but he also said nothing. Narat's gaze met Pulaski's. "She's right, you know," he said. "This is a time when we have to put aside our differences."

"It's getting very hard to do," Dukat said. "You

gave us all hope yesterday and today it's gone. That's worse than having no hope in the first place."

"But I already explained what this means," Pulaski said. "It means we have a chance."

"I don't see it," Dukat said.

"There's one option we haven't tried," Kellec said. He eased himself away from Pulaski's hand. "Katherine and I were discussing it when you so nicely knocked and asked if you could come in."

"Kellec," Pulaski said warningly.

"And what's that?" Dukat asked, obviously choosing to ignore Kellec's tone.

"Katherine says the *Enterprise* dealt with something similar over a year ago. Remember when I asked you if she could come aboard, I told you there were rumors about this?"

Dukat turned his flat gaze to Pulaski. "So you have records of this?"

"No," she said, "and that's the problem. What I do know of it is very sketchy. But it wouldn't take long to get the information. The *Enterprise* is the ship that's waiting to pick us up, just outside Cardassian space."

"What a wonderful opportunity to bring a starship to Terok Nor," Dukat said, and to Pulaski he sounded just like Kellec. She took a deep breath, forcing herself to remain calm. They deserved each other. All this fighting and lack of reason. No wonder no one knew how to solve the problems between their two planets.

"I wasn't suggesting that," she said, working very hard to keep her voice level. "I would like to contact the *Enterprise* and have them send the records here."

Dukat frowned, as if her response surprised him. Then he said, "I will contact the *Enterprise.*"

"I'm sorry, Gul," she said, slipping back into her diplomatic mode, "but they won't give this information to you. You're not a doctor."

"Then Narat—"

"They'll wonder why I haven't asked," she said. "It's a simple request, really. You can monitor it."

Dukat's reptilian smile filled his face. "That would work. You may make the request, from my office."

"Katherine, I don't think that's a good idea," Kellec said.

"Do you want the information or not?" Dukat asked.

"I think we need it," Kellec said. "I just don't see why she can't send the message from here."

"Because," Dukat said, "it will interfere with your work. Yours and Narat's. You may come up with a solution on your own, while she's gone."

"It's all right, Kellec," she said. "I'll be fine."

"You don't know what this man is capable of," Kellec said.

She sighed. "I think, at the moment, we all have the same goals."

Dukat tilted his head, and smiled mockingly at Kellec. "I think your wife—"

"Ex-wife," Kellec said.

"—is telling us we can resume our loathing of each other when the crisis is past."

Kellec crossed his arms. "Thanks, but I plan to continue my loathing all the way through the crisis."

"Then I'll remove you and place you back in the Bajoran section," Dukat said.

"Oh," Kellec said. "I promise the loathing won't get in the way of my work. But, unlike you, I can't shut off my emotions when dealing with others. I see the consequences of each action."

Pulaski put her hand on Dukat's arm and started to lead him out of the office. "Each moment we delay is a moment that we need," she said to him.

He let her guide him into the main room. Cardassians were returning at a rate of two or three a minute. He grimaced at their green skin, the flaking scales, and she felt a shudder run through him.

"I would hope," she said, because she couldn't keep silent, "that you watch Kellec's actions, instead of listening to his words."

"I'm keeping a close eye on his actions," Dukat said. "I know what kind of a man he is."

They stepped into the Promenade and Dukat relaxed visibly.

"What surprises me," he continued, "is why you married him."

She smiled. "He's brilliant man."

"He's a fool."

"He hates witnessing pain. The Cardassians have caused a lot of pain on Bajor."

"The Bajorans brought it on themselves," Dukat said.

"I don't think the Bajorans would agree with that."

"What do you know?" Dukat asked. "You haven't observed our people."

"No," she said, "and I'm not trained in the subject. All I see is hatred on both sides. One day that will hurt you all."

"If we live through this plague," he said.

"That's my responsibility," she said. "I plan to see that you do."

Chapter Twenty

THE IMAGE OF DOZENS OF DEAD bodies piled on top of a cart like so much deadwood came back again, superimposed on the image of the stars she was gazing at through the Ten-Forward window, and pushing the voices of the *Enterprise* crew into the background. But this time Beverly Crusher didn't try to push the image away the way she usually did. She let herself remember the limbs jutting awkwardly, the tags on their toes, and just the sheer *number* of dead piled high in the Archarian hospital because there was no more room in the morgue.

That was Crusher's first view of the plague on Archaria III and the image that stayed burned in her mind. Thousands more died before she had found a cure.

But the image of those bodies never went away.

Neither did the memory of sixteen of her crew-mates, including Deanna Troi, suffering the intense, crippling pain that seemed to twist from the inside, eating them alive like a monster Crusher couldn't see. And at the time couldn't fight.

It had taken Crusher some months to stop having nightmares.

But now the nightmares were back. The situation on Bajor seemed so similar to Archaria III. And she had helped Dr. Pulaski to walk into it basically alone. If only she had been able to go along, that would have been better than waiting here. But her request had been denied.

And she had been relieved. . . . She didn't want to face another plague. Not again. Not so soon. She didn't think she could handle another roomful of bodies piled on top of one another.

A gentle touch on her arm brought her back to the stars and the muffled conversation in the lounge. She turned and smiled at Captain Jean-Luc Picard, whose hand was resting comfortably on her arm.

"She's a good doctor," he said. He could still read her clearly. She had been annoyed at that a year ago. Then she discovered, in her short stint at Starfleet Medical, that she missed it.

Crusher nodded. Dr. Pulaski was. But even the best needed help at times. And it felt so frustrating not to be able to be there giving that help, instead of sitting here sipping Earl Grey tea.

"I know she's good," said Crusher. "That's not the problem. The problem is me. I hate waiting."

"Don't we all," the Captain said.

He was waiting too, waiting to hear from Pulaski. And he had served with the woman for the last year. He had to be worried. But in typical Jean-Luc fashion, he didn't say anything. He was willing to listen to her.

Over the last few days Ten-Forward had become Crusher's haven. Dr. Pulaski had left the medical areas in better shape than they'd been in a year ago, and it had only taken Crusher a day to get settled back in. Since the *Enterprise* was simply standing by on the Cardassian border, waiting for two weeks, there was very little for her to do. Being alone just wasn't what she needed at the moment, so she often sought company from whoever she found in the lounge. She didn't always talk. Sometimes she just let the buzz of conversation flow over her while she drank tea.

And thought of that pile of bodies on Archaria III.

She smiled at the captain, then took a sip of her tea, letting its perfumy flavor push the image of death back for a moment. "Thanks for joining me," she said.

He shrugged slightly. "We missed you last year. I missed you. I thought we might take this opportunity to get caught up."

She laughed. "And so I sit staring out the window."

"Sometimes," the captain said, "that's the best kind of catching up."

She smiled at him. She had missed him and the *Enterprise* a great deal. She had used Wesley as her main reason for returning, but in truth, there were many reasons.

"Dr. Crusher," Data's voice broke into the moment

over the comm link. "You have an emergency incoming call from Dr. Pulaski on Terok Nor."

She was on her feet and headed for the screen built into the wall of Ten-Forward before she answered. "Put it through to here."

A moment later she had dodged around two tables and was at the screen as Dr. Pulaski's face appeared. Behind her stood a stern-looking Cardassian.

Crusher managed not to gasp at what she saw. In just a few short days Pulaski looked as if she'd lived a dozen years, all without sleep. A week before, a neat, polished doctor had turned the medical area over to her; now Pulaski had deep circles under her eyes, her hair looked like it hadn't been combed in years, and a dark smudge of something streaked her neck.

And her eyes seemed almost haunted, as if she were seeing things no human should ever see.

"Dr. Crusher," Pulaski said, her voice level as always, "I need your help."

"Anything," Crusher said as Captain Picard moved up behind her.

"I need your records from the plague on Archaria III. It seems we may be dealing with something similar here."

Crusher nodded. "I was afraid of that."

"Can you send the records?" Pulaski asked. She was wasting no time. Crusher knew exactly how that felt.

Crusher glanced around at the captain, even though he would have nothing to do with this decision. The records of the plague on Archaria III were classified and under the direct control of Starfleet

Medical. And since she was no longer in charge of Starfleet Medical, it was no longer her decision as to whether or not to release those records.

"How bad is it?" Crusher asked, trying to buy herself a little time to think. To get a message to Starfleet Medical from this distance could take a day, maybe more. And there was always a chance—a strong chance, considering the location of the plague—that they might turn her request down.

"It's bad," Pulaski said. "I wouldn't be making this request if I didn't think those records might help."

"Understood," Crusher said. "I'll need to—" The image of the bodies on Archaria III floated back to her mind. She had been about to say she would have to get clearance from Starfleet Medical, but in that time how many on Bajor would die?

How many deaths would it cost for her to follow the rules exactly?

Even one was too many.

She would get permission from Starfleet Medical after the records were sent. She had a few favors she could call in yet. She'd make them understand.

But that would take time. Time Dr. Pulaski didn't have.

She faced Pulaski directly. "Doctor, the encoded records will be downloaded to you within the next minute. Please stand by on this channel."

Pulaski's relief was obvious. "Thank you."

"Is there anything more we can do?" she asked, half-hoping Pulaski would invite her to Terok Nor.

Crusher wanted to be busy. She could always say that the situation forced her to disobey the initial orders from Starfleet Medical.

"This just might be enough," Pulaski said. "Standing by."

The image went blank.

Crusher tapped her combadge. "Data, please download on the open line to Terok Nor all medical information from the Archaria III incident. Medical only. Let me know when you are finished."

"Understood," Data said.

She turned to the captain.

"I know I didn't follow procedure. I'll make it right with Starfleet Medical, though. It won't be a problem for you, Jean-Luc."

"I'm not worried about that, Beverly." His tone was warm. "I would have suggested you take the course of action you chose. It's clearly very bad there."

"How can you tell?" she asked.

"The Cardassian behind Dr. Pulaski," the captain said. "That was Gul Dukat himself."

Crusher instantly knew what the captain was saying. The image of the Archarian bodies came back. Crusher hadn't been able to save her, but maybe this time the bodies wouldn't be so numerous that they'd have to pile them in Terok Nor's infirmary.

"Data to Dr. Crusher."

"Go ahead," she said.

"All records have been sent."

"Thank you," she said.

She looked at the captain. "Now I guess it's time I faced the music with Starfleet Medical."

195

"We face the music," he said, taking her arm and heading her toward the door. "I was on Archaria III also. Remember?"

The image of the dead bodies came back again. Crusher squeezed the captain's hand in thanks. "How could I forget?"

Chapter Twenty-one

AH, THE SOUND OF CONVERSATION and laughter in his bar. Quark leaned against the back wall and closed his eyes. How he had missed this. It wasn't just the sound of the Dabo wheel and the silly girl's voice crying "Dabo!" or the clink of glasses, or even the silent accumulation of latinum as it made its way from his patrons' hands to his pockets. No. It was the feeling that he was in a viable business once more.

He was almost grateful to the plague. It had been such a traumatic experience that those who felt they had dodged it were coming into Quark's, wanting to drink themselves into oblivion. He was going to let them.

"Brother."

Of course Rom *would* interrupt Quark's reverie. Any time Quark felt that things were going his way, he had to be reminded of the presence of his stupid brother.

"What?" Quark asked, opening his eyes. Five more Cardassians were coming into the bar, laughing and slapping each other on the back.

"Brother, I have something to tell you."

"Well, it can wait," Quark said. "See those five? They're new customers and they need to buy drinks."

"Brother—"

"This is about making profits, Rom," Quark said. "Remember. 'A Ferengi without profit is no Ferengi at all.'"

"Brother, please don't quote the rules to me," Rom said. "I have something to tell you."

Quark leaned forward. "I'll make you recite every one of the rules if you don't get to work."

"Ah, yes, brother." Rom scurried toward the center of the bar, balancing a tray precariously on one hand.

Quark shook his head and began to make drinks. He already knew what three of those Cardassians would have. They were regulars, at least when they were well. And they were well now.

A Cardassian stood up in the back. Quark frowned. He had seen this before. He had a sinking sensation in his stomach. Maybe the lighting was bad. Maybe the Cardassian had spilled his drink. Maybe. There had to be some other explanation for the green color of his skin and the way he was swaying.

Quark slid out the side of the bar and hurried toward the Cardassian. If he got the Cardassian out of here before the man collapsed, there might be a chance that no one else would notice. Some kind of chance.

Any kind of chance.

Quark was halfway there when the Cardassian fell backwards.

All noise in the bar stopped. The Cardassian's companion stood and looked down at his fallen friend.

"This can't be right," he said. "He just got over the plague."

It was enough to start a stampede to the door. Quark grabbed at customers. "Don't believe them," he said. "I'm sure they misunderstood. Maybe he had been misdiagnosed. Surely—"

But no one was listening to him. They streamed out as if they were afraid they would suddenly topple over backwards, their skin a lovely shade of lime green. Even the Dabo girl had disappeared.

"Brother," Rom said.

Quark held up a hand. "Don't say a word to me. I don't want to hear it."

He headed back to the bar. It had taken five hours to fill the place up again, and only two minutes to empty it out. Except for the Cardassian on the floor. Moaning.

"Call a med team, would you, Rom?"

Rom gaped at him. "But brother, last time you made us—"

"I know what I did last time," Quark said. "There was no one in the bar then. Unless it was my imagination, we had a full bar this time. There's no hiding this one."

"All right, brother." Rom let his tray drop as he stared at the Cardassian.

Quark stared at Rom.

More specifically, Quark stared at Rom's ear.

On the lobe was a shiny pimple, with a whitehead that looked as if it could burst at any moment.

"Tell me, Rom," Quark said slowly. "A Cardassian dumped a case of Jibetian beer on your head."

"No, brother," Rom said, turning to him. "Well, not since the last time. No one has dumped anything on me."

"Then do you want to tell me where that pimple came from?" Quark asked, pointing.

Rom clapped a hand over the offending lobe. "I was trying to tell you."

"You were trying to tell me in a full bar. Now we have an empty bar. How did you get that—pustule—on your ear?"

Rom shrugged. "It grew there."

"Like hair."

"Or skin."

Quark nodded slowly. "And you're comfortable with that?"

"No," Rom said. "It itches. I was going to ask you if you had any cream left."

"I have some cream left," Quark said.

"I would like to borrow it," Rom said formally.

"And after you've applied it to your ear, you'll what? Scrape it off so that you can return it to me?"

"No," Rom said, obviously flustered. "I mean, I would—"

"You want me to give it to you," Quark said.

"Yes," Rom said. "But not all of it. Since you need it too."

"I don't need it," Quark said.

"Yes, you do," Rom said.

"No, I don't," Quark said. "I healed days ago. That's why I'm wondering what happened to you."

"The same thing that happened to you, brother. It came back."

Quark reached both hands up slowly and clapped his ears. Beneath his right hand, he felt a lump.

A pimple.

A pustule.

"What did you do to cause this?" Quark asked.

"Nothing," Rom said. "Maybe the cream didn't work."

"Obviously the cream didn't work," Quark said. He sank into a chair. "Not that it matters." He stared at the moaning green Cardassian on his floor. "No one will ever come here again."

Rom stared at him for a moment, then sat down beside him. "Things are bad, aren't they?"

Quark nodded. "And they're getting worse."

Chapter Twenty-two

PULASKI WAITED UNTIL KELLEC and Narat were seated in the small medical office's only two chairs. Governo and Marvig stood against the wall, and Ogawa was just coming in. The room was hot and stuffy, like almost everything on Terok Nor. With six of them, it was going to do nothing but get worse before this short meeting was over.

"Leave that door open," she said to Ogawa.

"Thank you," Governo said. Pulaski could see he was already sweating.

She had called this meeting the instant she got back to the medical area with the information from the *Enterprise*. It had taken fifteen minutes for them all to gather from different parts of the station, enough time for her to go over the data quickly. She didn't like what she saw, especially the final conclusion Dr.

Crusher had put in the notes after the crisis was over.

"Ready?" She glanced at everyone.

"Do it, Katherine," Kellec said.

She nodded to him. In all the years she had known him, she'd never seen him this worried. Or this tired. The human faces around her all had deep worry carved in them, and Narat was now starting to look more afraid than anything else. But Kellec looked so strained she would have thought him seriously ill if she hadn't known what he had been through.

"Here's what the *Enterprise* was dealing with on Archaria III." She brought up the information supplied by Dr. Crusher on the screen in front of them. The three-dimensional image of a virus slowly spun, showing all its sides.

"That's very different from what we're dealing with," Kellec said.

And it was. Its shape bore no resemblance at all to the viruses she had spent the last week studying.

"Completely," Narat said.

"At a glance, I agree," Pulaski said. "This particular virus would be harmless to any Cardassian or Bajoran—or human, for that matter. This one wasn't designed for Cardassians or Bajorans or humans. It was designed to strike at cross-species breeds."

"Designed?" Narat asked.

"Designed," Pulaski said, "just as the virus we're dealing with was designed."

"Did they ever discover who created that one?" Governo asked.

"No," she said. "They didn't."

"Too bad," Marvig said.

"So why is this important?" Kellec said. "I see no possible connection."

Pulaski knew when her ex-husband was getting impatient and might just rudely leave.

"I'll get to that in a moment, Kellec," she said. "There is a tie, believe me."

He made a face, but remained in his chair.

She took a deep breath and then touched the console. "This is how the Archaria virus was formed." She set the screen in reverse motion.

The screen showed a computer image of the DNA of the virus shifting, breaking apart, until finally all that was left was three prions, the smallest life-form known to science. Prions were so tiny that not even transporter biofilters could remove them, so light they could blow on a slight breeze, and strong enough to live through freezing cold.

"The three prions are harmless separately," Pulaski said, "but when all three were present in the body of a cross-species humanoid, they merged and somehow rewrote their own DNA to form a deadly virus. Watch again."

She set the screen in forward motion and the three prions joined, changed, and formed the deadly Archaria virus.

"Amazing," Kellec said.

"So if the virus was killed," Narat said, "but the three prions remained in the body, the patient was reinfected."

"Almost at once," Pulaski said.

"Which is what we're dealing with here," Kellec said.

"This is pure evil," Marvig said.

"Again," Pulaski said, "I need to caution you all that our patients getting reinfected is just a similar symptom. There might be a completely different cause, we don't know yet. But at least this gives us a starting place we didn't have before."

"So our next step is what?" Governo asked.

Pulaski pointed at the tables where the sick were. "We take a few patients, both Cardassian and Bajoran, and cure them of the virus. Then we watch the prions in their blood to see if this pattern, or something similar, occurs. Once we know that, we might be on the track to a permanent cure."

"We can hope," Kellec said.

"You'd better do more than hope, Doctor."

The voice spun Kellec and Narat around.

Marvig stepped further away from the door.

Pulaski had seen Dukat come in just a second before Kellec spoke. The Gul now stood in the doorway of the medical office. He nodded to her.

"Fighting has broken out in a dozen places on Bajor," Dukat said, not waiting for a response from Kellec. "If it spreads here I don't have enough healthy guards to contain it. And if I can't contain it, the Cardassian fleet will."

"They're getting afraid back on Cardassia Prime," Kellec said. "I thought the mighty Cardassian warrior never showed fear."

"Kellec!" Pulaski said, making her voice take on the command authority she'd learned over the years. "Now is not the time."

Dukat nodded to her. He didn't even bother to smile. He was worried now, and not at all interested in baiting Kellec.

"You'd better listen to her, Bajoran," Dukat said.

"At the moment I am the best friend you have. Find the final cure and find it fast. The Cardassian government will not allow this to reach Cardassia Prime."

Dukat turned and strode from the room.

Pulaski turned to say something to her ex-husband, but then stopped. His face was as white as she'd ever seen it. Narat was hunched so far over that he looked as if he were going to be sick.

Kellec glanced at Narat. "He means it, doesn't he?" Kellec asked.

Narat nodded.

"Means what?" Governo asked.

"Yeah," Marvig said, "what was that all about?"

"The Cardassian fleet will destroy this station and everyone on it—and all of Bajor—to stop this," Kellec said.

Again the Cardassian doctor nodded, as if destroying an entire planet's population was something they talked about every day.

For all Pulaski knew, maybe around here they did.

Chapter Twenty-three

KIRA SLIPPED INTO THE SECURITY OFFICE, looking both ways before closing the door. No one saw her go in, which was good. Very good.

The office was empty, of course. The constable was everywhere except where he was supposed to be. She didn't know how to summon him. Create a ruckus on the Promenade? Who would notice now that the disease was back? Only it wasn't really back—at least that's what one of the human medical assistants had told her.

It had never really left.

At least they had found a way to keep everyone from dying. That was a step in the right direction.

She made her way behind the desk and stared at the security console. Cardassian design, of course; but there had been modifications, modifications she didn't entirely understand. She threaded her fingers together, then eased them forward, cracking the knuckles. Since Odo wasn't here, she would just play with the console until he arrived. That would get his attention, and she might learn a few things in the process.

She placed a hand over the screen, wondering where to start.

"Touch that," Odo's gravelly voice said, "and you will spend the rest of your life in the brig."

"Oh, you frightened me," she said, but she moved her hand. Then she looked up. He was standing before her, his brown uniform trim as always. The door was closed, just as she had left it. Had he slid in under it? Or hadn't she heard him enter?

"You like to take chances, don't you?" he asked.

She gave him a half smile and shrugged. "One gets used to a certain level of danger."

"Maybe you do," he said. "But people who play dangerously around here more often than not get killed."

"Is that a threat?"

"From me, no," Odo said. "But if Dukat were to know you were here, then it would be. You need to be more cautious."

"Actually," she said. "That's why I'm here."

"You want me to teach you to be more cautious?" He actually sounded surprised. And then she realized he was making a joke. Not a very funny one, but it was at least an attempt.

"No," she said. "I need your help."

"Well," he said. "Isn't that an interesting turn of events."

She wasn't used to being a supplicant, especially

with someone in a position of authority in a Cardassian government. "I need to get off the station."

"I thought we discussed that," he said.

"We did," she said. "That's why I'm here. I need your help to leave."

"Why should I do that?"

"Because," she said. "Kellec Ton has asked me to go to the surface to help him with the research."

"Kellec Ton?"

"And his ex-wife Pulaski."

"Why would they want you to go, when Dukat has already sent a team below?"

She stared at him for a moment. He worked for the Cardassians but he had always struck her as different. How different, she didn't know. And she couldn't rely on a guess.

"They need independent confirmation of the Cardassian findings."

"They don't trust the Cardassian findings, you mean," Odo said.

"And with cause," Kira said. "The Cardassians started this thing."

"It seems to me," Odo said, "they shouldn't trust the Bajoran findings either."

She stared at him.

"But then, it would be the prudent course to get information from both sides and compare. Somewhere in the middle they would find the truth." He tilted his strange head at her. "Do you have written permission from Kellec Ton to leave the station?"

He was playing with her again. Why did this shapeshifter always make her feel off-balance? Because she had never encountered anyone like him before? Or because he knew how to get to her when no one else did?

"Of course I don't have written permission," she said.

"Then how do I know you're not making this up?" Odo asked.

"Why would I make it up?"

"Why indeed." He frowned, musing. "I suppose I'll just have to check with Kellec."

"Okay," she said. "And Dr. Pulaski."

"And Dr. Pulaski," he said.

He didn't move, though; he didn't try to use his console or leave the room, either. He just watched her for a moment and then, to her surprise, he attempted a smile. It looked as if he didn't make that expression very often. It came out as half a grimace.

"All right," he said. "You may go."

"As easy as that?" she asked.

"As easy as that," he said.

"It's too easy."

"It's what you wanted."

"Yes, but you didn't check."

"You weren't worried about it. That's confirmation enough for me."

"What about the quarantine?" Kira asked. "Aren't you worried I'll fly off somewhere else?"

"Why should I worry about that?" he asked. "Even if Cardassian space weren't so heavily patrolled, you would never try anything like that."

"Just two days ago, you were worried that I might leave here and infect someone else."

"Two days ago, there wasn't a Cardassian fleet surrounding Terok Nor and Bajor. You couldn't go anywhere besides Bajor if you were the most cunning pilot in the quadrant."

Kira sank into the constable's chair. "The Cardassian fleet? What are they doing?"

"Think about it," Odo said. "The plague is back."

"And they don't want it to spread to Cardassia Prime." Kira pounded a fist on the console. "Those bastards!"

Something beeped beneath her hand.

"I would prefer it if you take your anger out on something a little less sensitive," Odo said.

"Well, then, I guess my mission becomes even more urgent," Kira said.

"It would seem so." Odo rounded the desk. "I'll give you clearance. Then the fleet won't give you any trouble."

She looked at him. Those eyes. So sad. She wondered why she always thought of him as sad.

"That's the second time you've done me a favor. Why?"

He shrugged. "Maybe I'll ask for repayment one day."

"Maybe." She slipped from behind the desk. "Anyway, thanks."

"You're welcome," he said. "But be careful. If this disease is a designer virus, like they're saying, finding information about it won't be easy."

She nodded. "Thanks for the warning."

"And it might also be dangerous."

"That one I figured out on my own." She glanced at the door. Two Cardassian guards walked through the Promenade. "I hate to impose on you one more time," she said, "but do you think you could beam me to my ship from here?"

He sighed. "What's one more violation among friends?" he asked, and pressed the console a few times.

As the transporter beam caught her, she saw him look up. His expression was unguarded—and worried? No. That had to be her imagination. She vowed to shut that imagination off while she conducted her investigation on Bajor. She couldn't afford to indulge in speculation.

Especially since that's all her Cardassian counterparts would be doing.

212

Chapter Twenty-four

DISTANT PHASER FIRE ECHOED throughout the station. Quark had the doors to the business shut and bolted and was still hiding behind the bar. His ear was swollen and covered with blisters. It itched so bad he couldn't think, and he was doing everything he could with his hands to keep them from scratching.

"That's the last of it, brother," Rom said as he came out of their quarters. His right ear was bleeding again. Quark shook his head. If the bar had been open, if he had had any customers, if he had still been serving drinks, he would have forbidden Rom to come out in public. But none of that mattered anymore.

The Bajorans had started rebelling in the Bajoran section, shooting the remaining Cardassian guards. Gul Dukat didn't have the forces to keep the Bajorans in check. It would only be a matter of time before they

213

overran the station—and then Quark *really* didn't know what he'd do. The Bajorans weren't well known for having a lot of latinum.

Nog entered the bar behind his father. He was wearing the cap the Volian had made for Rom, attempting to follow Quark's edict not to scratch.

Quark sighed. He had hidden away all of the latinum, and had made Rom and Nog hide the expensive liquor. Now there was nothing he could do except—

"Aeeiieee!" He clapped a hand over his left ear and fell backwards. The itching suddenly got so intense that it was painful. Rom hurried to his side.

"Let me see, brother."

"You're not touching me with those infected hands," Quark said and rolled over, pressing his ear against the floor.

"I'll wash them first," Rom said.

"Just let us see, uncle," Nog said, crouching beside him.

Slowly Quark rolled the opposite direction so that they could see his left ear.

"Oh, my," Rom said.

"Oh, my?" Quark asked.

"Oh, my, my, my," Rom said.

"Oh, my, my, my, what?"

"Oh, my, my, my, my, my."

With his free hand, Quark shoved his brother. "Stop it! What do you see?"

"They're too big to be blisters," Nog said.

"What are?"

"The lumps, with pus, traveling toward your ear canal."

"Brother, you know how sensitive ear canals can be. If one of those gets down there and bursts . . ."

They all stared at each other. Then Quark got to his feet.

"I don't care who is shooting at whom, we have to get to the infirmary."

"People are dying, brother," Rom said.

"They're not dying anymore, stupid," Quark said. "They're just sick. And they aren't threatened with—" he couldn't suppress the shudder "—loss of ear function."

Rom's eyes got bigger. Nog put a hand on his hat. "That won't happen, will it, uncle?"

"Yes, it will," Quark said, "and it'll happen to me first. Let's go."

They walked to the door of the bar and peered through the glass design. The Promenade was empty.

"I think you should stay here, Nog," Rom said.

"Why?"

"It might be dangerous out there."

"No more dangerous than in here," Nog said, tugging on the hat.

"I want him treated too," Quark said. "I don't want to be reinfected."

He hit the door release and the glass doors opened. The silence was short-lived. He heard more shots and a few screams coming from far away.

"Follow me," he whispered. He motioned them out and let the doors close and lock behind them. He kept to the wall and crouched; at this level, no one would mistake them for Cardassians. Or Bajorans for that matter.

It took only a few moments to reach the infirmary. The stench was as bad as it had been before. Maybe worse. Quark let himself inside, and saw patients everywhere, mostly Cardassians, leaning against the wall in a semblance of a line. At the end of it, the male hu-man assistant was attacking them all with a hypo-spray.

A few Cardassians sat on beds, clutching limbs with phaser burns. Dr. Narat came out of the office and his gaze met Quark's.

"I don't have time for Ferengi nonsense," he said.

"Look," Quark said, shoving his ear in Narat's direction. "The infection has gotten worse. It's heading for the ear canal and when it gets there—"

"I don't care," Narat said. "You can wait. It's not life-threatening."

"Well, that depends," Quark said. "If this continues, my quality of life will be dramatically lowered."

"It's a minor problem," Narat said. "Go back to your bar. When things settle down, we'll worry about your ear infection."

"Ear infection?" The hu-man female stood in the office door. She wore clothes and looked much too efficient for a female.

"Yes," Narat said. "I'm trying to get rid of them."

"Let me see," she said. She walked over to Quark, who tilted his head up so that she could examine his ear.

Her fingers were gentle on his lobes. If he weren't in so much pain—

"Kellec," she said. "Come see this."

Kellec Ton came out of the office and frowned at her. "What?" he said. "It's just an ear infection. I treated it before."

"You did?" she asked.

"Yes, with some antibacterial cream."

"How long ago was that?"

"A few days."

"And it's come back, worse," Quark said.

"When did this start?" the female asked.

"When the Cardassians poured drinks all over me," Rom said, a bit too eagerly.

"When was that?" the female asked.

Rom frowned. "About the time that Cardassian turned green and—"

"About the time the plague started," Quark said. He didn't want Rom to admit they had carried a sick Cardassian out of the bar. Hu-mans, Bajorans, and particularly Cardassians wouldn't take well to that.

"Really?" the female said. She bent over his ear again. "Was it this bad when you saw it, Kellec?"

"No," he said.

Narat joined them. "What you're thinking is not possible," he said.

"What are you thinking?" Quark asked.

"A third species," the female said, not to him, but to the other doctors. "And of course it manifests differently. And not as seriously."

"That we know of," Kellec said. "This could just be the early stages."

"Are you saying we have the plague?" Quark asked.

"Come into the office and let's find out," the female said. She sounded remarkably cheery about the whole thing.

Rom grabbed Quark's arm. "Brother, I don't want to die."

"It's not high on my list either," Quark said.

"It's better than being green for the rest of your life," Nog said, looking around. Rom shushed him, and shoved him forward.

"We won't die, will we?" Quark asked Narat as he followed him into the crammed office.

"Oh, you'll die," Narat said. Then he smiled. "Someday, anyway. You just probably won't die of this."

"Some bedside manner," Quark mumbled, and clenched his fists so that he wouldn't scratch his extremely itchy ears.

Chapter Twenty-five

THE SOUNDS OF PHASER FIRE off in the distance echoed through the heat and choking stench of the Bajoran section. Kellec Ton had never thought he would ever hear the sounds of battle here. Clearly a few Bajorans had managed to get Cardassian guns and were holding off the Cardassian guards. All the Cardassian guards had been driven from the Bajoran section of the station. For all he knew, the fighters might even be making headway into the Cardassian section. But it wasn't a headway that was taking them anywhere except closer to their own deaths.

And his too.

He had no doubt that if the final cure wasn't found quickly, the Cardassians would destroy the station. And possibly even Bajor.

Yet he wasn't going to tell the fighters that. They were Bajorans, fighters against Cardassian rule. As

219

long as there was one of them left to fight, there was still hope.

Kellec moved quickly from one sick Bajoran to another, inoculating them with the temporary cure. It would get them back on their feet for at least ten hours. Then they'd be back sick again as the virus reformed and tore them apart. But at this point, ten hours was a very long time.

With luck Katherine and her people would find a final cure by then.

He checked his hypospray as he leaned over a young boy whose mother held him in her lap. She looked as flushed and sick as her son. He injected her first, then the boy. He had enough injections for a few more hours at this pace. He had brought supplies from the Cardassian medical lab, and his Bajoran assistants were helping him make more serum in the Bajoran medical area. But down here the process was much slower, the equipment nowhere near as good. There was no way they could keep making enough to maintain all the Bajorans alive until a final cure was found.

Since he'd come into the Bajoran section, the fighting had expanded from isolated sections and now covered the entire area. Most of it was between his position and the Cardassian medical lab. He doubted he could get through at this point; he'd face that problem when he completely ran out of serum.

Again, phaser fire echoed through the wide corridor as two Bajorans carrying another headed toward him.

"Doctor," one of them said, "can you help him?"

For an instant Kellec didn't realize the man they were carrying wasn't sick. He was wounded. A phaser had caught him in the left shoulder.

"Stretch him out here," Kellec said, motioning to an open place in the hallway beside the woman and her son.

They did as they were told, and quickly he inspected the wounded soldier. Phaser burn. Shock. But he would live, given a little time and care, assuming the entire station lived through this.

Kellec quickly gave the wounded soldier a shot against the virus just to be sure, then glanced up at the other soldiers. "Get him to the medical area. He's going to be fine. I'll check in on him in an hour or so."

"Thanks," the soldier said.

Kellec watched them carry him off. How crazy was this? He was temporarly curing his people of a deadly desease so they could keep fighting and dying. Sometimes it was hard to keep straight just why he was doing this.

The young boy took a deep shuddering breath, and then started to cry softly.

Kellec glanced at him. Both he and his mother were clearly recovering quickly, regaining the pale, hungry look of a normal Bajoran worker here on Terok Nor. More than likely, they were recovering for the second time.

He watched the mother comfort the child, then nodded. There was one of his reasons. The child. Kellec was fighting for a future for that child beyond working in an uridium-processing plant for a Cardassian dog. He'd keep his people alive long enough to see the Cardassians beaten, even if he had to die along with many others trying.

He moved on, injecting the temporary cure into Bajoran after Bajoran scattered along the wide hallway. And with each patient, he tried not to think about the fact that their only real hope for survival and winning this battle was Katherine and her crew.

They had to find the final cure and find it fast. But if there was anyone he trusted to do it, it was Katherine.

Chapter Twenty-six

IT HAD TAKEN KIRA LONGER than she expected to set up this meeting. She had been back on Bajor for more than a day, and three times she'd had to scramble for her life. The fighting here was intense and getting worse by the hour. The Bajorans saw weakness in the Cardassians and were fighting more and more directly, facing Cardassian guards head-on. She had never seen such ferocity in her own people—and she had always thought of them as extremely fierce—nor had she seen such desperation.

She had been feeling a bit desperate herself. Every time she stumbled, every time she felt even the slightest bit light-headed, she worried that she was getting sick. But so far, the disease had eluded her. She hoped it would continue to do so. There was no guarantee she would survive it if she caught it.

The plague was moving too swiftly. Too many

223

people were dying. They either didn't have access to the temporary cure, or they hadn't initally believed the cure was temporary and had disappeared back into the hills. Cardassian guards had taken to haunting medical areas, looking for resistance leaders, hoping to arrest them when they came in for the cure, and that was stopping people from seeking help as well.

The farther away from a city center she got, the less frequently she encountered anyone with a cure at all.

So many Bajorans believed their faith would protect them. So many thought this plague was a lie invented by the Cardassians. And so many more believed that if they just stayed away from other Bajorans while the contagion was on the planet they would be all right. All of that served only to increase the death rate.

And now Kira was a little too far away from the medical facilities for her own comfort. But she had been tracking information on the origin of this disease, and she had come here.

She loathed this part of Bajor. It was barren scrub land, so unlike most of the planet that sometimes she felt as if she weren't on Bajor at all. If she squinted she could see mountains in the distance—or perhaps she just imagined them and their comfort.

The resistance cell that operated out of this area was known for attempting to organize the other cells. It didn't work, but it did mean that the information that flowed here was usually reliable.

"Nerys?"

She turned. An old man stood behind her, his arms open. She slipped into them and hugged him hard. "Chamar," she said. "It's been a long time."

224

"Too long." He backed out of the hug. "You're looking well."

"For now," she said. "But I don't like what I'm hearing."

He nodded. "The plague. It is the final sin the Cardassians will commit against us."

She took his hands in hers. "Where are the others?"

His eyes were sad. "They have scattered. Some to their families in this time of need, and others to fight a more direct war against the Cardassians. There are only a few of us left here, and I am the one who offered to come meet you."

"You're well?" she asked.

"For now," he said, echoing her words. He took her arm and led her down a thin path into a copse of dying trees. Behind them was a sturdy hut that had been there as long as she remembered. And the nice thing about it was that unless you knew it was there, you couldn't see it.

He pushed open the door. The interior was neat. A single room with a table and some comfortable chairs, and a small area set aside for sleeping.

"Would you like something?" he asked.

"Whatever you have," she said, knowing she didn't dare push him. Chamar did things in his own time.

"You have been traveling."

"All over Bajor," she said, deciding not to mention Terok Nor. "I'm helping in the medical effort."

"You have become a doctor since I saw you last, Nerys?"

She laughed. "No," she said. "I'm doing research for them, which is why I'm here."

"To the point so quickly," he said, setting a mug of

juice in front of her. "You young people can wait for nothing."

So even in attempting to wait, she hadn't taken long enough. "I'm sorry, Chamar. It's just that every moment this disease lingers, we lose more Bajorans."

He nodded, looking tired. Then he closed his eyes. There was something he knew, something he didn't want to say. "What have you learned, Nerys?"

"That the first outbreaks happened at three different places on Bajor. The only things those places had in common were their space ports, the fact that they routinely sent ships to Terok Nor, and their high concentrations of Cardassians."

Chamar opened his eyes. "What else?"

"I heard rumors that Gel Kynled was behind this," she said. "I can't believe it. A Bajoran wouldn't do this."

He stared at her for a long time.

"I've met Gel," she said, "have you?"

"Once," Chamar said. "He wanted to serve in our cell. We threw him out."

"Why?"

"Because he walked up to a Cardassian guard and shot him at point-blank range—in front of witnesses. We had to risk good people to get him out of here. He was reckless."

"Yes," Kira said. "He was reckless. And he was dumb—he didn't have the ability to start anything of this magnitude."

"That's right," Chamar said. "If he were to spread a disease, he couldn't have created it. He would have had to buy it."

Kira felt as if someone slapped her. "You mean the

Cardassians sold him the virus and he released it? Not even Gel is that dumb."

"Was that dumb," Chamar said. "Some of the earliest reported deaths were in his cell."

"So he died of this thing?"

"No," Chamar said. "He was shot at curfew by a Jibetian trader about two weeks ago."

"A Jibetian?" Kira said. "I didn't know the Cardassians worked with the Jibetians."

"Some Jibetian traders are little better than mercenaries, Nerys. They sell both sides against the other."

"Do we know who this trader is?"

"No," Chamar said. "And we've tried to find out. I don't think we're going to be able to find the creator of the disease, at least not this way."

"And the Cardassians won't give him up."

"If he is, indeed, a Cardassian," Chamar said.

"Why do you doubt it?" Kira asked.

Chamar shrugged. "I believe the Cardassians are evil, and a threat to our people. But I also believe they are the most self-centered people in the quadrant. They would never sacrifice themselves to a greater cause."

"But what if it was an accident? What if they didn't know it would affect them?"

"Nerys, from what I've heard, this virus is insidious. Would someone who devised a killing machine like that not first make sure it wouldn't kill him?"

She leaned back in her chair. "I don't like what you're saying."

"I don't either," he said. "It's easier to believe the Cardassians would do this. And that is what we will tell our people, once this is solved."

"I had hoped I would be able to give the doctors more information than this," Kira said.

"If they are true researchers, each piece of information helps," Chamar said.

Kira shook her head. "You think someone sold Gel a biological weapon against the Cardassians and he actually chose to use it?"

Chamar stared at her for a long time. "Nerys, if I gave you a weapon, and told you that with only one use you could destroy the Cardassians forever, that Bajor would be at peace forever, would you use it?"

"I'd like to think not," she said. "That's genocide."

"Is it?" Chamar asked. "What lengths would we go to in order to get rid of the Cardassian menace? How many Cardassians have you killed for the cause?"

Kira flinched.

"What's a few more?"

She hadn't touched her juice. Now she pushed the glass away. "Are you saying Gel was right in what he did?"

"Gel wasn't a man who understood subtlety, Nerys. And he was given an opportunity. I don't know how many of us, having seen our loved ones die horribly and knowing that everyone we love might suffer the same fate, would let such an opportunity pass us by."

Kira stood slowly. "You're scaring me, Chamar."

"I scare myself sometimes, Nerys. But I have had years to think on this, and every time I do, I realize that we are not as noble as we believe."

"I would never kill my own people to get rid of the Cardassians," Kira said.

"I don't think Gel would have either," Chamar said. "Which is why I believe there was an outside agent. Think on it, Nerys. The promise of no Cardassians, a fanatic like Gel, and a weapon. Only what the creator of that weapon doesn't say is that it is a two-pronged weapon, which kills both sides."

"That's too hideous to contemplate," Kira said.

"Yes, it is," Chamar said. "Which is why I hope you—or someone—finds the creator of this disease."

She nodded. "First we have to stop it. I need to get a message to Kellec Ton on Terok Nor. Do you still have communication equipment?"

"In a safe place," he said. "Let me take you there."

He got up slowly. Kira watched him. The information she got wasn't much, and yet it felt like a lot. Almost too much. She thought she was used to the lengths people went to, used to the cruelty in the world. And then she was surprised, like this afternoon, when she discovered that someone could go a step further.

Chamar made his way to the door. Kira followed him. She would send the message to Terok Nor, and then she would go back to her own work. Before she joined the fighting, though, she had one more task. She needed to round up the sick and get them closer to the medical areas, to make sure they got treatment when treatment was available. And she knew the treatment would become available. She had to believe Pulaski and Kellec Ton would find a solution. They had to.

She sighed. Why was it so easy to destroy? And so very hard to rebuild?

She didn't know, and she doubted she ever would.

Chapter Twenty-seven

PULASKI STOOD AND FORCED HERSELF to move a little, loosening tight and tired muscles. She was sweating slighty in the heat of the contained room, and her eyes felt strained from far too many hours staring at data. "Got to pace yourself," she said to herself.

She did a few slow stretches, then moved over toward the door. Through the window of the office she could see most of the medical section. Her team had been the only ones still working in the area since Kellec and Narat had left, a few hours before. Pulaski hadn't wanted them to, but they'd both felt it was important to distribute the temporary cure to their people, keeping each side at least going for the short term.

But that left all the research on her. And she had felt the weight of it the moment Kellec left.

Ensign Marvig bent over a Bajoran, carefully monitoring the progress of the three prions with a medical tricorder. Her hair was pulled back and Pulaski could see a rip in one leg of her uniform. Marvig hadn't had time to go back to her quarters in the last thirty-six hours. None of them had. And with the fighting going on around the station, Pulaski doubted they could even make it now.

After getting the information from the *Enterprise,* it had taken them only a few hours to discover that it was three prions forming the virus that had cause this epidemic, too. Pulaski knew that was too much of a coincidence. More than likely, the same virus designer who had created the Archaria III plague had created this one. Who this designer was had to be solved later, although she wished it could happen now.

Who would do such a thing?

And why?

But she couldn't focus on that. Right now the focus had to be on stopping the virus's formation here and now.

Nurse Ogawa moved from Cardassian patient to Cardasian patient, doing basically what Ensign Marvig was doing—monitoring the progress of the three prions to see if they formed the virus again. Just twenty minutes ago they had decided to try the same idea Dr. Crusher and the *Enterprise* crew had come up with at Archaria III. They would know shortly if the *Enterprise* cure, as they were calling it, was going to work or not. For some reason she didn't think it would this time, since this was the work of the same designer. If she were designing a virus, and she hoped she would never go that crazy, she would make certain it didn't fall prey to the same cure a second time.

Still, she had to try. Maybe this one had been unleashed at the same time, but took longer to incubate.

Or longer to reach Bajor.

Although she doubted it.

Two of the Ferengi were still in the medical area, sitting on a lab table. The older one, named Rom, looked nervous while his young son seemed both defiant and very interested in everything around him. Ensign Governo was monitoring them for the same prion reformation. Somehow, Pulaski knew the answer was with the Ferengi. She just didn't know how they were involved. She knew the Bajorans infected the Cardassians with the prions that caused the virus. But who had infected the Ferengi? And why did it only give them blisters instead of killing them?

She shook her head and then stretched again. Too many unanswered questions.

A faint explosion lightly shook the floor, and Marvig glanced up, a look of fear in her eyes. Pulaski nodded at her in a reassuring way and Marvig half smiled and went back to work. Too bad it wasn't that easy with all these patients.

She just hoped Kellec was all right. She had no idea how bad it was out there, but at the moment, as long as the fighting didn't come in here, she didn't care. None of it was going to matter unless she found the cure for this virus.

Nurse Ogawa glanced over at her and shook her head no.

Pulaski moved out into the patient area. "Not working?"

"Virus is forming. The *Enterprise* cure isn't stopping it or even slowing it down."

"I'm afraid it's the same with the Bajorans," Marvig said.

"And the Ferengi," Governo said. But he didn't take his eyes off his medical tricorder.

"You mean we're still sick?" the older Ferengi asked, clearly panicked. He put his hand to his ears, as if he could protect them from the infection. The younger Ferengi put a hand on his father's leg to calm him down.

"I'm afraid so," Governo said, still studying the tricorder intently. "But just stay put and don't worry. We'll find the cure."

Pulaski wished she could be as sure as Governo sounded.

"Dr. Pulaski," Governo said, his voice sounding unsure, "this is really odd."

"What is?"

She was about to step toward Governo and the Ferengi when Narat stumbled through the door of the medical area, another Cardassian slumped over his shoulder.

Narat looked faintly green and very weak. And it took her a moment to understand who the other greenish-tinted Cardassian was.

Gul Dukat.

Acting like a well-trained trauma unit, her crew sprang into motion. She and Governo went to help Narat and Dukat while Marvig and Ogawa helped two Cardassians who were not as sick off the biobeds.

She took Dukat and levered him over and onto his back on the bed. He tried to help, but was clearly so weak his effort almost made it more difficult. Cardassians were heavy enough.

Governo grabbed Dukat's legs and lifted them onto the bed as Pulaski started the scan. The virus was throughout his system, extrememly far advanced.

"Why didn't you come in here earlier?" she asked.

The look of terror in Dukat's eyes surprised her, but he said nothing.

"Have you been injected with any of this cure before?"

He shook his head no, then closed his eyes for a moment at the effort.

She upped the dosage slightly and injected him. "Now stay still and try to rest."

His hand came up and grabbed her sleeve. "The permanent cure?"

"I'll find it if you let go of my sleeve," she said. "Now rest. And that's an order."

For a moment she thought he was going to get angry, then he nodded, let go of her, and closed his eyes.

On the bed beside Dukat, Narat had just gotten his injection of the temporary cure from Nurse Ogawa. He looked up at Pulaski. "Anything?"

She shook her head.

He sighed. "I was hoping." Then he closed his eyes.

She stared at the two Cardassians for a moment, then turned to Ogawa. "Monitor them closely. I want to know the moment the virus is clear from their systems."

"Understood," Ogawa said.

"Crystal, you continue monitoring the Bajorans."

"Yes, Doctor," Marvig said.

Pulaksi did a quick medical scan of Dukat. The

temporary cure was already attacking the virus. In fifteen minutes he'd be back to his normal, overbearing self. But that gave her fifteen minutes of time in which to work.

She turned to Governo. "Okay, what were you going to show me with the Ferengi?"

On the lab table, the older Ferengi actually flinched.

Chapter Twenty-eight

PULASKI WATCHED THE MEDICAL MONITOR as if it might
blow up at any moment. The Ferengi named Rom
squirmed on the biobed, even though no one was
actually touching him. She was instead looking at
what was happening in his body. Governo had noticed an odd reaction just before Dukat had come in.
But with the disruption of the now sleeping Dukat,
they had missed the timing on whatever Governo had
seen.

So they got the quivering Ferengi's permission to
reinfect him and then heal him again. It had taken
both the younger Ferengi and Governo a good twenty
minutes to convince him it would be safe. It wasn't
until the boy Ferengi offered to do it that the older one
caved in.

"Dukat's starting to come around," Ogawa said.

"Give him a light sedative," Pulaski said. "I want

him resting for at least another thirty minutes." Plus she wanted that long until she had to deal with him again.

"See it?" Governo said, his voice excited. He too was monitoring the ongoing prion activity in the Ferengi body.

"I did," Pulaski said. But she wasn't sure exactly what she had seen. It had happened so fast. But this time it was recorded, visual and all other data.

They both continued to monitor the forming of the virus until it was at its full stage, then she said, "Let's watch this on the screen in the office."

"Um," the Ferengi said.

Pulaski turned to him. She had learned in the last few moments that Rom was not very assertive.

"Um, would you mind curing me first?" he asked.

"Of course not," Pulaski said.

She nodded toward Governo, who hyposprayed the Ferengi. "There," he said when he was done. "All better."

The Ferengi's hands immediately went to his ears. His grin was wide enough to split his face. "Thanks."

Pulaski glanced at Narat. He was standing beside Dukat, monitoring his sleeping commander. Narat's color had returned to its normal healthy gray, just as Dukat's had. But Narat's stage of the infection had been nowhere near as advanced as Dukat's. With the gul, she was going to be safe.

"Narat, are you up to seeing something?"

"I think I should remain here," he said.

"All right." She was a bit relieved that he wasn't coming. She had kept so much from him in this research that she didn't want to blurt it out at the last minute. Still, she had to offer.

She followed Governo into the office. Right now Pulaski wished that Kellec were here. This was just the kind of thing she could use his knowledge on. But at the moment she was going to have to go it alone.

She quickly set the screen to start right before the strange event in the Ferengi virus formation, then started it slowly forward. Nothing seemed different. Three different and harmless prions were drawn together, just as in the other two races.

"Coming up right about now," Governo said.

As the prions started to join and alter their DNA, something different suddenly happened. The virus was formed, but also a fourth prion was formed and quickly expelled.

She froze the image on that prion, quickly isolated it and ran a computer diagnostic. The moment the data appeared, she glanced out the office window at the Cardassian doctor. Thank heavens he hadn't accepted her invitation.

"Amazing," Governo said, staring at the data. "That means what I think it means, doesn't it?"

She nodded. "That prion is the key prion in the Bajoran virus, which then mutates into the Cardassian virus."

"The Ferengi are carrying the catalyst prion that restores viral functioning even after it's cured." Governo said.

"Don't say that too loud," she said, glancing at where the nervous Ferengi and his calm son sat on the biobed, then at where Dukat still slept, with Narat standing beside him.

"Sorry," Governo said, his face white at what she was suggesting by the warning.

She stared at the data again. Her hunch had been

right about the Ferengi being critical elements in this. But that still didn't answer the question of how to stop the prions from forming the virus.

Out of the corner of her eye she could see Dukat starting to stir.

"Ensign," she said to Governo, "I want you to remain in here going over this data again and again. We need to find a way to stop those prions from coming together in the first place. No one else is to see this unless I give permission. Understand?"

"Yes," he said.

She headed out toward Dukat, who was now sitting up.

"Are we going to live or not?" the Ferengi asked.

"You're going to be fine," she said. "Just stay there and keep calm."

Then she turned to Dukat. "And how are you feeling, Gul?"

"I've been better," he said. His voice was raspy and his eyes were bloodshot. Some of his scales were still flaking, but he didn't seem to notice. "How's the research going?"

"We're making progress, but we haven't found a final cure yet."

He dropped down off the biobed and stood up straight, towering over her. For a moment he tested his own balance, then took a deep breath and nodded. Finally he looked at her. "Doctor, I need to talk with you for a moment. Alone."

She nodded and indicated the door of the medical area leading out into the wide hallway beyond. Normally she'd have escorted him into the office, but Governo was working in there, and she didn't want to disturb the ensign.

Dukat glanced at Narat, then turned toward the main door, leaving the Cardassian doctor looking puzzled.

Pulaski followed Dukat, watching his steps gain confidence with each stride.

In the corridor he turned to face her. Then with a quick glance around to make sure no one was close by, he said, "Doctor, I'm not sure how much longer I can contain this situation."

"I'm not sure I follow you," Pulaski said.

"Before I fell ill I managed to hold off the Cardassian fleet, saying we were on the verge of a final cure. They are expecting it soon."

"And if we can't come up with it we die," Pulaski said.

"I'm afraid so, Doctor," he said. "All of us. And more than likely all of Bajor."

For an instant the corridor seemed to spin. She took a deep breath and it stopped. "I had better get back to work and you had better try to buy me a little more time."

He nodded and without another word turned and headed off down the corridor, his stride long and sure.

She watched him for a moment, doing her best to keep her entire body from shaking. She had known coming here that she and her team might not get back alive. She had accepted that. But she had never expected also to have to save an entire planet.

Finally, she turned and headed back toward the medical office, ignoring Narat's stares. That extra prion in the Ferengi held the secret to the cure. And as Dukat had just made very clear, she didn't have much time to find it.

Chapter Twenty-nine

BAJOR FILLED THE VIEWPORTS of the docking ring as the sounds of fighting echoed down the corridor. Kellec Ton knelt in the hallway and quickly wrapped the burned arm of a Bajoran fighter, then injected him with a quick painkiller.

"You'll be all right," Kellec said, patting the man on the leg.

The man nodded weakly, as Kellec moved and crouched next to the woman leaning against the bulkhead two steps away. Plague, in its middle stage. The woman looked to be about Kellec's age and her skin had the rosy glow of the disease. Her face was dirty and she was starting to smell of rot. He quickly injected her with the temporary cure, and then monitored her as the medicine started to work. She was going to make it, at least for another ten hours or so.

"Rest here as long as you can," he said, and she nodded.

He stood and checked the level of his hypospray. He had enough for another thirty or so, then he'd be forced to try to make his way through the fighting to one of the medical labs.

Down the hall to his right the fighting was raging, as the Cardassian guards tried to retake this area of the docking ring. So far his people had held them off, but it didn't look as if that would last long. He'd been forced here by following the wounded and sick workers. It was like following a never-ending road of blood and death.

With the fighting echoing behind him, he moved down the large hall. A low moan caught his attention, coming from an alcove. Three Bajoran workers lay in the dark, against the wall. The smell in the small area made it seem as if they'd been dead for a week, but he could tell that two of them were still breathing. Barely.

He scanned them quickly. The two who were still alive both needed to be in one of the medical areas, but at the moment that wasn't possible. With all the fighting there was no one to take them there and no way to get there.

He gave both survivors full plague shots, then quickly checked them again. They might make it. He didn't have much choice but to leave them and keep helping others. At this point he'd done everything he could for them. They were so far gone that if they did recover they wouldn't even remember him being here.

He went back out into the main hallway, as a group of seven Bajoran workers moved past and turned into one of the docking-bay corridors. Two of them carried Cardassian weapons, while the others carried iron bars. Three of them looked as if they were in the early stages of the plague.

"Hold on," Kellec shouted. He ran up behind them and quickly injected one of the men who he could tell was quickly getting sick.

"You Kellec Ton?" A man with a bloody rag wrapped around his arm stepped forward.

"I am," Kellec said. Kellec pointed at the other one clearly coming down with the plague. "You need this." He held up his hypospray.

The man nodded and moved up to where Kellec could inject him.

Then Kellec looked at the rest of them. "Have the rest of you been given the plague cure in the last four or five hours?"

All of them nodded.

"We're getting out of here," the man with the bloody arm said. "Heading for Bajor. Help with the fighting there. You want to come along?"

"You won't make it," Kellec said, shaking his head.

"Sure we will," the man said. "That's a Cardassian ore freighter right there, and we have two pilots among us."

"And there's a very large Cardassian fleet surrounding the station," Kellec said, pointing out the viewport.

"That's what the Cardassians want us to think," the man said, laughing. "We'll just drop right straight down and be on Bajor before what ships there are out there even know we've moved."

Kellec shook his head. "Don't waste all your lives."

The man with the bandaged arm stepped right up into Kellec's face. "We're going home and no Cardassian sympathizer is going to stop us."

The blow caught Kellec squarely in the stomach, sending him backward onto the deck gasping for breath. He couldn't believe the man had hit him.

"See you, Doctor," the man said, motioning for the men to turn around and head into the freighter.

Kellec tried to shout no, but there was no breath left in him. His stomach felt as if it were holding his lungs in a death grip. No air was going in or out. His shout came out as more of a choking gag.

By the time Kellec could even get his lungs to take in a small amount of air, the men were in the freighter and the lock had rolled closed.

Kellec stumbled to his feet and moved over to a viewport just as the freighter disengaged itself from the station and turned toward Bajor. The planet looked so close, so large.

Maybe they would make it.

Maybe he had been wrong.

Three seconds later the ship exploded as two shots from Cardassian warships blew it apart like a child's balloon against a pin.

"No!" Kellec shouted, then dropped down onto the deck, his head in his hands.

He sat there for a few moments, until the sounds of fighting grew in the corridor to his right. He had to keep going, to keep curing people for as long as he could.

He pulled himself back to his feet, facing Bajor and the expanding cloud of wreckage from the ore ship.

"Stupid fools," he said.

Beyond the wreckage, against the blackness of

space, he could see three Cardassian warships. He knew, without a doubt, there were a lot more than that surrounding the station at this moment. He knew, without a doubt, those warships would blast this entire station if a cure wasn't found soon.

He picked up his hypospray and checked it to make sure it was still working, then headed in the direction away from the sounds of the fighting.

"Hurry, Katherine," he said to the walls and to the image of Bajor below him. "Hurry."

Chapter Thirty

PULASKI STARED AT THE IMAGE of the three prions on the screen. They seemed so harmless. The smallest living things known. She'd studied them in medical school. Everyone had. They were mostly of interest only because they were so small. Yet these three prions in front of her could mutate into a deadly virus when joined. They were far from harmless.

And one of them had been created by a biologically manufactured mutation in a Ferengi's body. It was no wonder the incubation period for this plague had taken so long. That special prion had had to travel through air or fluids from the Bajorans, then to a Ferengi, and then to a Cardassian, where it combined with two other naturally occurring prions to form a deadly virus.

Then that virus mutated into a deadly virus for Cardassians. Amazingly complex.

Yet it was an elegantly simple way to wipe out two races.

And so far impossible to stop.

Whoever had designed this had thought of almost everything. Even if the Ferengi were removed from the station and Bajor, the special prion was already here and multiplying in Cardassian and Bajoran bodies. She had no doubt that with the long incubation period it had already traveled to Cardassia. The Ferengi had been the start, but they were now no longer needed in the final deadly result.

She stared at that fourth prion. It revealed nothing.

She shoved her chair back and rubbed her eyes. She couldn't remember the last time she had slept or even eaten much more than a handful of nuts and a glass of water. But from her conversation in the hallway with Dukat two hours ago, she might not need to eat or sleep ever again. She didn't know how much time they had left, but she bet it wasn't much.

Behind her Governo, at another monitor, let out a long sigh.

"Nothing?" she asked.

"Nothing," he said. "I just don't understand what draws the three prions together. There has to be some sort of molecular attraction."

Pulaski looked at her assistant for a moment, letting what he had said sink in. He was right. There had to be something working between the prions that drew them together. And if she had to wager, she would bet that attraction was in that special prion created by the Ferengi mutation.

She'd been focusing all her energy on trying to find a way to kill the prions, not on why they went together. It hadn't even occurred to her to look in that area. It was lucky Governo had.

"There's just no way to isolate what that attraction might be at such a small, microscopic level," Governo said, "at least not without months of trial and error."

"We don't have months," she said. She doubted they even had hours left.

"I know," Governo said.

She stared over Governo's shoulder at the image of the prions on the screen. They were slowly working their way toward each other in the solution.

"I think the attraction comes from this one," Governo said, highlighting the prion with a red glow. Suddenly, staring at that red glow, Pulaski had the solution.

"What happens if we coat it?" she said.

"What?" Governo said, turning to stare at her.

"See the red highlight you have on that prion?"

He glanced around at it. "Yes?"

"You said you think the special prion is attracting the others in some unseen way. Right?"

He nodded.

"So what would happen if we coated all the prions somehow, and try to block the attraction, whatever it might be."

Governo nodded. "It might work. But first we have to find something that will stick to them."

Pulaski moved quickly to the door and out into the lab area. Narat was working over a sick Cardassian. Ogawa and Marvig huddled over a badly injured Bajoran.

"Listen up everyone," Pulaski said to her team. "I need at least a dozen blood cultures from all three races, virus-free but full of prions, set up at once. And then I need another dozen being set up right behind the first dozen. Make it fast."

"Did you find a cure?" Narat asked.

"We don't know yet," she said, heading for the nearest Cardassian to start drawing samples of blood. "And until we get these cultures set up, we won't know. You want to help?"

Narat had the common sense not to say anything more. But he instantly went to work beside her.

It took them thirty minutes to get everything set and ready to go for the first tests.

And another twenty minutes and seven failures before they found a molecular cousin of an iodine derivative that actually stuck to the prions, turning all of them the same shade of sickly brown. It was as if the prions had been dipped in dye.

"Now," Pulaski said, staring at the monitor in the office, "we need to find something that will ride on the iodine carrier, something that will block the attraction."

"I don't think we're going to need to," Governo said, his voice an octave higher than she had ever heard it. "Look at this!"

She watched the monitor where he was pointing. The sickly brown prions in the solution were moving past each other, not seeming to even notice. The attraction between them seemed to be gone.

"Color?" Pulaski said. "Could the attraction have been something as simple as color?"

"Or maybe they hate the derivative," Governo said. "At such a microscopic level, anything is possible."

They both stared at the prions for a few more long moments. But unlike what had been happening in previous tests, these prions were no longer interested in each other. And without that interest, they wouldn't form the deadly virus.

Governo looked up at her, his smile filling his face. "It's working. It's actually working."

Pulaski stepped back quickly into the medical lab. "How many more cultures from all three races are set up?"

"Six each," Ogawa said.

"I want to use all of them to test the iodine derivative. Quickly. Everyone monitor the cultures and put the computer on them as well. We don't want any prions to join."

Ten minutes later the tests, with the entire team watching closely, seemed to be conclusive. But she had to be sure—and at this point all normal medical procedures were long out the airlock.

"Now we try it in patients," she said.

Narat looked at her. That hesitation was built into both of them. But they had to get past it. They had to work quickly, or they would lose every chance they had. If the Cardassians blew up Terok Nor and then killed everyone on Bajor, they still wouldn't have stopped the plague. They would have committed genocide and a few days later gotten sick on Cardassia Prime.

And they would have unknowingly killed off their best chance to a solution.

Narat nodded.

Pulaski quickly mixed the iodine derivative with the cure and injected it into two Cardassians and two Bajorans, plus the older Ferengi.

Eighteen minutes later she had enough faith in their cure to call Dukat.

His face appeared on the screen. He wasn't the

strong, confident Cardassian leader he'd been when she'd arrived. Now he looked more like a tired street fighter. And when he saw her he didn't even smile.

"We have it," she said.

"And you're sure it's permanent this time?"

"As sure as I can be under these conditions."

He nodded. "Get some to Narat and start the distribution. I'll see what I can do to convince the ships outside."

"I will," she said.

He cut the connection.

Behind her Governo said, "Not even a thank-you."

She dropped down into the chair and took a deep breath. "Not yet," she said, staring at the blank screen. "If we survive the next few hours, then he might thank us."

She glanced at the Cardassians who were getting this new version of the cure, and the Bajorans, who were walking around again, and the Ferengi, who was clapping his ears and jumping up and down, clearly gleeful that he felt better.

Governo followed her gaze. She smiled at him tiredly, and said, "I think we have all the thanks we need right here."

Epilogue

IT TOOK TWO WEEKS. They were smarter than he thought. His observers had reported back, saying the virus had been defeated yet again.

He was glad he was doing test cases. He had underestimated the intelligence of his foes. But he wouldn't do that again. He would be very careful next time. And, if it took a few more attempts, he would make them. He wanted to do this right. He would do this right.

And one day soon, he would succeed.

When someone said lack of pain was the best experience in the world, Quark had never understood them. But after this week, he did. His ears no longer itched and, more importantly, the pustules were gone from his ear canal. The female doctor had pronounced him well before she left—and her casual fingering of his lobes had proven that he still had ear function.

His ears were operating in another capacity now. They were reveling in the sound of a full bar. The fighting had stopped, which was too bad for the Bajorans but did ensure that Quark's black-market business would kick back up soon. Cardassians crowded the Dabo table, spending hard-earned latinum. They were drinking to wonderful excess, and a few were so happy to be alive they were splurging on expensive liquors, many of which Rom did not even know the names of.

Rom would come back to the bar, tray in hand, and mangle an order, often so badly that Quark would have to go to the table himself to clarify. But he was in too good a mood to be angry. He'd let Rom get away with his incompetence today. Tomorrow would be another story. Tomorrow, Rom and Nog had to start saving their salaries for another gold-plated ear brush, one Quark had had his eye on for a long, long time.

They would give him the funds, of course, or even better, he would never pay them and use the money for that brush. Which he would then keep locked up—and he would wear the key around his neck. He didn't want to risk cross-contamination again.

No matter what that female doctor and Kellec Ton had said. They believed that someone, or something, had actually brought the virus to the bar. They believed that the Ferengi had been infected first. Quark had begged them and even tried to bribe them to prevent them from sharing that insight with Narat, and in the end they had agreed. Kellec Ton, to Quark's surprise, negotiated the bribe: He wanted Quark to help with the Bajoran resistance on the station. In small ways. Funneling in messages or supplies, or helping someone escape Odo's eye. Quark refused, until Kellec Ton reminded him that they could easily reinfect the Ferengi—and make certain the virus didn't spread beyond Quark, Rom, and Nog.

Quark didn't believe the threat. He didn't think Kellec Ton was that sort of man (and the hu-man female's attempt to hide her laughter reinforced that) but, on the off-chance that the threat was real, Quark agreed to those terms, for a time of limited duration. He suggested a week. Kellec suggested a month. They had compromised on two weeks.

Which was good enough for Quark. It protected his bar, his livelihood, and, much as he hated to admit it, his family. For it looked like Rom and Nog weren't going anywhere soon. And that meant that Quark had to teach them to be at least mildly competent.

"Brother," Rom said. "Gul Dukat would like a vodtini twisted."

"A what?" Quark asked, turning toward his brother.

"A vodtini twisted."

"And what is that?" Quark asked.

"A hu-man drink, suggested by the good doctor. Apparently she said that generations of hu-mans drank it after their workday was over to relax."

"A vodka martini with a twist?" Quark asked.

"That's it!" Rom said.

Quark looked over his brother's head at Gul Dukat. He was sitting at a center table, looking exhausted, but he was managing to laugh with a few of the guards. "Does he know what vodka does to Cardassians?" Quark asked.

"How should I know?" Rom asked.

"Tell him that if he wants to drink it, he has to take it outside. Tell him that the fumes are too much for my other patrons." Quark shook his head. "Who'd have figured the hu-man was a practical jokester."

Rom frowned. "Jokes, brother?"

Quark nodded. "Vodka and Cardassians," he said. "If they've never had it before, it turns them green."

"That doesn't seem very funny to me," Rom said, and went back to Gul Dukat's table.

Quark watched him. What he didn't want to explain to his idiot brother was that sometimes the point of practical jokes wasn't humor. Sometimes the point was to teach someone a lesson.

Apparently the lady doctor believed Gul Dukat had some lessons to learn.

How many times would she have to say good-bye to the *Enterprise?* Pulaski leaned back in her chair in the captain's ready room. The fish were swimming in their aquarium, and Captain Jean-Luc Picard had a clear glass on his desk filled with perfectly brewed Earl Grey tea. The faintly flowery smell of the liquid permeated the room.

Picard was standing behind his desk, looking out the portholes to the stars. The ship was heading back to Deep Space Five at full warp. Apparently someone there had a new assignment for Pulaski and wanted her to arrive on the double.

Just what she needed. More work.

Beverly Crusher sat beside her, nursing an old-fashioned cup of coffee. Pulaski was having one as well. It wasn't Cardassian or Bajoran. It was an Earth beverage, with a taste of home.

She couldn't believe she was leaving. Even when

she, Ogawa, Governo, and Marvig had boarded a Cardassian transport ship she hadn't believed she was going home. The trip to the *Enterprise* had been very different from the trip bringing them to Terok Nor. They were being treated like royalty, each with large cabins even though they weren't staying long enough to sleep in them, and the captain was treating them to a lengthy meal filled with things Pulaski had never seen before.

It all made her feel vaguely guilty about her parting recommendation to Gul Dukat. Even Kellec had given her a funny look when she gave it.

And it all sounded so innocent: a vodka martini with a twist. But she had done so because Dukat had annoyed—no, perhaps the correct term was angered—her, with his insistence on quotas and returning the station to normal. She had overheard him ordering double shifts and punishment for any Bajoran who still claimed weakness from the illness. He had also ordered harsh measures for the prisoners who had instigated the fighting.

He was putting Terok Nor back together the old way, ignoring Kellec's contribution and refusing to see that Bajorans were people, just like Cardassians.

It had riled her temper. And so she had sweetly told Dukat of a way he could rest at the end of his day.

At least she could be sure he wouldn't get sleep for one night. Maybe more. And if she ever saw him again, she could claim ignorance of vodka's effects on Cardassians.

"Are you sure you've told us everything?" Crusher was saying, her tone sympathetic. She had been through one of these plagues too and she had said, when Pulaski got off the transporter pad, that she would be there any time Pulaski needed to talk. "You have a strange expression on your face."

Pulaski smiled just a little. She wouldn't admit to the vodka remark, not in front of Captain Picard, but she did say, "I guess I am a bit surprised by the level of hatred between the Cardassians and the Bajorans."

"I think I can understand the Bajorans' reaction," Picard said, returning to his chair. "After all, the Cardassians have been occupying their planet for some time now."

"Yes, but they worked together on Terok Nor for a brief time, and then even that fell apart." Pulaski sighed. Not even the coffee was helping her bone-deep exhaustion. "And now both sides are blaming the other for the plague. The situation has grown worse instead of better."

"I can't help but wonder if that wasn't the designer's intent," Crusher said.

"What do you mean?" Picard asked.

"Well, we can assume that this plague is related to the one we dealt with on Archaria III," Crusher said. "It almost seems like a second trial of an experiment."

Pulaski looked at her. She had had the same thoughts.

"After all, it didn't respond to the same solution, and the stakes were escalated. There were three species involved. There was a new method of delivery. And—" Crusher paused to look first at Pulaski, then Picard "—this one had the added benefit of destabilizing a precarious region. So if this second trial failed, perhaps the designer saw a benefit in worsening the Cardassian-Bajoran situation."

Picard picked up his glass cup. "Who would do such a thing?"

"A monster," Pulaski said.

"But why?"

"I don't know," Crusher said. "And I'm not sure I want to find out."

"Surely you want to catch this person or persons," Picard said.

"I do," Crusher said, "but on my terms."

"Terms?" Picard asked.

Crusher nodded. But before she could respond, Pulaski spoke. "I understand what Dr. Crusher is saying. We weren't able to track the designer from the scant information we received from our sources on Bajor, and I take it, you had no more success on Archaria III."

"That's right," Picard said.

"Which means that the only way we'll be able to track this monster down . . ." Crusher said.

"Is if there's another plague," Pulaski said tiredly. "Let's hope that his experiment is over and he leaves us in peace."

"Unpunished?" Picard asked.

Pulaski nodded. "Unless we can find him before he causes more deaths." She closed her eyes. "I don't want to see any more death."

She felt a hand on her arm. She opened her eyes to see Crusher looking at her with concern. "You really should rest before you go to your next assignment. If you want, I'll contact Starfleet Medical and ask them for a leave—"

"No." Pulaski smiled. "Work is always better for me. But if you both will excuse me, I do think I'll go to my quarters now. I hope you won't be offended if I sleep most of the way back to Deep Space Five."

"Not at all," Picard said.

"We'll wake you so that you'll have enough time to get your notes together before the briefing with Starfleet Command on Deep Space Five," Crusher said.

"No need." Pulaski stood. "They're already together. I like to finish my tasks before going to bed. I sleep better that way. Good night all."

She heard them say good night as she stepped from the ready room to the bridge. Commander Riker sat in the captain's chair, and he smiled at her as she walked past. Data said hello and Geordi, who was at the engineering station on the bridge, asked her if she was doing all right.

"I'm fine," she said, and stepped into the turbolift. What she didn't tell them was how much she'd miss them, just like she would miss Kellec. It seemed as if her life was about moving away from the people she cared about.

She sighed. If there was one thing she had learned in all her years in Starfleet, it was that every time she left one group behind, she found another—different but just as good—ahead. She knew that. But it seemed as if she would never find a group quite like this one again.

Or perhaps she was just tired. Things always seemed better after she got a little sleep.

Pocket Books
Proudly Presents

Double Helix #3

RED SECTOR

Diane Carey

Coming in July from Pocket Books

Turn the page for a preview of
Red Sector. . . .

"Animals," Ensign Stiles grumbled. "I'd like to get you disrespectful slugs on starship duty for five minutes, just five minutes. . . ." He buried himself in padded insulation as he pulled his flak vest over his head, then slipped into his gauntlets, adjusted his sidearm, and led Perraton out into the coach's main seating area.

Here, five other members of Oak Squad were already suited up and looking at him from inside their red-tinted helmet shields. Jeremy White, Bill Foster, Dan Moose, Brad Carter, Matt Girvan—their names and faces swam before his eyes like a manifest, and for a moment he thought the blood was rushing out of his head. Midshipmen and ensigns, all in training for what would eventually become specialties, now they were assigned to Starbase 10 in the Security Division, under their senior ensign—Stiles. At twenty-one, Eric Stiles was the old man of the outfit. Perraton was next, at twenty years old and forty-two days junior to Stiles' ensign stripes. Knowing that they had heard the ribbing he took from the wings, Stiles felt his face flush. He had to lead the mission. He'd gotten himself into this on purpose. He had to address them as a commander. Nobody to hide behind. They'd seen the landing. His dream of a crisp textbook military approach and regulation landing had gone up in an ugly puff. Now the squad members were blushing and snickering, burying grins, trying not to look right at him—that was hard to take!

"Heads up." His voice cracked. "There's a riot going on outside. Some kind of local political trouble. The embassy is beam-shielded, so we have to go in the security door. As we approach, the guard will drop the door shields. We'll have to go in and come out in single file. We're going to put the dignitaries between us, at two or three in a row. There are about twenty of these people, so the seven of us'll be just about right. I'll go last, with the ambassador right in front of me. He's the primary person to guard, and if he gets so much as a hangnail, somebody's gonna answer to me in a dark alley. After we get—shut up, Foster!"

"I didn't say anything!" Bill Foster protested.

"Quit snickering! This is . . . this is—"

"Serious," Perraton supplied.

"I know, Eric," Foster muttered.

"You call me 'Ensign,' mister!"

"Aye-aye, Ensign Mister."

"I want the rest of this mission to go like clockwork! I don't want a single twitch that isn't in the rule book! Don't snicker, don't scratch, don't burp, don't slip, don't do anything that isn't regulation!"

A hand was pressed to his shoulder and drew him backward a step on the plush carpet.

"Everything'll go fine, Eric," Perraton mildly interrupted. "We're ready when you are." His short dark hair was buried under a white helmet with Starfleet's Delta Shield printed on the forehead, now obscured by the raised red visor. The shield glowed and sang at Stiles. Starfleet's symbol.

And Stiles had to make it look good. In the echo of Perraton's mental leashing, the symbol now lay heavily upon him. If he couldn't yell at his men and tell them they were scum, how would he keep them in shape?

He huffed a couple of steadying breaths, but didn't lower his voice. Now that he'd gotten up to a certain level of volume, it was hard to reel in from that. He took a moment to survey the squad—bright white helmets, black leggings, white boots, red chest pads against the black Starfleet jumpsuits, and the bright flicker of a combadge on every vest. Elbow pads, chin guards, red visors . . . looked fair. Good enough. The uniforms made up for the inadequacies he saw in the people.

Time to go.

"There are riots going on," he repeated, "but so far nobody's tried to breach the embassy itself. Our job is to clear a path between the coach and the embassy and get all Federation nationals out. These people don't have a space fleet, but their atmospheric capabilities are strong enough to cause a few problems. I won't consider the mission accomplished until we're clear of the stratosphere. When we get out of the coach, completely ignore the people swarming around unless they come within two meters or show a weapon. Clear?"

"Clear, sir!" Carter, Girvan, Moose, and Foster shouted. Perraton nodded, and White raised his rifle. Had they accented the "sir" just a little too much?

Stiles stepped between them and the hatch. "Mobilize!"

Perraton took that as a cue, and punched the autorelease on the big hatch. The coach's loading ramp peeled back and lay neatly across the brick before them. Instantly, the stench of molotov cocktails and burning fuel flooded the controlled atmosphere inside the coach. At Stiles's side, Perraton coughed a couple of times. Other than that, nobody's big mouth cracked open. Stiles led the way down, his heavy boots thunking on the nonskid ramp.

They broke out onto a courtyard of grand proportion with colonnades flanking it on three sides and the diplomatic buildings on the fourth side—a battery of fifteen embassies, halls, and consulates. Most of them were empty now. The Federation was the last to evacuate. Two of the colonnades were in ruins; part of one was shrouded in scaffolding while being rebuilt. Most of the buildings had signs of structural damage, but generally the Diplomatic Court of PojjanPirakot was a stately and bright place, providing a sad backdrop for the ugliness of these protests.

A quick glance behind showed him the positions of the five fighters landed around the coach. Their glistening bodies, streamlined for both aerodynamics and space travel, shined in the golden sunlight. There was Air Wing Leader Bernt Folmer, their best pilot, code "Brazil," parked like a big car in front of Greg "Pecan" Blake. Behind the coach the tail fin of Andrea Hipp's "Cashew" fighter caught a glint of sun. On the other side, hopefully parked nose to tail, were Acorn and Chestnut, brothers Jason and Zack Bolt—but Stiles didn't bother to check their position. He only hoped they were in sharp order.

All around were angry people waving signs, some in a

language he didn't understand, others scrawled in English, Vulcan, Spanish, Orion Yrevish, and a few others familiar from courtesy placards all over Starfleet Command where multitudes wandered.

The ones in English jumped out instantly before Stiles's racing mind. OUT, ALIENS ... LEAVE OUR PLANET ... GET OUT, STRANGERS ... ALIENS UNWELCOME ... CURSE ALIENS ALL ...

Some of the people were calling out in English, too, though clumsily and without really understanding the arrangement of nouns and verbs. The anti-alien message, though, arrowed directly through to the team.

To the music of enraged shouts from the people rattling gates and creating a din by banging small silver knives on the iron posts, Oak Squad broke into a jog and flooded into a broad shield of sunlight glaring between the embassy and the consulate next door. The doorways and lintels were heavily reinforced with titanium T-girders, and titanium bands swept around every building, two on each story, like shiny ribcages. Stiles glanced around at his squad, making sure nobody pulled ahead of the formation. This had to be crisp. The ambassador was watching from some window inside that embassy. Everybody was watching.

Fifty meters . . .

Oak Squad thundered forward relentlessly, their phaser rifles tight against their chests. As Stiles led his men across the patterned brick, he saw that just the raw heat from the coach's VTOL thrusters had scorched some of the bricks nearly black and pitted them beyond repair, destroying the geometric design in the historic courtyard.

His boots felt secure and thick as he crunched over the litter of broken glass, smashed fruit, and rocks that had been thrown by the rioters, who were now milling around the fighters and the coach. These Pojjan people were stocky and thick, with strong round cheekbones and bronze complexions tinged with an olive patina, reminding Stiles of Aztec paintings seen under a green filter. They wore various clothing, from the men's ordinary shirts and pants or the women's shiftlike dresses to the brightly beaded tribal tunics and leggings he'd seen on travel posters.

The travel agencies might as well rip those posters up. Nobody was going to want to come to this dump anymore.

He cast the rioters a threatening glance or two, but

although some were touching the ships' landing struts they weren't doing anything destructive. Not yet anyway. If anything happened, the escort pilots would zap them. So he kept moving forward at a pace, letting the natives swerve out of his way. He led the squad manfully through a large puddle of fuel, some of which was still gulping out of a discarded and dented container. Their boots splattered it and freshened the stench.

Thirty meters.

Cries of anger, protest, and insult at Starfleet's intrusion into their courtyard grew louder, as the squad jogged across the brick plateau. Stiles didn't understand the Pojjan language, but some of these people were shouting in English or Vulcan and waving get-out-of-town banners in English, apparently smart enough to know how to get to the Federation personnel.

It's getting to me. I'm allowing it to shake me. Just do the job, get the people out of the embassy, into the coach, and lift off. Ignore the crowd. Just ignore them.

At his right elbow, Travis Perraton was watching a gang of Pojjan teenagers on the other side of the embassy fence. A flash of flame—the teenagers were lighting up a fuel-soaked towel.

"They can't throw that this far, can they?" Blake asked from behind Stiles.

"They don't have to," Perraton said. "We're jogging toward puddles of kerosene."

"Gasoline," Midshipman Jeremy White corrected from the flank.

"Stinks," Dan Moose added, then cast to the man on his left, "Make room, Foster."

"Sorry."

"Bag the noise," Stiles snapped, turning his head briefly to the right. "Don't splash through the gas. If we get it on our uniforms, we're in big trouble."

And that was his error—that one glance over his shoulder. A stunning force struck his left shin just below the kneepad, driving his entire leg out behind him. Blown forward by the force of his own movement, Stiles let out a single strangled yell, leaped forward over a slick of gasoline, and crashed to the bricks just beyond the slick. Though he evaded the gas, he slid sidelong into a pile of garbage dumped on the courtyard. Managing to thrust his arms out, he somehow kept from landing on his phaser rifle, which instead clattered to the brick and butted him in the face shield, then scratched across his bared jaw. If his visor had been up, the rifle would've taken out his teeth.

A blunt force rammed into his lower back—a boot—as Carter tumbled over Stiles, crumpling to the bricks on top of the garbage. Carter rolled and ended up on one knee.

With his jaw and knee throbbing, Stiles tightened his body, twisted onto his side, and brandished his weapon at the laughing crowd as his face flushed with humiliation. They were laughing at him. His fantasy of a clockwork mission had just cracked and blown up before his eyes.

Bile rose in his throat, a rashy heat down his legs. His lungs tightened as he felt slimy garbage soak into his uniform and the stench of petroleum knot his innards. The sky wheeled above him, cluttered with white helmets and flashing red visors reflecting the afternoon sun.

Smiling, Perraton reached to pull him to his feet. "Nice going, lightfoot."

"Don't help me!" Stiles blurted.

As if bitten, Perraton retracted his hand. Stiles rolled to his feet, now smudged with the gummy remains of garbage and mudballs.

When he got to his feet, Stiles staggered a few steps in the wrong direction and was forced to endure the foolish chickenscratch of turning around and struggling back to the front of his squad, and the further embarrassment of realizing his men were deliberately slowing down so he could get in front. He slammed his way between them, elbowing Perraton and White cruelly out of his path. He didn't need their charity!

At the gates, two Pojjan guards immediately opened the iron grid and let them in without a word. The embassy's medieval-looking carved wooden door, three guys wide and set between two gargoyles, also opened automatically.

No, not automatically—this door was manual. Another guard or servant of some freaky nationality Stiles didn't recognize was now peeking around the door's iron rim like a shy cow peeking out of a barn. He was an elderly man, with bent shoulders and bright green eyes set in a jowly dark face with stripes painted on it. More tribal weirdness.

Moving far enough into the heavily tiled foyer, Stiles suddenly felt ridiculously out of place. The foyer was splendid, its mosaics of gold and black chipped stone and glossy ceramics portraying some kind of historic battle scene and the coronation of somebody. Must be from way back, because this wasn't a monarchical culture anymore. Was it?

The guard pushed the big door shut and swung a huge titanium bolt into place to lock them safely inside, then turned to the clutch of evac troopers and gasped, "One minute! I'll get the ambassador's assistant!"

And he disappeared into a wide archway that was two stories tall.

Oak Squad stood in the middle of the gorgeous tile floor, their uniforms scuffed and stinking, and looked around.

"I'd hate to be the guy who cleans the grout," Perraton commented.

White grunted as he scanned the mosaic on the ceiling. "How long you think we'll have to wait?"

"Not long," Stiles filled in. "They called for us to come get them, so they're probably ready to leave. And they're Vulcans, so you know they're efficient."

"How do you know they'll be stiffs?" Moose asked.

"Because Ambassador Spock's a st—a Vulcan. They like to have their own kind around. They understand each other better than we do."

"Oh, right," White drawled. "They do everything better than we do."

Stiles scoured him with a glare. "Don't start on me, Jeremy."

He turned away, but in his periphery he noted Perraton's quick motion to White, erasing any further annoying comments.

Though they stood in this wide foyer feeling dirty and small, they were not alone. Sounds of footsteps and voices leaked from the depths of the embassy halls, and twice Stiles saw ethereal forms slip from one office to another. Did they trust him to get them out safely? Had they seen the botched choreography of the landing? Did they wonder whether the ensign in command was competent enough to handle this?

He gripped his phaser rifle until his hands hurt and shifted from foot to foot, halting only when a young woman—a human—skittered through the grand main door and into the huge foyer. Stiles didn't pay attention. The small-boned woman, with tightly wrapped brown hair, tiny pearl earrings, and a twitch in her left eye, went directly to the tallest of them—Jeremy White—and breathily said, "I'm Miss Theonella, Ambassador Spock's deputy attaché. Are you Ensign Stiles?"

She had a tight foreign accent that sounded Earth-based, but Stiles couldn't pinpoint the country.

"He's over there, ma'am," White told her, and gestured.

Stiles stepped through the cluster of Starfleeters and took his helmet off, revealing his sweat-plastered blond hair. "Eric Stiles, ma'am. I'm here to evacuate the entire embassy. Nobody should be left behind."

"We understand." Miss Theonella rubbed her tiny pink palms as if kneading bread dough between them. "All embassy envoys, functionaries, ministers, delegates, and clerks will be going, as well as four Pojjan defectors who lost their homes in the last Constrictor. They're being given asylum here and we have clearance for them to be evacuated with us. In all there are thirty-five of us."

"Thirty-five!" Perraton blurted. Then he instantly clammed up, but the number twenty kept flashing in his eyes like beacons.

How could seven of them safely escort thirty-five dignitaries through fifty meters of rioting?

"We're prepared, ma'am," Stiles shoved in, more loudly than necessary, before anyone else could speak up. "About the landing . . . the ambassador is probably wondering why we were so . . . out of formation. . . ."

"What?" Miss Theonella's white temples puckered and her brows came together like pencil points. "We can't see the courtyard from here. There are only reception rooms on the court side of the building. Was there some reason you wanted us to be watching you? Was there a signal?"

He stared at her, caught between relief and disappointment that nobody had been watching. "Uh . . . no, no signal."

Preoccupied, the thin young woman simply said, "Continue to wait here, please, Ensign. I'll get the ambassador."

Again the evac squad stood alone, holding their rifles, standing in the middle of the gleaming tile floor, listening to the drumming chants of angry people outside in the square and trying to imagine how they were going to hustle thirty-five dignitaries through that. The unpleasant possibility of rushing half of them out to the coach, then coming back for the second group—Stiles winced. Two trips through that courtyard full of alien-haters? Was that safer than one big rush? If he ordered two separate groups, would the angry people see that as their last chance to get them and attack the second group?

"Wonder why they hate aliens?" Dan Moose voiced.

Matt Girvan checked his rifle. "I hate you too."

Stiles noted that his men were looking at the windows and doors, but his own eyes were focused on the long hall of offices into which Miss Theonella had disappeared. The ambassador was in there somewhere.

"Ambassador, ambassador," he murmured. "Don't you think that's a flaming word? I *love* that word. *Ambassador . . .*"

"Yeah, nice word, Stiles," Brad Carter muttered. "Everybody's got a pet word. Mine's 'glue.'"

Moose put his gauntletted finger to some of the tiles on the wall. "I've always been fond of 'meat' myself."

"Give me 'meat,'" Perraton echoed. "I want 'meat.' You're right, Dan, great word."

"Stiles's pet word is 'Vulcan.' You like that word, Jeremy?"

"Eh, y'met one stiff, you met 'em all."

"As you were!" Stiles erupted when he saw activity down the hall. "I don't want you guys prattling when the ambassador—Is that him? I think I see him! Travis! Look—it's him! He's coming down the hall! What should I do?"

"Don't curtsy, for God's sake," Perraton muttered.

All the men turned to face the hall to their left as a crowd of elegant dignitaries bobbed toward them. In the midst of them was the tall instantly recognizable figure of the famous Ambassador Spock.

Bow? Kneel? Handshake?

"Don't faint! Eric, stand at attention!"

Perraton's anxious whisper boomed in Stiles's ear like a foghorn.

"Stand at attention!"

"Attention. . . ." Stiles planted his boots on the tile, but wasn't able to get them together. He squared his shoulders, raised his chin, held his breath, clutched his rifle, and forced an appearance of adept steadiness and control. Cool. Calm. Military. Crisp. In control. In charge. Confident. Smelly.

The ambassador and his party approached them, but Spock wasn't looking at them. Instead his dark head was bowed as he spoke to Miss Theonella, who was clipping along at his side. The ambassador listened, nodded, then spoke again while a male attendant slipped a glossy blue Federation Diplomatic Corps jacket around the boss's shoulders.

The sight was a shock—Stiles had expected the flowing ceremonial robes that Vulcan seniors were usually seen wearing, but now that he saw Spock in the trim gray slacks and dark blue jacket with the UFP symbol on the left side, that outfit seemed to make more sense for a spaceborne evacuation. Robes might be harder to handle on boarding ramps and in tight quarters.

Why hadn't he thought of that?

Though Spock—tall, narrow, controlled—possessed all the regal formality common to his race, his famous form was somehow less imperious in person than Stiles had anticipated, his angular Vulcan features more animated, and framed by the fact that he was the only Vulcan in the bunch. Of course, Stiles had only seen still photos or staged lecture tapes. Seeing Spock in real life was very different—he wasn't stiff at all.

As they approached, he could hear Miss Theonella's thready voice.

". . . and the provincial vice-warden will be sending his prolocutrix as proxy to speak for the entire hemisphere at Federation central. Also, sir, the consul general's wife and children are waiting in the Blue Room, and Chancellor De Gaeta's wife is in his office."

Miss Theonella finished her sentence just as she and the ambassador and their party came into the foyer.

"Thank you, Karen, very good work," Ambassador Spock said gently, countering her quivering report with his silky baritone voice. "Suggest to the Sagittarian military attaché that he post a Pojjan communications sentry, and that person must speak both Bal Quonnot and Romulan."

That voice! That famous voice! Stiles had been hearing it all his life! Historical documentaries, training tapes, mission interactives, holoprograms—now he was here, in person, right in the same room with that voice!

"This is Ensign Stiles," Miss Theonella added with a gesture. "And the evacuation escort men, sir."

The ambassador scanned the team, then fixed his gaze at Stiles. Directly *at* him. Right in the eyes! He was looking right at him!

Those eyes—like blades! Black blades!

Stiles tried to take a breath, but all he got was a gulp of

garbage fumes from his soaked trouser leg. As his lungs seized up, he felt the boink-boink of Perraton's finger poking him in the back.

Report, you idiot!

"Ev . . . Evacuation Squad reporting as you requested, sir! Ensign Eric J. Stiles, Starfleet Special Services reporting, sir! One G-rate transport coach, evacuation team, and five fighter escorts, sir!"

The ambassador's black-slash brows went up like bird's wings. The chamber fell to silence. Stiles's fervid report echoed absurdly.

Calmly Spock said, "At ease, Ensign."

His deep mellow voice took Stiles utterly by surprise.

"Aye-aye, sir!" Stiles choked.

"We'll be ready within five minutes," the ambassador told him fluidly, then turned to the attendant who'd put the jacket on him. "Edwin, please bring out the consul general's family and Mrs. De Gaeta and turn them over to Ensign Stiles."

"Right away, Ambassador."

As the man left, Spock turned again to Miss Theonella. "You have our records and diplomatic pouches? The legal briefs and service files? Personnel manifests?"

She held up a stern black pilot's case with a magnetic lock, hanging from a strap on her shoulder. "All here, sir."

"Very well. We should also bring the jurisdictional warrants. They could be confiscated and used to gain passage into restricted areas."

"I'll get them, sir."

"No, I'll get them." The ambassador turned to leave, then paused and gazed briefly at the tiled floor, thinking. "Stiles . . ."

"Here, sir!"

Spock looked up at the inflamed response. Coolly he repeated, "At *ease*, Ensign."

Stiles shivered, glanced at Travis Perraton, and again met the ambassador's eyes. "Yes, sir . . ."

"Are you by chance related to—"

"Yes, sir, I am, sir! Starfleet Security Commander John Stiles, Retired, is my grandfather, sir! He served with you under Captain James T. Kirk, Stardates 1709 to 1788 point 6 as Alpha-Watch navigator aboard the *U.S.S. Enterprise,* Heavy Cruiser NCC 1701, commissioned stardate—"

"I recall the ship, Ensign."

"Oh . . . oh . . . aye, sir. . . ."

"You have a long line of Starfleet service officers in your family heritage, I also recall."

"Yes, sir! Several active-duty servicemen lost in the Romulan Wars, sir! A captain, two lieutenants, two—"

"Commendable, Mr. Stiles. Carry on." Spock turned to the little gaggle of people behind him and said, "All of you please stand by until everyone else arrives. Then you'll take your instructions from Ensign Stiles as to how you will arrange yourselves during the actual evacuation. As you know, the building is beam-shielded, and therefore we must go out the door and board the transport coach on foot. Unfortunately, our general safety compromises our safety during emergency evacuation. Karen, keep them in order. I'll return momentarily."

With that he disappeared down a different hallway and into an office, leaving a confused clutch of embassy persons standing here in the foyer, wide-eyed and obviously frightened. By nature, the two groups divided to opposite sides of the foyer, embassy folks over there, Oak Squad over here.

Stiles let himself be tugged aside, and barely registered the low mutters of his men around him through the afterglow of his meeting with Spock.

"Beam-shielding," Matt Girvan grumbled. "There's planning. What if they had to get out under more dangerous conditions than mudballs and molotovs?"

"It's beam-shielded so assassins or terrorists can't beam *in*, freak."

"Why couldn't they make it one-way?"

"Too unstable. Sucks too much energy to maintain over time."

"Doesn't matter. We'll get 'em out. Eric'll carry them all on his back if he has to."

"If he doesn't choke up a lung first."

"We'll be lucky if he doesn't make us bow backward out of the room."

The team laughed. A cluttered sound, muffled . . . like a storm coming.

Beside Stiles, Perraton raised his helmet visor and smiled with genuine sympathy.

"You okay, Eric?" he asked.

"He's having a coronary," Jeremy White diagnosed. "Anybody know mouth-to-mouth?"

"Not me."

"No chance."

"Uh-uh."

"Let him die."

Stiles felt his lips chapping as he breathed in and out, in and out, like a landed fish. He'd just met his hero and he didn't know if he'd liked it.

And it wasn't over. In fact, it was just beginning. He'd have to do everything perfectly from now on. No more botched formations. No more stammering. He had to be perfect. Smooth.

"Put your helmet on, Eric," Perraton suggested privately. "Ambassador's coming back."

In a sudden panic, Stiles drew up his helmet so fast that he clipped himself in the eye before getting the thing back on his head.

"Ouch," Perraton supplied for him. "Another souvenir of your first mission. A shiner."

Noting Stiles's wince of anguish, Perraton straightened the helmet and put the scratched visor up.

"Ease up, lightfoot," he said. "He's just a guy."

"Just a guy," Stiles rasped. "He's a hero, Travis . . . a Starfleet icon . . . the first Vulcan in Starfleet . . . Captain James Kirk's executive officer . . . I've heard every story a hundred times all my life—do you know how many times he participated in saving the *whole* Federation? And even the Klingon Empire?"

"Doesn't matter now. Anyway, the hard part's over. You met him, you survived, and the experience didn't suck out your brains. He was a Starfleet man for half a century. He knows the drill. So get a perspective. Here he comes."

Do the job. Do the job.

The ambassador flowed back into the foyer, now carrying a slim red folder and followed by more than a dozen people and his attendant Edwin. Suddenly the foyer was swarming with civilians. At least they were mostly adults, a few teenagers—Stiles didn't relish the prospect of herding toddlers through that mess out there. He stiffened as the ambassador came directly to him.

"We're ready, Mr. Stiles."

"Yes, sir . . . how would you like to do this?"

Spock handed the folder to Miss Theonella. "Pardon me?"

"I . . . I figured you'd have some preference about . . . what order you want them in and . . . how to do it."

The ambassador thought about that briefly, his dark eyes working, as if he hadn't considered such an option. After a moment he vocally shrugged. "Your mission, Ensign."

Over Spock's shoulder, Perraton smiled and gave Stiles a thumbs-up.

Sustained by that, Stiles forced himself to rise to the demand. "Uh . . . if you people would form a line, two by two, and Oak Squad situate yourselves between them, uh, one every . . . uh—"

He paused, tried to do the math, but couldn't remember how. His brain *had* been sucked out!

Maybe he wouldn't have to count and add and divide—his men were already arranging themselves into position. Perraton was taking the lead, and motioning the others into the queue at intervals.

"I'll take the rear guard," Stiles said. "Ambassador, would you mind coming back here with me, sir?"

"Thank you, Ensign, I will."

"All right, let's—no, no, you can't do the door." Stiles motioned to the funny-looking butler who was still standing his post at the door, waiting to open it for everybody. "Travis, put that man in line behind Girvan and you do the door. Then fall in."

"Copy that."

"Okay, phaser rifles ready."

"Ready!" his men shouted.

"Rifles up!"

"Up!"

"Very well!"

Stiles took one more look at Ambassador Spock's steady form in line before him, at the large UFP shield printed on the back of the blue jacket. The stars of the United Federation of Planets swam before his eyes.

He drew a breath. His voice echoed under the high tiled ceiling.

"Mobilize!"

Look for
Red Sector
Available in July
Wherever Books Are Sold

STAR TREK®
Strange New Worlds III
Contest Rules

1) ENTRY REQUIREMENTS:

No purchase necessary to enter. Enter by submitting your story as specified below.

2) CONTEST ELIGIBILITY:

This contest is open to nonprofessional writers who are legal residents of the United States and Canada (excluding Quebec) over the age of 18. Entrant must not have published any more than two short stories on a professional basis or in paid professional venues. Employees (or relatives of employees living in the same household) of Pocket Books, VIACOM, or any of its affiliates are not eligible. This contest is void in Puerto Rico and wherever prohibited by law.

3) FORMAT:

Entries should be no more than 7,500 words long and must not have been previously published. They must be typed or printed by word processor, double spaced, on one side of noncorrasable paper. Do not justify right-side margins. The author's name, address, and phone number must appear on the first page of the entry. The author's name, the story title, and the page number should appear on every page. No electronic or disk submissions will be accepted. All entries must be original and the sole work of the Entrant and the sole property of the Entrant.

Contest Rules

4) ADDRESS:

Each entry must be mailed to: STRANGE NEW WORLDS, *Star Trek* Department, Pocket Books, 1230 Sixth Avenue, New York, NY 10020.

Each entry must be submitted only once. Please retain a copy of your submission. You may submit more than one story, but each submission must be mailed separately. Enclose a self-addressed, stamped envelope if you wish your entry returned. Entries must be received by October 1st, 1999. Not responsible for lost, late, stolen, postage due, or misdirected mail.

5) PRIZES:

One Grand Prize winner will receive:

Simon and Schuster's *Star Trek: Strange New Worlds III* Publishing Contract for Publication of Winning Entry in our *Strange New Worlds III* Anthology with a bonus advance of One Thousand Dollars ($1,000.00) above the Anthology word rate of 10 cents a word.

One Second Prize winner will receive:

Simon and Schuster's *Star Trek: Strange New Worlds III* Publishing Contract for Publication of Winning Entry in our *Strange New Worlds III* Anthology with a bonus advance of Six Hundred Dollars ($600.00) above the Anthology word rate of 10 cents a word.

One Third Prize winner will receive:

Simon and Schuster's *Star Trek: Strange New Worlds III* Publishing Contract for Publication of Winning Entry in our *Strange New Worlds III* Anthology with a bonus advance of Four Hundred Dollars ($400.00) above the Anthology word rate of 10 cents a word.

All Honorable Mention winners will receive:

Simon and Schuster's *Star Trek: Strange New Worlds III* Publishing Contract for Publication of Winning Entry in the *Strange New Worlds III* Anthology and payment at the Anthology word rate of 10 cents a word.

There will be no more than twenty (20) Honorable Mention winners. No contestant can win more than one prize.

Each Prize Winner will also be entitled to a share of royalties on the *Strange New Worlds III* Anthology as specified in Simon and Schuster's *Star Trek: Strange New Worlds III* Publishing Contract.

6) JUDGING:

Submissions will be judged on the basis of writing ability and the originality of the story, which can be set in any of the *Star Trek* time frames and may feature any one or more of the *Star Trek* characters. The judges shall include the editor of the Anthology, one employee of Pocket Books, and one employee of VIACOM Consumer Products. The decisions of the judges shall be final. All prizes will be awarded provided a sufficient number of entries are received that meet the minimum criteria established by the judges.

7) NOTIFICATION:

The winners will be notified by mail or phone. The winners who win a publishing contract must sign the publishing contract in order to be awarded the prize.

Contest Rules

All federal, local, and state taxes are the responsibility of the winner. A list of the winners will be available after January 1st, 2000, on the Pocket Books *Star Trek* Books website, www.simonsays.com/startrek/, or the names of the winners can be obtained after January 1st, 2000, by sending a self-addressed, stamped envelope and a request for the list of winners to WINNERS' LIST, STRANGE NEW WORLDS III, *Star Trek* Department, Pocket Books, 1230 Sixth Avenue, New York, NY 10020.

8) STORY DISQUALIFICATIONS:

Certain types of stories will be disqualified from consideration:

a) Any story focusing on explicit sexual activity or graphic depictions of violence or sadism.

b) Any story that focuses on characters that are not past or present *Star Trek* regulars or familiar *Star Trek* guest characters.

c) Stories that deal with the previously unestablished death of a *Star Trek* character, or that establish major facts about or make major changes in the life of a major character, for instance a story that establishes a long-lost sibling or reveals the hidden passion two characters feel for each other.

d) Stories that are based around common clichés, such as "hurt/comfort" where a character is injured and lovingly cared for, or "Mary Sue" stories where a new character comes on the ship and outdoes the crew.

Contest Rules

9) PUBLICITY:

Each Winner grants to Pocket Books the right to use his or her name, likeness, and entry for any advertising, promotion, and publicity purposes without further compensation to or permission from such winner, except where prohibited by law.

10) LEGAL STUFF:

All entries become the property of Pocket Books and of Paramount Pictures, the sole and exclusive owner of the *Star Trek* property and elements thereof. Entries will be returned only if they are accompanied by a self-addressed, stamped envelope. Contest void where prohibited by law.

Look for STAR TREK Fiction from Pocket Books

Star Trek®: The Original Series

Star Trek: The Motion Picture • Gene Roddenberry
Star Trek II: The Wrath of Khan • Vonda N. McIntyre
Star Trek III: The Search for Spock • Vonda N. McIntyre
Star Trek IV: The Voyage Home • Vonda N. McIntyre
Star Trek V: The Final Frontier • J. M. Dillard
Star Trek VI: The Undiscovered Country • J. M. Dillard
Star Trek VII: Generations • J. M. Dillard
Star Trek VIII: First Contact • J. M. Dillard
Star Trek IX: Insurrection • J. M. Dillard
Enterprise: The First Adventure • Vonda N. McIntyre
Final Frontier • Diane Carey
Strangers from the Sky • Margaret Wander Bonanno
Spock's World • Diane Duane
The Lost Years • J. M. Dillard
Probe • Margaret Wander Bonanno
Prime Directive • Judith and Garfield Reeves-Stevens
Best Destiny • Diane Carey
Shadows on the Sun • Michael Jan Friedman
Sarek • A. C. Crispin
Federation • Judith and Garfield Reeves-Stevens
The Ashes of Eden • William Shatner & Judith and Garfield Reeves-Stevens
The Return • William Shatner & Judith and Garfield Reeves-Stevens
Star Trek: Starfleet Academy • Diane Carey
Vulcan's Forge • Josepha Sherman and Susan Shwartz
Avenger • William Shatner & Judith and Garfield Reeves-Stevens
Star Trek: Odyssey • William Shatner & Judith and Garfield Reeves-Stevens
Spectre • William Shatner

#1 *Star Trek: The Motion Picture* • Gene Roddenberry
#2 *The Entropy Effect* • Vonda N. McIntyre
#3 *The Klingon Gambit* • Robert E. Vardeman
#4 *The Covenant of the Crown* • Howard Weinstein
#5 *The Prometheus Design* • Sondra Marshak & Myrna Culbreath

Star Trek: The Next Generation®

Encounter at Farpoint • David Gerrold
Unification • Jeri Taylor
Relics • Michael Jan Friedman
Descent • Diane Carey
All Good Things • Michael Jan Friedman
Star Trek: Klingon • Dean W. Smith & Kristine K. Rusch
Star Trek VII: Generations • J. M. Dillard
Metamorphosis • Jean Lorrah
Vendetta • Peter David
Reunion • Michael Jan Friedman
Imzadi • Peter David
The Devil's Heart • Carmen Carter
Dark Mirror • Diane Duane
Q-Squared • Peter David
Crossover • Michael Jan Friedman
Kahless • Michael Jan Friedman
Star Trek VIII: First Contact • J. M. Dillard
Star Trek IX: Insurrection • Diane Carey
The Best and the Brightest • Susan Wright
Planet X • Michael Jan Friedman
Ship of the Line • Diane Carey

#1 *Ghost Ship* • Diane Carey
#2 *The Peacekeepers* • Gene DeWeese
#3 *The Children of Hamlin* • Carmen Carter
#4 *Survivors* • Jean Lorrah
#5 *Strike Zone* • Peter David
#6 *Power Hungry* • Howard Weinstein
#7 *Masks* • John Vornholt
#8 *The Captains' Honor* • David and Daniel Dvorkin
#9 *A Call to Darkness* • Michael Jan Friedman
#10 *A Rock and a Hard Place* • Peter David
#11 *Gulliver's Fugitives* • Keith Sharee
#12 *Doomsday World* • David, Carter, Friedman & Greenberg
#13 *The Eyes of the Beholders* • A. C. Crispin
#14 *Exiles* • Howard Weinstein
#15 *Fortune's Light* • Michael Jan Friedman
#16 *Contamination* • John Vornholt
#17 *Boogeymen* • Mel Gilden

Star Trek: Deep Space Nine®

Star Trek®: Voyager™

Flashback • Diane Carey
Pathways • Jeri Taylor
Mosaic • Jeri Taylor

#1 *Caretaker* • L. A. Graf
#2 *The Escape* • Dean W. Smith & Kristine K. Rusch
#3 *Ragnarok* • Nathan Archer
#4 *Violations* • Susan Wright
#5 *Incident at Arbuk* • John Gregory Betancourt
#6 *The Murdered Sun* • Christie Golden
#7 *Ghost of a Chance* • Mark A. Garland & Charles G. McGraw
#8 *Cybersong* • S. N. Lewitt
#9 *Invasion #4: The Final Fury* • Dafydd ab Hugh
#10 *Bless the Beasts* • Karen Haber
#11 *The Garden* • Melissa Scott
#12 *Chrysalis* • David Niall Wilson
#13 *The Black Shore* • Greg Cox
#14 *Marooned* • Christie Golden
#15 *Echoes* • Dean W. Smith & Kristine K. Rusch
#16 *Seven of Nine* • Christie Golden
#17 *Death of a Neutron Star* • Eric Kotani
#18 *Battle Lines* • Dave Galanter & Greg Brodeur

Star Trek®: New Frontier

#1 *House of Cards* • Peter David
#2 *Into the Void* • Peter David
#3 *The Two-Front War* • Peter David
#4 *End Game* • Peter David
#5 *Martyr* • Peter David
#6 *Fire on High* • Peter David

Star Trek®: Day of Honor

Book One: *Ancient Blood* • Diane Carey
Book Two: *Armageddon Sky* • L. A. Graf
Book Three: *Her Klingon Soul* • Michael Jan Friedman
Book Four: *Treaty's Law* • Dean W. Smith & Kristine K. Rusch
The Television Episode • Michael Jan Friedman

Star Trek®: The Captain's Table

Book One: *War Dragons* • L. A. Graf
Book Two: *Dujonian's Hoard* • Michael Jan Friedman
Book Three: *The Mist* • Dean W. Smith & Kristine K. Rusch
Book Four: *Fire Ship* • Diane Carey
Book Five: *Once Burned* • Peter David
Book Six: *Where Sea Meets Sky* • Jerry Oltion

Star Trek®: The Dominion War

Book 1: *Behind Enemy Lines* • John Vornholt
Book 2: *Call to Arms . . .* • Diane Carey
Book 3: *Tunnel Through the Stars* • John Vornholt
Book 4: *. . . Sacrifice of Angels* • Diane Carey

Star Trek®: My Brother's Keeper

Book One: *Republic* • Michael Jan Friedman
Book Two: *Constitution* • Michael Jan Friedman
Book Three: *Enterprise* • Michael Jan Friedman